DR. ELLEN

BY

JULIET WILBOR TOMPKINS

WILDSIDE PRESS

DR. ELLEN

DR. ELLEN

I

THE girl appeared disproportionately happy, even absurdly so. Amsden had watched her during the somewhat stupid finals of the tennis tournament that afternoon, his attention caught by an impression of surface brilliance that made her seem of another race from the young women about her in the little hot grandstand. The brilliance was not of colour, for the faint powdery blondness of her hair found little contrast in her light hazel eyes and even paleness; it was the breathless happiness shining out that made her seem so vivid. She was full of eager laughs that spilled over at the lightest touch. Her eyes followed the balls back and forth with joyous abandon; she cried out at tense moments, and beat her parasol on the platform in applause. She seemed to have an inordinate capacity for trivial excitements, vaguely repelling in a young woman who was clearly out of her teens.

Later, Amsden, who had paused near the door of the ballroom, found her looking on there with the same intensity, and extracting from the conversation of Will Wallace a stimulating charm which to Amsden's positive knowledge did not exist. Had she been fifteen! But time had marked her twenty-three or four at least; besides, she was evidently with Christine O'Hara, and Christine was no missionary to débutantes. Amsden's eyes followed the latter's light red curls about the ballroom until they paused near an open window, then he crossed to her with a deliberate slowness that was not at all a stroll. In all his actions there was a neat precision that precluded any impression of loose-jointed carelessness.

Christine's smile at his approach had a histrionic quality. "Me to be so honoured!" it said as she turned from a red and shiny partner some seven years her junior — the tournament dance was not a socially brilliant affair.

"What are you doing here?" she demanded in mock alarm. "Don't you know that grown men under fifty are not allowed in the ballroom?"

Amsden smiled indulgently at the broad, plump face in its frame of little curls. He could not trouble to be playful himself, but he had no objection to Christine's gambols so long as they made no demand on him. A delicate skin and amusing little brown eyes would have made her pretty if she had not used her face much as a more frankly coy generation did its fan, peering through it for effects, presenting it always at a meaningful angle.

"Who is that rapturous young woman you have with you?" he asked.

"So that is what brings you — not me at all," said Christine inevitably, though more by way of doing her duty by the situation than in any expectation of a response. "It's Ruth Chantry," she added. "Didn't you ever know the Chantry girls?" Her eyes were wandering restlessly among the dancers as though marking future partners. A little girl of twelve with long, pink legs was whirled by, waltzing exquisitely, with the bland air of one who has partners in abundance. "How absurd to let that child sit up," Christine exclaimed impatiently.

"Was there an older Chantry girl who had some sort of a tragedy?" Amsden asked.

"Yes, Ellen. Ruth has a tragedy, too, let me tell you."

"She looks it."

Christine laughed. "What you are seeing is a momentary escape. That girl has been cooped up in a little cabin off in the Sierras for three solid years — not one day in town, even. What do you think of that for tyranny?"

"Who is the tyrant?"

"Oh, Ellen — Mrs. Roderick, she is. She chooses to live there, and Ruth has to live with her. I'd go mad. I can't stand Ellen, anyway. She's su-per-ior!" The word crinkled her expressive nose. "Come and meet Ruth, if you like," she added briskly, as the music came to a halt and various partners were set free. "I want her to have a good time."

Amsden followed somewhat reluctantly. The missionary spirit was not strong in him, and the girl interested him as an abstract fact rather than as a personal acquaintance. Moreover, he was impatient of being detained in this absurd ballroom, full of undistinguishable young women and crimson tennis heroes. All this belonged to a phase he had passed too long ago for a trace of charm to linger, and yet too recently for any reminiscent sympathy.

Ruth Chantry showed herself as glad of meeting Amsden as she was of everything else. Her light hazel eyes were brimming with smiles.

"I am not dancing because I solemnly promised not to get overtired," she explained; Amsden had suggested a waltz as the easiest way of meeting the situation, feeling himself helpless to cope with so much enthusiasm. "It's not that I don't love it!"

"Then you are an invalid?" he asked, taking the chair beside her. She laughed, and showed a brown forearm under the ruffles of her thin white dress.

"Does that look like an invalid? I was one, three years ago," she added. "At least, I had been very ill, and my sister got so in the habit of laying down the law, she can't get over it." There was a trace of impatience in her tone that interested Amsden, who was always curious about human relations that did not touch himself.

"Is your sister here to-night?" he asked with a glance towards the dancers. She laughed.

"Fancy Ellen — out there!" Her delight at the idea brought a smile of sympathy that asked for an explanation. "My sister is a doctor," she said in answer. "She rides about the mountains on a cavalry saddle, with saddle-bags full of medicines and instruments, and the poor women have to hide their beloved patent medicines under the mattress when they hear her coming — they are deadly afraid of her. Everyone is afraid of her," she added resentfully.

"Is she so stern?" Amsden asked. The picture had appealed to him.

"Oh, no, not stern at all — very calm and kind and firm and fine and just." Her vivid face had clouded. "Don't you think that superiority frightens people more than anything else?"

"I think it makes them very cross," he said with amused understanding. She expanded delightedly.

"Only one can't admit it; it sounds so small and mean!" she exclaimed. And so there was a secret between them already. "Don't you hate to be big and just and broad-minded?"

"I never tried." It was pleasant to humour her, and see the satisfaction well up in her hazel eyes.

"How nice! I am always trying — like the frog who tried to swell up into an ox. He didn't really want to be an ox, I am sure, but his family expected it of him."

"Might one not be a very modest ox who mistook himself for a frog?"

She shook her head. "Oh, no. I was born with all the comfortable little feminine vices — I am vain, you know, and jealous, and petty, and unreasonable, and cowardly, and I have been shamed out of showing them all my life. You don't know how horrid it is to be high-minded every day!"

This burst of confidence was so earnest that Amsden was moved to laughter. "I can't imagine anything more awful," he admitted, whereupon she laughed too.

Christine O'Hara paused in front of them, histrionically pouting. Christine would have defined feelings as facial expressions designed to add piquancy to conversation — if she had been given to definitions.

"He never laughs when he is with me," she complained. "How did you make him, Ruth?"

Ruth reflected. "Why, I told him the tragedy of my life," she decided.

"Well, I dare say that is awfully funny," said Christine. She had taken Amsden's chair and he stood in front of them, free to escape, yet for once in no hurry to take advantage of it. "But I have a tragedy that is funnier yet. We are going to be one man short on our drive to-morrow. I don't suppose you would come," she added to Amsden.

"Why not ask me and see?"

Christine asked him with elaborate formality, but Ruth Chantry smiled up at him like a happy little girl. Such enthusiasm was perhaps vaguely repelling in a young woman clearly out of her teens; but Amsden had forgotten that.

II

PHILIP AMSDEN had gone to the tennis tournament at San Rafael because he was tired of being told that he was overworking. Of course he was; he did not need outside advice to know that. A young architect in a big city is inevitably overworking if he can claim such a position as Amsden had reached at thirty-three. He was not an enthusiast at life, but success, worldly and artistic, had seemed to him, as he put it, "worth the trouble," and he had aimed towards this with quiet singleness of purpose. This deliberate choice, excluding many elements inevitable to the lives of the men about him, was beginning gradually to enclose him in a sort of shell which might in time become one and inseparable with the man himself; as yet he was half indifferently conforming to what the world demanded of him. A sincere respect for his art and an amused contempt for the conditions to worldly success made the outer conforming comparatively easy, and, as yet, little harmful; his spirit was still that of one who lends himself for an evening to a children's party. This implies, and quite truthfully, a certain conceit. Amsden felt himself civilized above his community. It was definitely within his intentions, however, that the community should not be unpleasantly conscious of the fact, with the result that he was usually described as a "quiet, likeable sort of a chap," or "a pleasant fellow to have round." Of women younger than himself he saw little, for a sharp experience three years before had left him with several generalizations, the chief being that love is a power vastly exaggerated by novelists. The memory of his brief, inglorious engagement could still make him wince. It had been a nightmare of analysis, for, instead of finding love by forgetting it, they had cornered the poor butterfly at the first flutter and investigated it conscientiously until not a stirring of its wings survived and they were left with only their empty questions between them. "Do you love me?" is the natural song of the true lover, but "Do I love you?" is a blight and an enemy to joy. When the end came, they had kissed each other very sadly and gone home to tears and bitterness; and both had waked up the next morning vastly relieved. So had ended the first lesson, and Amsden had gone in for success, believing that he had done with illusions. Personally he was grave, slight and scholarly looking, with the refining mark of a long New England ancestry in his face, tempered by some sturdier reflection of his California heritage. He was not robust, but his grey eyes behind his glasses had a look of quiet strength. It was easy to fancy Amsden living well into the eighties with all his senses intact.

Monday morning he was back at his San Francisco office, but obviously not overworking. A mood of pleasant idleness seemed to have come back with him. The fact that he was to dine that night at the O'Haras' would usually have depressed him, but to-day it seemed an agreeable prospect. Pictures of Ruth Chantry, floating before his vision, filled him with paternal kindliness. She had a curious wet shine in her eyes when she laughed, and her almost colorless hair looked as if it would cling to one's finger like a baby's. Amsden smiled indulgently at the recollection, tipping back from his work-table with his hands in his pockets. There was a pleasant lack of intellectual effort in talking to her. He had come back from that long driving trip as unwearied as if his companion had been a merry little dog. The exhausting researches into life and character that had been a part of his brief engagement had left Amsden with a deep antipathy to intimate feminine conversation. Those hours of feverish analysis, the endless letters of minute explanation, could oppress him even yet with the burden of their weary futility. They had not taught him to think less, for he was essentially of those who wonder at this world until they die; but they had left a mental nausea for intensity, so that his chosen companions of the past few years had been practical men of affairs or sports, and two little nieces who could be made entirely happy by being abruptly turned upside down, or having ten-cent pieces dropped down their backs to be gloriously jumped out. Ruth Chantry's demands did not seem much more complicated.

Amsden came into the O'Hara drawing-room, top-

heavy with the sombre grandeur of the black-walnut-
and-cornice period, to find the two girls absorbed in
putting together a cut-out picture from a Sunday
paper. Christine was fond of being discovered at
some naïve occupation. She could scarcely spare
attention for a nod to her guest, but Ruth frankly
deserted and sat beaming at Amsden, while Mr. O'Hara
declaimed at him from the hearth-rug on the blunders
and stupidities of architects, and Mrs. O'Hara nervously wished he wouldn't. Mrs. O'Hara entertained
in a constant tremour lest somebody should not like
something that was said, and hovered about the conversation of her husband and daughter much as the
wet-sponge deputy hovers about the Christmas tree at
an infant festival. Amsden smiled reassuringly at her
soothing interjections.

"Oh, architects are used to being attacked, Mrs.
O'Hara," he said. "We don't mind so long as you
can't do without us."

"And sometimes we can that," broke in Mr. O'Hara.
"Miss Ruth, didn't your sister do all her own archi-
tecting for that house of yours up by Gallop?"

"And a good deal of the building, too," said Ruth.
"Ellen has a passion for climbing on beams and pound-
ing nails. She takes it all out that way."

"Takes what all out?" asked Amsden, more to see
her grow vivid with the ardour of explanation than in
curiosity for her answer.

"Oh, exuberance, you know. When other people
would be excited or joyous or angry all over, Ellen

seems to get it just in her right arm, and she smashes it all down into a nail without moving a muscle anywhere else." The shine that had haunted Amsden all day was already in her face. "Ellen never goes to pieces over things, you know. I think she is made of one solid piece, while I am a million little blocks."

"Put together with very bad mucilage," added Christine, whose absorption in her cut-out picture had died for lack of notice.

"Put together with fire and dew," thought Amsden with an inexplicable impulse of pity.

"Well, Ellen Chantry is a fine girl," declared Mr. O'Hara. "I'll not say I'd be wanting a lady doctor about me —" Mrs. O'Hara looked hasty apology at Ruth — "but it's a fine sight to see a woman with brains who doesn't spend her whole time over trash and parties, like Christine here. Well, Mr. Wallace, we are glad to see you, heartily glad; we're all getting savage with hunger."

"Indeed, Mr. Wallace, dinner has only just been announced," urged poor Mrs. O'Hara.

Mr. Wallace, a kindly young man of the fat-boy order, who was always called on when one more man was needed, and who always came, laughed his apologies and took his place happily by Christine, whom he considered "a great old sport." The two kept the talk in their hands during dinner, and Amsden, who had no personal misadventures to relate and little love of "guying," would have found it unrelievedly dull if

Ruth Chantry, beside him, had not been so exquisitely happy. She laughed till her eyes were little hazel slits of light, giving herself up whole-heartedly to the gaiety of the hour, yet without once slipping into silliness. Her spirit infected them all.

When Mrs. O'Hara rose, Ruth clung to the sides of her chair and looked pleadingly at her host.

"Oh, don't make us go off alone while you smoke!" she begged. "Just think, this is my last night. Please let me stay!" They laughed at her earnestness and settled back in their chairs.

"That you shall, my dear!" Mr. O'Hara patted her hand. "And why shouldn't you stay another week with us?"

Ruth shook her head. "If you knew the struggle I had to get this week! And it does make it hard for Ellen," she added conscientiously. "Ying won't answer the telephone, so there is no one to take messages when she is off. And as Ellen is the only doctor in or near Gallop who is always sober —" She broke off to smile at the general laugh.

"You're a good girl," commented Mr. O'Hara.

"Well, Christine is coming up to spend August; I have that ahead," said Ruth contentedly.

"I am going to take my vacation in August," suggested Wallace. "Why can't I come, too? I could put up somewhere near you, couldn't I?"

"Oh, Will, how perfectly lovely!" exclaimed Christine.

"And there is Mrs. Dorn not a quarter of a mile

away — she will make you as comfortable!" said Ruth, excitedly. "Do you really mean it?"

"Certainly. Say, Amsden, why don't you come, too? It's bully country, and you need a vacation, don't you?"

"Oh, Mr. Amsden, you must!" cried Christine. He turned amusedly to Ruth.

"Shall I?" he asked, not in the least intending it. It was as though the heavens opened and the glory shone through.

"Oh, will you?" came breathlessly. Amsden could have caught her up in his arms and laughed and cried over her, she seemed to him so infinitely young and pathetic.

"Of course I will!" he said quickly.

III

THE stage was nearly empty as it wound up the last mile towards Gallop. Amsden, perched on top, well behind the driver, spread his arms along the back of the seat and gave himself up to the sense of being floated between a new heaven and a new earth, silently rejoicing that a delay in his affairs had forced him to make the trip alone. All about him towered the peaks of the Sierra, cutting sharply into the pool of thin gold left by the sunset. From the mouths of darkly green cañons came breaths of clean, primeval night and the sounds of running water, and down every slope drifted the fragrance of sun-steeped pines, not crowded together in the blurred mass of forests, but standing apart in solitary dignity, each lifting to the sky its separate effort of symmetry and grace. The evening cool deepened, pouring deliciously over his hands and face as a great star splashed out just above the northern peaks. Amsden, his head thrown back, was so merged in the greatness of the earth that his individual life was a forgotten triviality. His spirit seemed to rise and hover above an oblivious body, the city and the quest of success were as remote as his childhood. He had not taken a vacation for three years, and had

14

almost reached the dangerous point of not desiring
one: the revulsion from city limitations left him buoyant, as though he had just escaped some bodily danger.
The night was like a purifying river rushing through
him. So deep was his absorption that he did not notice
the stopping of the stage, and felt a shock of disappointment, childish in its intensity, as he realized that
someone had mounted to the seat beside him. He
moved over, not taking his eyes from the miracle overhead; but the enchantment was broken, and he was,
after all, only a tired traveller on top of a stage-coach.
He straightened up with a stretch and a sigh, and
looked at his companion, a man of lean middle-age,
with grey hair floating above his coat collar, humorously plain, but with something likeable in his eccentric
features, palely freckled, and in the grave friendliness
of the little nondescript eyes. Amsden felt a primitive
desire to have this man like him.

"Nice night, isn't it?" he said, as their glance met.
The man considered a moment.

"Well, yes, sir, I reckon it's a nice night down here
on top of a comfortable stage-coach, with nothing to
make trouble," he said, a faint southern cadence giving
his voice an unexpected warmth. "Up there where
I've been," he dipped his head towards the slope they
were leaving, "it ain't so nice. I've been burying a
child — little girl of five. Her folks waited thirteen
years for her, and they won't get another. Pretty
rough!" He passed his hand heavily over his forehead and eyes, then turned to Amsden with subdued

intensity. "I'm a preacher, after a fashion, but I don't know any comfort that takes hold in an hour like this. Do you?"

"No," said Amsden, with a startled sense that life up here might be as near and naked as the great blazing stars that seemed to hang close above their heads.

"Pretty soon they'll see that it was the Lord's will, and not anyone's fault," the man went on, staring absently before him. "But just now —" he broke off with a quick sigh. "Life in the mountains is all like that, somehow. Trouble never gets very far off. Why don't more people come and try to help?"

The thought of Ruth Chantry, whose girlhood was being sacrificed to her sister's missionary impulse, checked Amsden's rising sympathy.

"Most people have obligations somewhere else," he said slowly. "The first debt is to the happiness of our own people. One has no right to sacrifice a mother or a sister — not to a thousand mountaineers."

The man turned to him eagerly. "Not if the mother or the sister is worth more to the world — that's right, sir. You've got to get off and look at these things from a distance. Where's the biggest value? You decide that the best way you can, and then go ahead. Your mother might be worth more to humanity than all the women in the Sierras put together: then you stick by her life and minister to it as long as you live. That's your job."

"But suppose the value were not to humanity, but to her and to me and to one or two others," Amsden was beginning in vigorous protest when a shout and a waving hat from the road brought the stage to a creaking halt.

"Hello!" called the boyish voice of Will Wallace from the dimness. "Stand and deliver! You up there, Amsden?"

"Hello!" Amsden rose, kicking a stiff knee. "How are you, Wallace? Is this where I get down?"

"Yes. Leave your luggage. Say, driver, put his bag off at Mrs. Dorn's gate, will you? They will be watching for it. You are to come up to the cabin for supper," he added, as Amsden dropped in the road beside him. "Bet you're ready for it. Hold up till I light this lantern: you'll need it if you don't know the trail. I lost five square feet of skin before I got over being a tenderfoot." Amsden laughed, feeling suddenly very jovial and human, and accepted the lantern. As the stage lumbered off, he waved to the solitary figure on top.

"Good-night! See you again, I hope," he called.

"Good-night, sir. I hope so," came the hearty answer.

Wallace led the way up a winding trail, free from underbrush, but made treacherous by smooth slabs and jutting ledges of rock. Absolute night seemed to have shut down about them since the lighting of the lantern. Wallace showed an astonishing nimbleness.

"The dark here is of the best quality black velvet; none of your flimsy, semi-transparent stuffs," he explained. "It's a great old place — bully. You'll like

17

it. You want to get in the good graces of Ying, first thing you do; then you're all right. Can't he cook!"

"But surely those two girls don't live here alone with a Chinaman?" Amsden asked.

"Oh, Ying brought 'em up. He has been in the family thirty years — beats any guardian angel you ever saw for devotion and chaperonage." Wallace chuckled at some recollection. "Besides, Ellen Chantry would be equal to six Chinamen," he added. "She's off most of the time, doctoring — and you won't be so awful sorry."

"Why?" Amsden was becoming decidedly curious about Mrs. Roderick.

"Oh, I can hit it off with her all right. (Look out for this rock here — it has got some of my left shin on it yet.) Ellen's a nice, quiet, sensible sort of girl, so far as I can see. But she shuts the others up, somehow. We never get really howling when she's around, don't you know? And then it is pretty mean, the way she keeps Ruth glued up here summer and winter. I guess she's sort of selfish. There, see that light up ahead, to the right? That's the cabin. Bet you're glad." And he lifted a shrill "Whoo-oo!" that went echoing off among the cañons. A door opened, showing a glowing square of light, and a feminine "Whoo-oo!" answered. A few minutes later Amsden stood blinking in the doorway of a big, low-ceilinged room, rosy with firelight, and Ruth Chantry was welcoming him as a prisoner might welcome deliverance.

"You did come, after all! And I have worried about it day and night," she cried.

"But of course I came," he said in unmistakable satisfaction.

Any tired traveller must have felt the charm of the place. Evidently this was literally a living-room, for at one end stood a supper table, across a corner hung a hammock piled with red cushions, low bookcases full of pleasantly worn volumes lined the wall on either side of the arched fireplace, and against the opposite wall a staircase mounted to the rooms above. The walls were of redwood, set in wide panels and wholly free from ornament except for brass sconces holding candles; the chimney looked a rough pile of rounded and irregular stones, the rugs were skins of animals. Christine O'Hara, with a blue-checked apron over her white dress and the firelight making a halo of her light red curls, was setting the table with a busy-house-wife air, too domestic and important to give more than a passing handshake to the newcomer, though her energy flagged visibly when Wallace led him off down a porch and through a side door and offered him the freedom of a civilized bath tub.

"Better grab your chance," he suggested. "At Mrs. Dorn's you'll have to wash in a doll's tea-set. We won't have supper till Ellen gets in, anyway."

Amsden accepted the offer gratefully, and twenty minutes later came out with renewed self-respect, pausing on the porch for a deep breath of the sharp, aromatic night. A sound of hoofs drew his eyes to the road that passed beneath him to a rough outbuilding. As his sight adjusted to the dark, he saw a tired horse with drooping head and a rider who sat with hanging reins, her face hidden under a felt brim, but her whole attitude showing abstraction. The horse paused at the shed door, but she did not dismount until a reproachful whinney roused her. Then she swung herself down from her masculine saddle, patting his neck as though in apology, and called:

"Ying!" A wire door somewhere in the rear creaked open.

"Al'light! You put him inside — I come plesently," answered a voice in the imperative accents of Americanized China. "You hurly up now — supper all get spoiled."

Woman and horse vanished obediently into the shed and Amsden turned to the living-room.

"Evidently that is the superior Ellen," was his comment.

Christine had told him what the world knew about Ellen. She had perhaps good right to be unlike others. Nine years before she had stood at a window and seen her husband instantly killed by a car. Her child had been born in the hour of his funeral, its own tiny funeral following a week later. When it was time for Ellen to emerge again, people found that she had no intention of emerging, but was wholly absorbed in studying medicine. It was natural that such an experience had left her a little queer, and they were glad that the poor girl had something to take her thoughts. When she began to practise, they even sent for her to attend their protégés or their maids — and were a little shocked that she came in blue serge rather than in the permissible black and white. But the maids and the protégés flourished, and the profession began to take Dr. Roderick so seriously that even her old friends were impressed. She seemed actually about to achieve a career when Ruth's serious illness made a trip to the mountains advisable. There she had taken up work among the mountaineers, and had become so absorbed in it that she could not be dragged back to civilization even for a day.

"At least, Ruth believes that is why she stays," Christine added. "I am not so sure! There is something queer about it."

Ruth, poor girl, starving for young life, was forced to stay on there year after year. Christine had visited her every summer, but when a return visit was suggested, Ellen always found means to prevent it, not caring, doubtless, to be left up there alone. Of course Ellen did a great deal of good — outside her home.

"Missionaries never do consider their families," Christine ended indignantly. "Someone ought to interfere. Ruth can't do it herself because — oh, well, if you knew Ellen! But someone ought to."

And Amsden quite agreed that someone ought. It was nothing to him personally; he was simply moved by the abstract principle that anyone who could be made happy as easily as Ruth Chantry, should be made happy.

Mrs. Roderick was something of a surprise when she came into the living-room a little later. Her thin, white gown was of an antiquated simplicity, but there was about it, or her, a distinction that all Christine's insertion and embroidery could not achieve. Her hair had the blond shininess of stubble in the sun, parting smooth and straight over a wide, sunburned forehead and serene grey eyes; nose and chin were roughly modelled, but the mouth had been exquisitely and delicately finished, and the lips rested together without a tremour of self-consciousness or a pinch of self-concealment. She was not large, but a splendid Saxon strength showed in her shoulders and arms and throat. It occurred to Amsden as she came towards him that she would have made a magnificent figurehead for a Viking ship.

"But it is a heavy face, beside Ruth's," he decided instantly.

Her welcome was courteous but not especially cordial: not cordial at all, he decided presently, finding her eyes fixed on him unsmilingly as he looked up laughing from some naïveté of Ruth's. He felt that he was being "lumped," as he expressed it, with Wallace and Christine O'Hara, and coolly resolved that if Ellen had not discernment to recognize the difference, he would not help her out. The others had never known him "so nice and jolly" as he was at that first supper. Yet what Wallace had said was true: Ellen Chantry's presence spread an impalpable constraint. Christine laughed artificially, was defiant in her little arts and graces, over-pouting and over-gleeful. Ruth's gaiety was robbed of its shine, and Amsden, feeling a subdued apprehension in her, realized that she was instinctively trying to act as a screen between her friends and her sister's judgment. The dimming of her spirits angered him. What right had this calm, blond woman to dominate a tableful of independent beings! He devoted himself exclusively to Ruth until the light was relit.

If Ellen depressed them, it was quite evident that something depressed her. She took part — very simply and pleasantly, it must be admitted — when she had to, but seemed relieved when they left her to eat her supper in peace. It was an exceedingly good supper. Wallace watched Ying bear away the empty dishes with a sigh of contentment.

"I wish Ying could give Mrs. Dorn a lesson or two in cooking," he said. "She means awfully well — but when she fries chops, she fries them for keeps: you could shingle the roof with them. And I'm sure she makes her hot cakes out of Rory's saddle blankets."

"Rory?" queried Amsden.

"Yes, Rory Dorn: her mother named her Aurora," Wallace explained. "She thought it went so lovely with Dorn."

"She breaks horses for her living," Ruth added. "She is great fun, the only real companion I have up here."

"I met a strange character on the stage to-night,"

said Amsden, "a preacher of some sort: queer, lanky chap, but very likeable."

"Oh, Mr. Gilfillan;" Ellen turned to him with real interest. "He is a fine man. I don't know what I should have done without him this past year." Christine O'Hara had looked up with compressed lips.

"I hope to see him again," Amsden went on. "We had begun an interesting discussion — the rights of the missionary spirit over family obligations. We did not agree in the least, but I liked him." His tone was wholly without personal intention, and his eyes met Ellen's with no faintest acknowledgment of a coming struggle. Yet his heart had a quickened beat as he dropped sugar in his coffee.

"Well, I think one's family ought to count before everything," Christine began defiantly, but lost courage in the ensuing pause and jumped up. "I have sworn off on coffee," she exclaimed. "Let's have some music." She opened the piano, and began to play with dashing inaccuracy. Catching Ruth's eye, she signalled her to follow, and under cover of a rattling march, demanded:

"Who is this Mr. Gilfillan?"

"Oh, a broken-down minister — Methodist or Baptist, or some such queer kind. He came to Gallop for his health last fall, and now he is as daffy about the mountain people as Ellen is. He saves their souls or mends their roofs, just as it happens. He takes it very seriously, you know — comes up to 'consult' with Ellen about twice a day."

Christine looked skeptical. "Perhaps they're in love," she suggested.

"Chris-tine! He says 'ain't' and 'tasty,' and he wears a beard — a little beard under his chin!"

"Oh!" It was a note of apology, but Christine's eyes were still speculative.

"How old a man is he?" she asked presently.

"I don't know — forty, fifty;" Ruth's tone was thoroughly indifferent.

"Well, I should like to know why she stays, just the same," said Christine, as Wallace joined them, leaving Amsden alone at the table with Ellen Chantry.

"Don't wait for me. I always linger over my coffee," she said with calm and courteous indifference. Amsden felt a flash of resentment. Why should she assume that he had nothing whatever to give her? Was it because he came as Ruth's friend? Oh, she was superior, abominably so. He had no feeling on his own account, knowing that he could prove his value if he cared to; his resentment was all for the slight to Ruth — dear, fine and sensitive spirit, whom this woman of coarser fibre could not possibly appreciate. Some of the ancient stubbornness of his New England forebears showed in his grave and scholarly face as he settled more firmly in his chair. To Ruth Chantry, over by the piano, a sense of his strength came at that minute like a shock of pain. She could have fallen on her knees by his chair, crying out, "Be kind to me! Never be angry with me!" His eyeglasses, the firmly shut, reserved mouth, the lines of his coat on his lean, muscular shoulders, were suddenly become precious, endowed with an appeal no one could miss. She glanced with quick jealousy at Ellen, but was reassured by her evident absorption in her coffee and her thoughts.

Amsden presently broke in on this absorption.

"It has been a great pleasure to know your sister, Mrs. Roderick," he said in the tone of one who expects cordial assent. "She is a very unusual girl." There was a hint of surprise in Ellen's face, quickly banished.

"I think she is a very pretty girl," she said assentingly.

"She is so alive, so joyous," he went on. "Most of us have the spirit civilized out of us — there is something primeval in her capacity for happiness. It makes one long to give her everything she wants."

"That is scarcely the way to keep people happy, is it?" Ellen asked after a slight pause.

"Oh, life denies us so much; I don't believe we need to deny and discipline each other especially, do you?"

"I suppose we are sometimes the instruments through which life does its disciplining, the whip with which it beats its victim," she suggested, a hint of resentment in her voice, to Amsden's secret satisfaction.

"Isn't that rather a dangerous doctrine?" he asked. "It would be a selfish person's excuse for riding over another, wouldn't it?"

"Possibly — if you take it that way," she answered, with a faint shrug. "General doctrines have to be fitted to the weakest link in the chain; but the stronger can have their mental reservations, I suppose — we can trust ourselves with dangerous creeds."

"Yes, if we are willing and able to justify them. When we are a law unto ourselves, we lay ourselves open to challenge." Amsden looked squarely into her eyes. "Don't you agree with me?"

Her serene face was impenetrable. "No, I don't think I do," she said. "The challenge would have to come from a very high authority before I, for one, would —"

"Ellen! Don't you hear the telephone?" Ruth's voice broke in impatiently, to Amsden's disappointment. He was keenly enjoying the encounter. Mrs. Roderick left the room and her voice could be heard through the door, direct and business-like. In a few moments she came back to say good-night.

"I am called out," she explained.

"Oh, don't go," said Wallace, good-naturedly. "Say you have a patient here and can't leave." Amsden had risen.

"It is so very dark — isn't there some way in which I can go with you?" he asked, honestly concerned.

"Oh, I am used to it," she said indifferently. Her fingers were already at her belt buckle as she left the room.

"Ellen really likes going about; she would rather do that than be frivolous with us," Ruth assured him. "Besides, she is blue to-night. She has just lost a patient, some child she was treating; that always upsets her."

Presently they heard the bang of the barn door and a horse's tread under the window. Christine O'Hara sprang up from the piano stool.

"Now let's have some fun," she exclaimed.

IV

Ruth came down the stairs the next morning singing, though the song stopped when she saw Ellen at the breakfast table below. Ellen looked up pleasantly.

"Did you sleep?" she asked with a keen glance at her sister's face.

"Of course. Why not?"

"I didn't know but that so much company would be too stimulating," said Ellen, pacifically, pouring out her coffee.

"I am not so childishly excitable as you always seem to think;" Ruth spoke evenly, without open resentment. "I enjoy my friends, of course; anyone would whose life was completely cut off from them."

"Especially a person like you, whose friends are so very fond of her," assented Ellen. "Would Christine like her breakfast in bed?"

Ruth unbent a little. "Oh, no; she is dressing. What did you think of Mr. Amsden?" she added, a trifle defiantly. Ellen hesitated.

"Why, he seemed to me — an interesting personality," she said. "He has a certain distinction; I don't know whether it is his mind or his nice, clean-cut features. He is clever, isn't he?"

"Very; and one of the best architects in the city. He is very good family, too."

"Yes, I think one feels that," Ellen admitted. "Is he perhaps — a little conceited?" Ruth's face clouded instantly.

"I am sure I have not found him so. But then I am not especially discerning — I am glad to say."

Ellen looked discouraged. "Well, you know him better than I," she apologized, rising. "It was only an impression. I will tell Ying to make a fresh omelette for Christine."

Ruth, left alone, stared unseeingly at the morning beauty outside.

"She is always in the right, and always patient and magnanimous — and I am always nasty," she muttered. "Oh, I hate living with her, I want to go!" There were tears in her eyes, but she blinked them away as Ellen came back. The latter wore a khaki skirt that could be adapted to cross-saddle riding by unfastening a row of buttons, and she had put on a loose khaki coat over her white shirt-waist. There was power, a rough beauty even, in her very lack of grace as she stood pinning a felt campaign hat over the smooth straw-shine of her heavy hair. Ruth, conscious of it, felt a pang of apprehension as she saw two masculine figures coming up the trail. Anyone must see that Ellen was wonderful — oh, why couldn't the woman go, if she was going, and not stand there like an embodiment of vigour and simplicity, beside which others must inevitably shrink to triviality!

"Go, go, *go*," beat through her thoughts as she leaned back impassively, helpless before the laws of civilized demeanour.

"I have not much to do this morning," said the unconscious Ellen. "I shall be back early. You needn't bother about the telephone; I doubt if anybody rings up."

"We are all going for a walk;" Ruth's tone showed that she had had no intention of bothering about the telephone. The men were mounting steadily. Ellen turned to go, then came back.

"Do be a little careful, Ruth," she urged. "You know how done up you were when you came back from the city. I want you to be out of doors all you can, but do take it easy. Remember that you have always had more spirit than strength."

"Very well, I will;" anything to get rid of her. Ellen went to the door, then paused.

"They are coming now, your visitors," she said. "I think I had better wait and say good-morning to them." Ruth made no answer. It seemed to Amsden, as he came in, that her smile had a tremulous quality.

"Poor little soul, always 'way up or 'way down," he thought. Ellen's vigorous calm seemed unfeeling, by contrast. Ruth, conscious of approval, expanded happily, though she was dimly aware that the danger was only put off.

"He has not discovered her yet," would have been her thought if she had stopped to analyze. She felt a glow of satisfaction that both men, after speaking to

Ellen, came and dropped down by her, and was magnanimous enough to keep her eyes from her sister, lest she should seem to triumph. The latter bore her humiliation with stoic cheerfulness, and even followed them across, a thing Ruth could never have done. She made the coffee pot her excuse, touching it experimentally with her palm.

"It couldn't be hotter," she said. "Won't you have a cup? I am sure Mrs. Dorn's coffee isn't as good as Ying's." They accepted gratefully.

"Mrs. Dorn's coffee is no rich, brown, nourishing drink," said Wallace, with a sigh. "It is an evil black, and so strong it tips the cup over if you aren't careful. She told me that she paid fifteen cents a pound for it, and that it had a lot more flavour than coffee that cost twice as much. She's dead right — it has."

"Perhaps she concentrates on it too hard," Ruth suggested. "You know she is a psychic? When Rory's horses are too unruly, she sits at the window and concentrates on them — and then Rory always conquers."

"That's a mother's tender care with modern improvements," said Wallace.

"Her grandmother would have sat at the window and prayed," Amsden added. Ellen turned to him interestedly.

"Which method should you prefer?"

"I think I should back Rory's young muscles and lower jaw. I saw them both at work this morning."

"At breakfast?" queried Ruth.

32

"Oh, we breakfast by ourselves," put in Wallace. "We get coffee and mush, then, fifteen minutes later, the cream and sugar come with the meat, and when everything else is eaten, we get petrified slabs of toast. Rory hovers about and soothes us as she would a skittish horse. She patted my neck yesterday — honestly."

"What did you do?" asked Ruth.

"I'd hate to tell you. Hello, Ying. Did you make that omelette for me?" Ying grinned.

"Maybe Miss Clistine let you have it," he suggested, putting a tiny and perfect omelette at Christine's place.

"No, she won't!" called the latter's voice from the stairs, and Christine came rushing down in farcical alarm. Ellen rose.

"I must be off," she announced.

"Why not come for a walk with us?" asked the kindly Wallace. Ellen hesitated with a glance towards Ruth; but her eyes were averted, her lips compressed in a disapproving line.

"No, I must not cut work this morning, I am afraid," said Ellen. A few moments later Amsden saw her ride below the window, and it occurred to him that her serene face was sad when she was alone. He stared after her, wondering how far she had outgrown that tragedy of nine years ago.

"Mr. Amsden has scarcely said a word this morning," declared Ruth, a shade of impatience in her voice. "Is he one of those silent-till-noon persons?"

"He's a queer sort of a duck. I don't make him out so very well," said Wallace.

"Oh, I read him like a book," Christine asserted. "What puzzles you?"

Wallace considered, Amsden looking on in amused gravity.

"Well, when you see him from across the room, he looks sort of stuck-up; but when you go over to punch him for it, you find he's a darned nice chap, nothing lofty about him. You go off pleased and friendly, and then, next time you glance across, hanged if he doesn't look just as stuck-up as ever!"

Ruth had never seen Amsden laugh so thoroughly; but he said nothing.

"What you see is just his glasses and his cameo profile, and a sort of New England repression about him," Christine explained. "All you have to do is to stay on the same side of the room with him. That wouldn't be so hard!" she added with a glance of mock coyness at Amsden.

"Wow, Christine!" exclaimed Wallace. "If you hit me with a glance like that, I'd never be the same man again."

"Well, that might not be a bad thing," Christine returned, a species of repartee that gave Wallace unbounded delight.

The morning was half gone before they started, pausing first on the porch before a view that silenced even Wallace for a moment. The cabin clung to a comparatively open hillside, the mighty tents of the

Sierra towering about them like a giant encampment, encircling a gentle stretch of vivid green meadow far below. To the south, at the mouth of a winding cañon, lay the town of Gallop, started by miners, but long ago handed over to lumbermen and stock-raisers. A trail dropped abruptly from the cabin to the stage road beneath, while a rough road wound down more gradually towards the town, half a mile away. On the distant slopes sharp eyes could see occasional signs of human habitation, the brown dot of a cabin or a curl of smoke.

"Oh, but it must be lonely here in winter," Amsden exclaimed, thinking only of those distant dots. Ruth turned to him hotly.

"You don't know, you have no conception — there is no such loneliness in the world!" she said in a low tone. The other two had gone on ahead.

"Why don't you just walk out of it?"

"What could I do? I have no other home."

"Aren't the O'Haras always begging for a long visit?"

"Yes, but —" she hesitated, then spoke impetuously, "don't you see that that takes clothes? I couldn't lead their life in denim and flannel. And I have no money. Ellen knows I can't accept without clothes, and she doesn't offer them to me; and I won't ask her. So, you see, it is hopeless."

"It is very hard," said Amsden, thoughtfully. "Why can't I give them to you?"

She laughed with suddenly restored gaiety. "Will you?"

"Of course. I have plenty of money. How many do you want?"

"Let me see: I think five gowns would do, and an evening cloak, and two hats — or three? Could you afford three?"

"I think so. I should like a black velvet one on your hair. Are they — 'worn'?"

"Yes, always. Oh, wouldn't it be fun!" She broke into a little skip.

"Why on earth shouldn't I give that child five hundred dollars, if I want to?" was Amsden's thought as he followed. "It is a very stupid world." Whatever Ruth's thoughts were, her hazel eyes were brimming with light.

All Gallop seemed to be out on the sidewalk this morning, and Amsden thought something must have happened, until Ruth explained to him that this was Gallop's perennial state. The main street of the little town had made a sincere effort to present a civilized appearance. The half story was prolonged to seem a whole story by flaring sham fronts, occasional bursts of yellow or pea-green paint vied with whitewash and blackening pine, and electric lights of intermittent habits lighted the streets by night. Close by ran the swift flood of Juniper Creek, the logs bobbing at its edges offering ceaseless temptation to boys and terror to mothers. In the soft dust of the road dogs curled in placid sleep, occasionally dragging themselves resentfully out of the way of some unaccommodating cart. Mountain horses nibbled restlessly at the hitching-posts while their masters joined the sidewalk discussion.

It seemed to Amsden that the rough groups fell into silence at their approach, and that the silence was not a friendly one; once he caught a flash of open hostility in the eyes of a woman who turned to stare at them. Ruth was entirely unconcerned, and he tried to think it merely the natural animosity of the free-born American towards his "betters" — he used the word in quotation marks, even in his most secret thoughts. He would have liked nothing better than to get on friendly terms with these hulking mountaineers, clanking their spurs in and out of the general store. While Christine and Ruth were buying striped candy and weighing each other, he paused beside a man who was, oddly enough, buying some coarse black material not unlike crape. The gloomy, handsome face under a shock of black hair appealed to him.

"This is a busy town you have here," he said, leaning against the counter. "About how many inhabitants are there?"

The man looked at him, turned back and counted his change, sliding it deliberately into a pocket, took up the parcel, gave him another cool look and walked away. A boy lounging near grinned. Amsden felt the colour rise as it had not in ten years, and he started impetuously after the man.

"Say, better let him alone," interposed the boy, with an emphasis that made Amsden pause. "That's the father."

"The father? What father?" he asked sharply.

"It's Ned Spaulding," explained the boy, as though that ought to enlighten anybody.

Christine came fluttering across, a stick of candy in each hand.

"What is it? What is it? Me see, too. Is anything happening?"

"Nothing, whatever," said Amsden, shortly. "Let's get out of this," he added. "Can't we go into the woods somewhere?"

Ruth would have left the town at once, but Christine insisted on exploring the hardware shop, and was with difficulty kept out of the "hotel." It seemed to Amsden that they were meeting hostility on every side in glances and small rudenesses — the blocking of the sidewalk, curt answers to pleasant greetings; but the others noticed nothing, and he tried to argue down the impression as the effect of his own recent snub.

"What father? What did he mean?" he still wondered. Ruth's voice demanded his attention.

"Look, there's the new doctor, Dr. Pocock," she said, nodding to a sign. "Did you know that Ellen has a rival?"

"I hope he gets all her patients away so that she has to go back to the city," said Christine, joyfully, then clapped spread fingers over a scared mouth as a turn of the road disclosed Ellen.

She was standing beside her horse, deep in conversation with a lean, middle-aged man whose floating

38

grey hair and pale freckles identified him as Amsden's friend of the stage-coach. She seemed to be holding forth on some subject, and now and then her clenched hand came down sharply on the saddle. Mr. Gilfillan was listening with bent head, nodding gently at intervals. Ellen glanced at them unseeingly and paid no attention to their greetings.

"Well, how is that for a cut!" exclaimed Wallace as they passed on. Christine O'Hara narrowed her eyes.

"Mr. Gilfillan seems to be an absorbing person," she said with a small laugh.

Amsden glanced back curiously. A single vehement sentence had reached him: "I won't have Ned Spaulding think I am afraid!" Obviously this man Spaulding was making trouble in the town of Gallop.

V

ELLEN'S morning had been a strange one, with the baffling quality of a bad dream. The first manifestation had brought only amusement. Two little girls, who usually beamed shyly at her greeting, and who had been known to watch for her passing with hot, tight handfuls of drooping wild flowers, met her cheerful "Hello!" with a stiff mutter, their eyes lowered, their lips primly set. They seemed to draw their little bodies up and away from her, making a wide circuit into the grass by the road. The full realization of all this did not come to Ellen until she had passed, when she turned in her saddle to look back. They were staring after her, hand in hand, but at her friendly wave they wheeled without response and ran down the road.

"What has struck them? Is it a game?" Ellen wondered.

Her first visit was to the blacksmith, a difficult patient, who in the intervals of his groanings insisted on having in his neighbours for entertainment — not the best regimen for rheumatic fever. His wisp of a wife seemed more nervous and deprecating than usual this morning, though there were no visitors to be hustled out.

"He's so well, dear — you'll hardly need to be coming much more," she stumbled, opening the sick-room door.

Ellen, after studying her patient, had her own views on this subject. She frowned over unexpected developments.

"What have you been doing to yourself?" she demanded. The gentle obstinacy of her patient's face gave no prospect of explanations and his wife was suddenly moved to ransack the closet. Ellen's glance happened to fall on a strange bottle lurking behind a newspaper. Her frown deepened as she picked it up.

"How does this come to be here? I have not prescribed it." Her tone was imperative, and Mrs. Larsen backed reluctantly from the closet floor, rising slowly from her heels.

"Well, you see, dear, the other doctor was doing such wonders, we thought we'd have him just take a look, as you might say. Two heads is sometimes better than one," she explained soothingly. "And he seemed to think that bottle would help the poor man. You wouldn't have me deny him any chanst of easing the pain, dear — you wouldn't, now. It's done him a power of good."

Ellen stood staring at the bottle with compressed lips until the silence grew rather awful; then she put it down and spoke gently, with clearing forehead.

"Come into the other room and we will talk it

over," she said reasonably. She seated herself and made the other sit down while she talked with simple directness.

"Now you know I can't go on with the case if you don't trust me," she ended. "If you give foolish and harmful medicines when my back is turned, don't you see how you undo my work?"

The woman burst into weak tears. "It's him, dear," she sobbed. "He will have the new doctor, and I can't refuse him. You've been awful good to us, dear, and — and he might have been far worse without you. I keep telling him that. But he says it stands to reason that a man doctor knows more than a lady. Not that I'd ever believe a thing against you, dear. Whatever happened, I'd know you done your best. We all make mistakes."

Ellen rose. "I will come back any time you send for me," she said gravely. "Remember that. Goodby." She held out her hand and the woman clasped it fervently, but her face showed her relief.

"Good luck to you, dear," she said.

Ellen's mood was bitter as she mounted her horse. For three years she had given her best to these people, and it was no mean best. And now all her patient skill availed her nothing against the flashy pretensions of an utter stranger. She had met Dr. Pocock shortly after his arrival several weeks before, introduced at the post-office by a grinning townsman as "t'other doctor," and had felt instant dislike of his brisk, rotund person and ever smiling face, the short, fat hand ungloved with impetuous zeal to meet hers. He was very well dressed, from the Gallop standpoint, and the fact gave distinction to the brotherly equality of his manner. A pleased group was clustered about him when she made her escape; he had their names correctly already.

Even in that brief meeting he had made her — and perhaps others — feel that it was courtesy to a woman, not respect for a colleague, that kept his bristling pompadour uncovered. That he had taken over the case of the blacksmith without a word to her declared his professional status, in her mind. His object in settling here was clear enough; there was plenty of money to be made out of the lumbermen and ranchers if one chose to impose on their ignorance. It was not the prospect of a diminished practice that troubled Ellen now, but dread of the humiliating discovery that skill and devotion could be forgotten in the presence of a new and plausible personality.

"Oh, well, the Larsens are silly idiots, anyway," she finally dismissed the matter, turning her horse into a rough wood road — to his evident reluctance, for, once started in that direction, there was no rest until they had mounted to the solitary log cabin of the Flannerys.

Tranquillity came back to Ellen as they zigzagged up the wall of the cañon. Now they were in dense pine woods, the small, fine growth of land that has once been timbered, now they paused in a clearing to look down the broad expanse of the valley beyond, its peaks, a solemn bivouac, cutting sharply into the deep blue above, the smoky violet haze starting out from their shadowed sides as though it might presently roll forth in an active cloud. Passing from the hot sun to the shade was like a plunge into cold water. Ellen threw back her chest to it with a deep breath of satisfaction. She was sorry when a last turn brought her to a dilapidated log cabin.

"How is the boy?" she asked, swinging herself down at the kitchen door where Mrs. Flannery sat in an appalling confusion, the special properties of kitchen, laundry, and nursery piled knee deep about her as she serenely rocked and read a newspaper.

"Fine as a fiddle," was the cheerful answer. "But he's just dropped into a nap — perhaps you'd better not be disturbing him? He don't sleep so awful good."

"I am afraid I shall have to," said Ellen, unsuspectingly. Mrs. Flannery heaved herself out of her rocker and led the way into the adjoining room, where a thin little boy lay in one corner of a huge bed, wide awake, and looking wistfully towards the door. Ellen took the child's temperature, her hand resting on his wrist. She did not look satisfied.

"Are you doing everything I told you to, Mrs. Flannery?" she asked, and repeated her instructions.

"Every last thing, doctor," affirmed the mother. "Sure, I'd know what you say is right. I'd not be neglecting it."

Ellen returned to the kitchen and, finding an inch of space on the table, wrote a prescription.

"I want you to have this filled right away," she said. "Shall I take it down for you?"

"Oh, no, don't you bother." Mrs. Flannery took the paper carefully between a perspiring thumb and forefinger. "One of the boys'll be going right down. They'll see to it."

Ellen repeated her directions and went away, feeling vaguely dissatisfied. Even when she had mounted she did not ride off, but, after a thoughtful moment, turned to the kitchen door. She was just in time to see Mrs. Flannery lift a lid from the stove and drop in the unmistakable piece of white paper she had been holding between thumb and forefinger. There was a red flicker, and she replaced the lid with a satisfied nod.

Ellen backed quietly away and rode off unseen, her mind a tumult of anger and pain and bewilderment. Why she had not turned on Mrs. Flannery and demanded an explanation she could not tell; perhaps because under all her righteous indignation there was a strange clutch of fright. What did it mean? There was something stronger than a rival skill at work, some element of antagonism. She remembered the two little girls who had suddenly rejected her friendliness that morning. What had they heard and believed? She rode slowly down again, too troubled to notice the beauties of the way.

Her next visit led her to a white house on the outskirts of the town, a prim little place with a New England flavour about it, incongruous and even pathetic in contrast with the loose carelessness of its neighbours.

Ellen dismounted with a sense of relief, feeling that here at least the adverse influence must have failed, since Miss Finch had summoned her only the night before. Mr. Finch was overseer of a distant mine, and he had established — cached, he called it — his five motherless children here under the rigid care of a sister from New Hampshire, with a special request that Ellen should keep an eye on them. Little Number Five's attack of the night before had not been serious, and her call was more friendly than professional.

Miss Finch came out on the porch to meet her, and something in her stern, dutiful face made Ellen pause at the foot of the steps.

"Benjy isn't worse?" she asked quickly. Miss Finch shook her head, but she made no motion to open the screen door behind her.

"Dr. Ellen, I ain't one to beat about the bush," she said, her voice as hard as the hands folded over her apron, and yet, like them, a little tremulous. "I don't judge you, one way or the other; though I do say, to let a little girl die when you might have saved her comes pretty close to murder. However, I don't judge. But I'm responsible to my brother for these children, and I can't take no risks with 'em. I can't feel they're goin' to be experimented on and then neglected. I do my duty, and all I ask is that others do theirs."

Ellen, standing beneath her with a foot on the lowest step, had grown pale, but her steady eyes did not falter.

"What child have I allowed to die, Miss Finch?"

"Spaulding's little girl was buried yesterday afternoon. They waited thirteen years before that child come, Dr. Ellen — I guess you don't know what that means! I met Ned Spaulding to the grocery store this morning, and he says, 'If that was a man doctor, I'd kill him like a dog,' he says. I ain't judging —"

"How senseless — how unjust!" Ellen's eyes were blazing. "That child had the best treatment I could give, the most modern. I did my human best. What do they know about it!"

"Well, wasn't you off gallivantin' with a young city feller the day she died, so's they couldn't get you?"

Ellen, after a bewildered instant, remembered that Wallace had ridden a mile or two with her when she started on her rounds that day. She had left her visit to the Spauldings till the last, not knowing of the sudden change for the worse, and had arrived too late. Neither father nor mother had shown any hostility then.

"Oh, it is all so wickedly unfair," she exclaimed, turning away. "I shall go to Ned Spaulding at once and —"

"Dr. Ellen, you better not." Miss Finch came down the steps and followed her to the gate. "What's done is done, and you better keep away from Spaulding for a while. Explanations ain't goin' to help much; he just idolized that child, and I declare to you he's pretty near off his head. 'Tain't goin' to mend matters for you to listen to him now."

"But what right has he to say I mismanaged or neglected that case? What does he know?"

47

"Well, the day after the baby died, he had a talk with the new doctor, Dr. Pocock, and he says —"

"Oh!" Ellen's mouth shut ominously. "Now I understand." She swung herself into the saddle and rode away without another word, leaving Miss Finch looking uncertainly after her.

"Well, anyhow, I'm glad there's a man to call on now," she decided.

Ellen would have gone straight to Dr. Pocock, with no purpose clearer than a boiling need to "have it out," if she had not encountered the calming presence of Mr. Gilfillan. He let her tell the whole tale without interruption, gently nodding his bent head at intervals.

"I know, I know," he reassured her when she had finished. "After I buried the little girl yesterday, Spaulding let it all out to me. Poor fellow, he's half crazy; I said what I could, but I don't reckon he listened much, and he's been talking all over town."

"It is that Pocock," interposed Ellen. "I was just going to him."

"Well, some"; he nodded soothingly. "But so far as I can make out, he hasn't said anything you could take a hold of. If I was you, M'z Roderick, I'd wait a few days — just wait. It don't do to go at things when everybody's red hot."

"But to stay at home and let them say —"

"Well, I'll be here, you know;" the nondescript little eyes seldom looked at her, but now they were raised for an instant, and their simple loyalty made the long, eccentric face beautiful. "I reckon I can say

it better than you could. You just wait," he counselled.

"I suppose you are right," she admitted reluctantly.

"I'll kinder keep an eye on things, and report to
you. Oh, I know it's hard." His hand rubbed and
patted the horse's flank, as though his sympathy must
express itself in some visible form. She took the
hand and held it for a moment.

"You are the best friend anyone ever had," she
said. Her eyes were misty when she rode away.

VI

At six that afternoon Amsden, fresh and clean in white flannel, leaned on the window-ledge of his shaky little room in Mrs. Dorn's cottage, smoking a cigarette and amusedly watching Rory in the yard below. It had been a lazy, out-of-doors day, and he had left Ruth an hour before with no consciousness of having had seven whole hours of her company — as high a compliment as he could have paid a girl in his present state of mind. He was inclined to exaggerate the importance of the fact that she did not tire him; the memory of the last woman he had known well was still oppressively fresh. A pleasant sense of well-being was on him. He enjoyed his own bodily cleanness, his quieted nerves, the consciousness of a good supper and a friendly evening ahead. He was thoroughly glad that he had come.

Down in the yard Rory had tied a nervous young horse to a tree and was cautiously harnessing him into a heavy breaking cart. Half of the colts of the neighbourhood passed through her dexterous hands, hands seemingly endowed with something stronger than mere will power and muscle. Amsden wondered at the way the horse quieted under her touch and voice, dropping from paroxysms of rebellion to trembling meekness. Evidently he was new to the bondage of shafts, for every time they touched his restless flanks he plunged wildly.

"Rory, come in to your supper," called the voice of Mrs. Dorn from within.

"I can't leave. Bring me some out here," Rory called back. They always addressed each other in the shout of command, but were the best possible friends. There was a voluble protest, broken by an abrupt, —

"Oh, quit jawin', Mama, I'm hungry;" and presently Mrs. Dorn appeared carrying a tray, which she set down on the well-curb with a threatening —

"You'll ruin your stomach, Rory Dorn. Why don't you let the beast go and eat your meals like a Christian?"

"He's a wild one," said Rory, biting into a doughnut. "You'll have to concentrate good and plenty on him, Mama, the first time I take him out." There was dry humour in her tone.

"Oh, you can pull fun; but you'd never be alive this day if it hadn't been for me," protested the mother.

"And that's true enough," said Rory, gravely.

"Well, I'm glad you admit it," grumbled Mrs. Dorn unsuspectingly as she turned away. Rory grinned, but said nothing.

The girl perched herself on the well-curb and talked soothingly to her charge as she ate, occasionally springing up to go to his head. She was a graceful little person with a mass of chestnut hair, and a small, shrewd face that would have been pretty but for a slight aggressiveness expressed in the lower jaw. She had a slangy way of using her slim, hard hands, and a hobgoblin grin that were the joy of Wallace's life.

"How soon shall you be driving him?" asked Amsden from above. She looked up and greeted him with a friendly wave of the mutton chop in her right hand.

"Oh, three or four days," she said.

"You won't go alone, surely?"

"Well, yes," said Rory, thoughtfully. "If anyone was fool enough to go with me, they'd be too big a fool to be much help, d'you see?" Amsden laughed.

"Shall I come behind and pick up the pieces?"

"Indeed, the pieces wouldn't be much use to me. You can leave them lie."

"Your friends might like them as souvenirs."

Rory flung the remains of her chop neatly in the path of a prowling cat, who started violently and galloped off, tail streaming askew.

"Old fool — that was a present, not a brickbat," she commented. "I've not the luck with cats I have with horses; they always misunderstand me. Steady, boy, steady! What ails you, now? Friends?" she added, looking up at Amsden. "I haven't got one."

"Why not?"

"Well, I ride about now and again with Ruth Chantry; she's a nice little thing, though she don't know much. There's not another girl here that I'd

52

bother my head about except Dr. Ellen; and she has no time to throw away on me."

"But how about men?"

Rory with two expressive hands pushed away the idea, her face averted, her nose crinkled.

"Now Heaven deliver me! I've no use for the men."

"But why not?"

She wagged her head. "Naw, naw. Not for me. I'd like to see them abolished."

"What's that?" Wallace's head, wet and glistening, appeared at the next window. "Abolish us? Oh, now, Rory, you'd be the first to call us back."

"If you took the horses with you; not otherwise."

"World without men, ah me!" Wallace chanted, unconcernedly plying two hair brushes. He was coatless, and his full-moon face above his fresh white linen looked pleasantly pink and ten years younger than it was. Rory eyed him ironically.

"That's my idea of Heaven," she retorted.

"Oh, come off! Why are you so down on us, anyway?" She considered, with a dawning grin.

"Because you're such fools about us — if you must have it."

"Wow — help! I'm no fool about girls, Rory — honestly."

"There's time yet," was the dubious answer. "But you're making the colt nervous with all this talking. I must have quiet in my schoolroom!" She began to take off the harness with soothing words and strokings, and Amsden's suggestion that it was nearly supper time made Wallace withdraw. When they passed through the yard a few moments later, there was no one in sight but the cat, creeping back upon the bone with the stealthy triumph of one who outwits the enemy.

Ellen Chantry had not appeared that afternoon, except once in distant outline, mending the shed · roof.

"Something has gone wrong," Ruth had surmised, as the sound of echoing blows reached them, and Amsden wondered anew at the incidents of the morning. She was seated by the fireplace when they reached the cabin, looking gentle and feminine in her antiquated white lawn; it was only when she came to meet a difficulty that Amsden saw his figurehead for a Viking ship. He took a low seat beside her in the glow of the newly lighted fire, which was snapping excitedly, its foundation of twigs still curling in crimson effigy. Wallace wandered out for a friendly conversation with Ying, and the two sat in silence, Amsden determined that she should be the first to speak.

Her beginning was perfunctory. "Have you had a pleasant day?"

"Pleasanter than you have, I fancy," he said quietly. He was not going to be kept to mere surfaces with a person like Ellen Chantry. Superior she might be, conceited, selfish; but her importance was unmistakable, and Amsden was impatient for the struggle that lay somewhere ahead of them. The issue might be Ruth's captivity, or it might be some question as yet unraised; all he knew was that he never saw this woman without an overwhelming desire to match his strength against hers.

She gave him a startled look. "Why do you say that?"

"We saw you down in the town this morning talking to your friend the preacher. You were evidently very much disturbed."

She seemed to be waiting for more. "Is that all?" she asked finally.

"Except that last night you were miles away from us all, absorbed in some very serious thoughts. Or was it just that we bored you?"

"I have a good deal on my mind," she said gravely, after a pause. "To-day my work has — troubled me. Last night — I am sorry if I seemed abstracted, but I have a puzzling responsibility. Doctors are apt to have problems," she added with a faint smile.

"And does our being here complicate them?"

"I did not know you and Mr. Wallace were coming until the day he arrived," she said inconsequently. "Ruth — did not think to speak of it."

"Would you rather not have us?" His tone was wholly disinterested.

Her eyes searched his face, then turned back to the fire. She went on hesitatingly, seemingly ignoring his question.

"Mr. Amsden, there is a thing I want to speak to you about. Ruth has been growing very discontented with the life here, and I hope you will try — I mean, please do not make her any more so, if you can help it."

Amsden bent forward to push back a log that had rolled down between the andirons.

"But has she not perhaps a right to discontent?" he asked presently. "She is very young, very alive; what she wants may not seem to you exalted, but isn't it, after all, an honest necessity to her?"

"Perhaps," said Ellen, coldly, and there was silence until the sound of an opening door and Ruth's ecstatic laugh brought an involuntary smile to Amsden's face. He glanced up, to find Ellen's eyes fixed on him with an anxiety that made him suddenly sorry for her.

"I am not going to trouble you or to make anything harder for you," he assured her, rising. "One can't help caring about her happiness, that is all." She stood up, facing him.

"You are not in love with her?"

"Oh, good Lord, no!" His startled sincerity was scarcely courteous, and he sent a glance of apology after it, but she was smiling.

"Then it is all right," she said enigmatically as the girls appeared on the stairs. Ruth looked sharply at the two by the fire, but they were evidently glad of the chance to turn away from each other.

"It is good to see you again, after this long separation," Amsden said, holding out his hand. She took it up gaily.

"Why, you are not changed at all! You look scarcely an hour older. I should have known you instantly, anywhere."

"Oh, don't say you have forgotten me!" burst in

Christine, with a histrionic zeal that smothered the little comedy. Amsden smiled at her tolerantly, and dropped Ruth's hand.

"I think we are all forgetting supper," Ellen said, leading the way to the table. "Where is Will?"

"I heard his voice in the kitchen," began Christine as they took their places. Then she gave a squeal of laughter that made them all turn to the opening door. Wallace strode gravely in, clad in the stiffest and whitest of Chinese garments, a pigtail of black ribbon dangling down his back, a platter held high in front of him.

"You no come so late to supper!" he commanded, with a sharp wag of his head. "Heap too much company here — you send 'em home." He planted the platter before Ellen with a bang — Ying's own gesture on occasions of displeasure. "Supper leady hour ago — all spoiled!" he added. Their laughter doubled when they saw Ying's yellow face grinning in the doorway. Somewhat to Amsden's surprise, Ellen enjoyed it even more than the others. Wallace shuffled out with so good an imitation of Ying's independent swing — head tilted back until the pigtail hung clear of his blouse — that she had tears of laughter on her cheeks. He came back with two covered dishes which he planked down beside the platter.

"You alla time laugh — te he! No good!" he stormed. "Alla same fool. I no cook for you. I go to-night. You get 'nother boy!" With which he dropped into his own place and beamed round the table. "Wouldn't I make a pretty good chink?" he demanded. "Ying, I've got you pushed off the earth." Ying had come in with a dish, grinning sheepishly, and departed as quickly as possible.

"How you dared do it!" Ruth exclaimed. "He might have been furious."

"Oh, we're great pals, Ying and I. He didn't mind." Wallace's easy good nature expected — and generally brought forth — the same quality in others. "People don't get mad as easy as people think," he added confidently out of his experience.

"I'd like to know how you got that particular black ribbon," Christine interposed with a scrutinizing eye on his pigtail. He chuckled.

"I'll never tell."

"Well, you will find people do get mad, if you are not careful. Did you take it off that hat in the hall?"

"I'll put it back, Christine, honestly, just the way it was before. I know exactly how the bows went."

"If you aren't the worst!" was her pouting comment. "Very well, then, you shall retrim it."

After supper they brought a work-basket and the denuded hat and prepared to enjoy his struggles; but he insisted on retreating to the kitchen with the materials and being left alone.

"You will make me nervous, looking," he protested.

They found themselves rather quiet without him — dull, was Christine's version as she sought solace at the piano. Ruth looked at Amsden with happy expectancy, much as his little nieces did when he came in with pleasant possibilities in his pockets. Response was not easy, for he was wondering with growing irritation why Ellen Chantry had been delighted to learn that he was not in love with her sister. Discrimination against him as a husband would be childish; he had a presentable physique, a fair income, a sound preference for decency. The less unflattering explanation, that she was anxious to keep Ruth single, seemed a little too selfish to be plausible — "even of a missionary," he added. Ellen had seated herself under the lamp with a book, calmly aloof: "Amuse yourselves, young people, but don't disturb me," Amsden read into the action. Good heavens, the woman was only thirty or thirty-one, several years younger than himself. Could nothing reach her consciousness through that lacquered shell of superiority?

"You look so stern," Ruth complained from a nest of cushions. "I'm frightened to death." He dropped down beside her on the couch without abating his gravity.

"And so you should be. Little girls ought always to fear their elders."

"Do you know how old I am?" Her tone was indignant.

"Yes; you are going on ten. Nell and Poppy are eight and six, but I think you would like them. I will bring them to play with you some day."

"Ah — your little grandchildren?" Amsden's laugh admitted that she "had him."

"I wish they were," he added.

59

"But you don't wish you were a grandfather!"

"Why not? It looks like a peaceful and happy state, to me. And I should not be an unpleasant old man, with spots on my clothes and bad table manners, like so many of them; I shall make a point of becoming a neat and well-behaved grandfather."

"But you would miss the very best of it." Ruth was excitedly earnest. "Why, everything is ahead of you now — don't you see? The next ten years are all that I care about. After that, I'd as lief die as soon as possible. Or even live up here," she added, the light leaving her face.

"You want it so much — I wish you could have it, instead of me;" his voice was quick with sympathy. "I would gladly give you my share."

"You mean — of town?"

"Town life and social things and opportunities for marriage," he said boldly. "I would let you have them all, freely, if I could keep my work."

Ruth's eyes were on her fingers, busily braiding the fringe of a steamer rug into tight pigtails.

"But don't these things mean anything to you?" she asked with an evident effort.

"Very little. But perhaps that is just because I am ignorant and narrow. I have thought of very little but putting up buildings for the past three years."

"And before that?"

"Before that I was engaged to be married."

Ruth drew a quick breath. "It was broken?" she asked in a hushed voice.

"Oh, yes — wisely for both of us;" his tone was cheerfully matter-of-fact. "But it took some of the glamour off the possibilities, you see." She looked relieved.

"It made you ready to skip a few courses and go on to salad," she suggested.

"What is that about salad?" Christine broke in, leaving the piano. "Are you planning a picnic?"

"Let's," said Ruth. "Why can't we go off on one to-morrow? We do picnics beautifully, Mr. Amsden — not a bit like other people's."

"But I like picnics, anyway," he protested. "Food is so good when it is relieved from table manners. I'd rather lie on the ground with a chicken leg in one hand, a jelly glass of beer in the other, than go to the grandest dinner ever served."

"And yet you plan to be a refined and tidy grand-father," Ruth reminded him in a quick aside, and they smiled at each other.

"There are both drumsticks and beer in the house," said Ellen, who had looked up from her book. "I will tell Ying to make you some sandwiches, if you like."

"Why don't you come, too?" asked Amsden, out-wardly amiable. "A day with the children will do you good." Ellen hesitated, glancing at the others, who apparently had not heard, as they were talking together.

"I should really like to come," she said simply. "Ruth, may I go on your picnic to-morrow?"

"Why, of course," was the neutral answer. "We must tell Will. Do you suppose he is still struggling with that hat? There he is," she added as the door opened.

Wallace had returned to his own clothes, and he held the hat up proudly for inspection. The ribbon had been replaced with surprising dexterity, but he had not stopped at that; a bright red apple rested against the crown, and from a bunch of parsley opposite, a tooth-brush rose stiffly like an aigrette, while a cluster of tiny carrots drooped under the brim, which was caught up on one side with a sponge. The ornaments had been put on with ludicrous skill; the hat really possessed an air.

"Ladies, I zell you zis loafly hat for von tollar ninety-eight zents. You vill not find any hat like it for der zame money, nor for any oder money. It is a pargain! Notize der —"

"Oh, Will, stop!" implored Christine, hysterically.

"I can't laugh any more," gasped Ruth. "Try it on, Christine — oh, heavenly! Will, what would it take to keep you all the year round?"

"A rich wife, I guess," said Wallace, beaming frankly at his success. Ruth looked startled at this interpretation of her question, then sighed regretfully.

"That cuts me out," she said. "I haven't a cent."

"I have," suggested Christine, with a very avalanche of meaning. Wallace looked inquiringly at Ellen.

"Any more offers? No? Well, Christine, you get the prize. This does not imply any lack of merit in the other competitors; but where only one may be chosen —" he broke off and stared at her reflectively; Christine looked very pretty at that moment, with candle-light shining through her little frame of light red curls. "I don't know but what it might be rather a good idea," he said, in frank surprise.

Christine flouted and laughed at him. But late that evening, in the seclusion of her own room, she stared critically into the mirror with a candle held close to her throat. Not that it was yet a question of obvious hollows; but Time had undeniably chucked her under the chin and left two finger marks.

"After all, I'm twenty-nine," she mused.

VII

"Ying has made us enough sandwiches for an army," Ellen said, rising from the breakfast table as the two girls came down the next morning. "I will go and pack them. We couldn't have a more perfect day to picnic."

"It may be rather warm," Ruth objected.

"Not up the cañon. Or are we going to Lone Cedar?"

"Oh, anywhere," was the listless answer.

As Ellen went out with her strong, assured step, Ruth's eyes met Christine's, then fell away guiltily. They sat down in silence.

"How is it that she can leave her patients for a whole day?" Christine asked presently, in a carefully meaningless tone.

"I am sure I don't know." Their eyes met again, and then Ruth let an unwilling laugh escape. "Christine, we are hateful," she admitted.

"If there were another man, it wouldn't make so much difference," Christine said, relieved at this invitation to frankness, but availing herself of it with caution. "Wouldn't Mr. Gilfillan do?"

"Mercy, no; we couldn't have him. I dare say he

eats with his knife. Our only hope is in a patient's sending for her."

"We might bribe some small boy to fall ill. Aren't people different, Ruth! If I saw a nice little square party all arranged, I shouldn't want to come along as fifth — should you?"

"Nothing could hire me. But Ellen doesn't think of things like that much. You know, Christine, she is really a great deal nicer than we are!"

"I dare say. But no one likes her any better for it. Wouldn't you rather be human and popular, like us?"

"I don't know;" Ruth spoke worriedly. "I hate myself a good deal of the time. I can't live up to Ellen's standards but I can't quite ignore them, and they keep me uncomfortable. I wish I could live with some one who — who — well, a little horrider than I am. You, for instance."

"Thanks! But this isn't doing anything about our picnic."

"But can we do anything?"

"I don't know. We might."

They fell into depressed silence. Presently Ruth rose and carried the fruit out to the pantry, where Ellen was packing sandwiches into a pasteboard box.

"We might as well take some of these peaches," Ruth said. "They will go in the other knapsack, on top of the beer." Her heart was beating nervously with some unacknowledged purpose. "I will wrap them in paper. How many?"

"Why, five, don't you think?"

"You are really going, then?"

Ellen's hands paused and she looked up, but Ruth was carefully rolling a peach in tissue paper, and did not meet her eyes.

"Why, I thought I would," she said slowly. "I haven't had a day off for a long time." Ruth took up a second peach in silence; Ellen waited a moment, then spoke with a touch of sharpness; "Would you rather I did not go, Ruth? You have only to say so."

"Why, not at all." Ruth laid her peaches in the knapsack with exaggerated care. "Why should I? I don't think you will have a wildly exciting time, three girls and two men always make an awkward combination. But if you don't mind that — Oh, dear, these things are going to get jammed. I must put in some cardboard."

Ellen stood very still, her hands resting on the table. When she spoke, a moment later, her voice was clear and quiet as usual.

"I think, on the whole, I do mind that. I believe I will back out."

"Don't unless you really mean it," Ruth urged hurriedly. "You know Will likes you immensely — he always says so. And Mr. Amsden is always nice and friendly. I don't see why you shouldn't have a very good time, Ellen." Her face had suddenly flushed.

"No; on second thoughts, if I can't have a man exclusively to myself, I doubt if I should enjoy it."

If Ellen was sarcastic, there was nothing in her face or voice to betray it as she turned away. "I had not taken everything into consideration."

"Well, it is just as you like," Ruth said with urgent cordiality. "We should love to have you, you know. I suppose, of course, there is danger that you might be called to some patient."

"True," Ellen assented, and the door swung after her. Ruth finished packing the two knapsacks with hands that trembled visibly. As she gathered them up, tears started to her eyes.

"Oh, I wish I were good, I wish I were different," she whispered miserably. She could have flung her arms about Ellen and begged her to come. "And yet if she did I'd be crosser than ever," she acknowledged. "I can't help it, I can't! If I only could go away from her!" She did not return to Christine until she heard masculine voices on the porch. Then she announced Ellen's defection curtly, presenting a resentful blankness to Christine's glance of gleeful congratulation.

It was not to be a strenuous day. Lone Cedar lay two miles to the north, with only one difficult cañon to cross if they kept to the ridge back of the house. Wallace in the gaiety of his heart mounted his stick and galloped off up the trail, and Christine cantered after him, discreetly side-saddle on hers. Amsden felt the exhilaration of the morning as keenly as they, though his only outer admission of it was in the strong thrust of his hands into his coat pockets, his alert, contented eyes and lips drawn to a soundless whistle.

Perhaps it would have been better if he could have taken a little of it out in capering; that might have left him less sympathetically conscious of Ruth's dejection as she plodded silently after them, her eyes evidently blind to the brightness of the day.

For the first half of the way he ignored her mood, hoping her spirits would find the way up of themselves, keeping near her with a friendly hand for difficulties, but not forcing her to talk. It did not depress him — only filled him with a warm desire to pet and laugh at her as he did at Nell and Poppy. He had no intention of showing this, but life was very strong and sweet this morning, and the footing down the side of the last ravine was treacherous, keeping him close beside her. The trail went in abrupt jumps, winding through a thicket of dwarf oak, whose rigid little twigs snapped their faces and caught at their clothes. He had just freed her hat from one when another plunged into the soft mass of her hair.

"Wait; don't move. Let me undo it," he said. As she stood patiently with head bent towards him, Amsden for the moment forgot everything but the appeal of her dejection. He broke away the twig, then let his hands slip down to her shoulders.

"You poor little soul — what is it?"

She seemed to crumple in his arms, then slipped from them into a heap in the path, her face buried in her hands.

"Don't. I'm such a pig," she sobbed.

His eyes were still full of laughter, but his voice was

sufficiently grave as he gently rubbed her shoulder with his palm.

"Tell me about it. I don't believe you have been very — piggish."

"Oh, I have!" She controlled her voice, but kept her face hidden. "I wouldn't let Ellen come. I mean, I showed her I — didn't want her to. It hurt her feelings. And she is always so good to me, — so — so — I am always the horrid one. And I *can't* seem to help it."

The tragedy seemed to Amsden very funny and pathetic and endearing. He sat down beside her, still with his palm against her other shoulder.

"Why didn't you want her to come?" he asked.

"I don't know. It just isn't so much fun when she comes. I am mean to say that! But you know she really is better than the rest of us, and we aren't so comfortable." She glanced quickly about, and caught him smiling. "You are making fun of me!"

His laugh admitted it. "You foolish child! Are you spoiling a whole beautiful day for one little tiff?" This aspect of it evidently brought comfort. Hope of exoneration shone in Ruth's lifted face.

"But Ellen would have wanted me to come to her picnic," she persisted faintly.

"Oh, bother Ellen!" He jumped up, holding down his hands to her. "There is no law about wanting people, so long as you wanted me. Now let us have no more nonsense, little sister." She put her hands in his and looked earnestly up at him.

69

"Do you honestly like me best — better than Ellen?"
she asked breathlessly.

"Why, of course. You are my intimate friend."

The last remnant of a shadow cleared away magically
as she scrambled up.

"I *am* glad."

She led the way recklessly, catching herself by rocks
and branches when her feet threatened to run away
with her, laughing back at him for approval at every
narrow escape. He found her delightful, yet his mood
had unaccountably chilled. He felt a dim alarm at
the memory of the past few minutes.

"Next thing I know, I shall be making a fool of
myself," he decided. He was not sorry when they
caught up with the others.

Across the ravine the trail joined an old wood road
that mounted Lone Cedar by easy stages. Near the
summit it passed a comfortable looking cabin with
scarlet curtains in the windows, and an attempt at a
garden. In one corner of this a man knelt, working
with a trowel; a woman sat on a stump close by, watching him, her hand on the head of a brown setter. There
was a curious dejection about all three.

"Wow! Did you ever see such dismal-looking
beggars?" Wallace exclaimed. "You'd think it was
a funeral."

"Why, it is," interrupted Ruth. "Don't you see —
that is a grave, and he is planting things on it. A
child's grave." Her tone was gently awed.

The man lifted his head and looked at them, a quick,

sullen look, but long enough for Amsden to recognize the stern face, dully white under a shock of black hair. He remembered the explanation of the snub that had been dealt him: "That's the father. It's Ned Spaulding." So Spaulding had lost a child, and was perhaps bitter against all mankind for the time being. Poor old chap! The explanation took the sting from the memory.

When they had stood in the clean wind under the dwarfed and twisted cedar that gave its name to the peak, and stared their fill at the mountains humping along to the north like a grand old line of camels, they turned back to a sheltered hollow, sun-steeped and aromatic, cushioned deep in needles, and lunched luxuriously to the distant pine music.

"Gee! I'd like to stay here forever," sighed Wallace, rolling over and stretching to express his content. "I'm so full of loving-kindness and chicken and goodness and innocence and beer — oh, it's great! Amsden, what do we go back for, anyway?"

"Well, I have a thing called a career, down there."

"Wouldn't you give it up like a shot if you could? If you didn't need the money?"

"No."

"Bet you would. What's the good of success, anyway?"

"It makes the game worth the candle, I suppose. One must aim at something."

"Do you want it inside or outside?" Ruth asked

thoughtfully. "I mean, so that you can say to your-self, 'I have done good work,' or so that others will say, 'There's Amsden, the architect?'"

He smiled at her lazily over his folded arms.

"I want it so that my grandchildren may be both rich and proud."

"Well, you'd better hurry up about those grand-children," Wallace put in. "You're getting on — and there are preliminaries."

"I don't care for the tone this conversation is taking," said Christine with mock primness, and brought the talk back to the eternal guying.

Amsden slipped off into his own thoughts, his head on his arms. His city ambitions seemed at the present moment rather trivial. And there was something in what Wallace had said — about the preliminaries. He believed that he could forego a wife cheerfully enough, but some day there must be little girls in his house, like Nell and Poppy. A boy, too; only not a serious, sensitive little chap, such as he had been; he preferred the robust, puppy order of boy. He looked reflectively at Ruth, ecstatic at that moment over some nonsense of Wallace's. Perhaps it would not be making a fool of himself, after all.

It was a sense of a flaw in his content rather than any tangible sound that made him presently glance over his shoulder. His start drew the eyes of the others after his to a pine tree not twenty feet away, against which leaned the gaunt form of Ned Spaulding. From his relaxed attitude, he might have been standing there some time. Christine gave a startled squeal, and the men rose to their feet.

"Jolly, ain't you," said Spaulding; his voice was hard and hostile. "Hevin' a party. It's a wonder the doctor ain't with you. She's goin' to hev more spare time now for gallivantin', with a real doctor here for the sick folks — them that ain't dead of neglect already."

The girls shrank back, frightened. Wallace would have blustered, but Amsden interposed with temporizing quietness.

"You're Spaulding, Ned Spaulding," he said. "You have had a great loss. It's — hard lines." The man eyed him with fierce contempt.

"Yes; when your only child is murdered and you haven't got no redress — yes, you might call it hard lines."

"Murdered!"

"Yes, murdered — by an ignorant she doctor. Let a baby choke to death. Never did nothing for her poor throat, pretendin' to treat her some other way — that warn't so much trouble for the doctor! She might just as well hev strangled that child with her two hands — I wish to God she had. Then I could —"

"Beg your pardon, Mr. Spaulding, sir, but your wife is needing you down at the house," broke in a quiet voice. Mr. Gilfillan had come noiselessly over the pine needles and paused deferentially at a distance from the group, a lank, homely figure, who spoke with eyes averted, as though from a gentle desire to make it easier for others. "She thought you might be up here somewheres and I was glad to fetch you for her. Sorry to interrupt, sir."

Spaulding hesitated a moment, then turned and plunged down the slope without a word, leaving the minister to follow, his ancient frock coat flapping patiently about his knees.

The sunny content of the afternoon was shattered. They began to gather their belongings in uncomfortable silence.

"Well, I suppose a doctor can't help making mistakes," Christine said, evidently with an idea of being comforting and magnanimous. "Probably she tries to take more cases than she can manage."

"It is more likely that the man does not know what he is talking about," said Amsden, with an incisiveness that surprised himself. "I cannot imagine Mrs. Roderick careless of any responsibility."

"You bet," Wallace confirmed him.

Christine was never one to cling to the unpopular side.

"Oh, of course not; I didn't mean that," she assured them.

"But it's dreadful to be a doctor," said Ruth with a sigh. "I wish she would give it up. I wouldn't stay in a profession where such horrible things could be said of me."

"I never did believe in it for a woman," agreed Christine.

Amsden turned impatiently away from them. "They

are only girls," he tried to reassure himself; but his disappointment betrayed how far his musings had led him. After all, the merry-little-dog ideal of companionship might have serious limitations when life presented big issues. He was glad that the girls elected to walk together, leaving him free.

As they passed the Spaulding cabin, Mr. Gilfillan came out. Amsden paused.

"I will follow you, if you don't mind," he told the others; "I want to have a talk with the preacher."

"Oh, certainly; don't mind us," said Christine, with an exaggerated toss of her head; but Ruth smiled brightly to show that she was not in the least hurt.

The two men were oddly contrasted as they met. Amsden's neat outlines, his fine, scholarly face, his reserved grey eyes with their look of quiet strength, gave him every outer advantage over the shambling, palely freckled Southerner in his grotesquely loose clothes, his long features suggesting that they had received a sharp pull downward at some early period, his dingy little eyes never looking straight ahead. Nevertheless, there was no patronage in the younger man's interest. He had a suspicion that this lanky preacher might be of a vastly higher civilization than himself, in the broadest sense of the term.

"Do you do all your visiting on foot?" he asked as they fell into step.

"Not usually, sir. But my little mare has had a hard year, and I am giving her a rest. These friends of mine are in great trouble," he added, with a motion of his head towards the cabin. "I come up as often as I can."

They hesitated before the topic, then Amsden took it up.

"I have seen that Mrs. Roderick was upset about something. I suppose Spaulding has been attacking her right and left."

Mr. Gilfillan nodded regretfully. "Pretty much. They don't treat diphtheria like they used to, and he allows his child was neglected because there wasn't a lot of throat washes and medicines. I reckon he'll see it different when he's more ca'm. It takes time — takes time."

"It must be maddening to have to fight stubborn ignorance as well as disease," Amsden said thoughtfully. "I should think Mrs. Roderick could really accomplish more down in the city." Mr. Gilfillan was silent a few moments, his hand on the little beard that had roused Ruth's scorn. A turn of the road showed them a diminishing vista of peaks, sharply blue in the distance.

"I reckon it ain't always the number of folks you help that counts," he said slowly. "You see that mountain to the right, the bare one? It's a cattle range, and about half-way up there's a cabin with a woman in it. She's nigh twelve miles from a neighbour, and four years ago, when the snow was over your head, she had a baby — came before 'twas expected. They sent to Gallop, but the doctor was drunk —

76

couldn't do anything with him. The parson went up and buried the child; most buried the mother, too. But she pulled through somehow. Now what do you reckon it means to that woman to know that M'z Roderick's just waiting for the word to come up and help her through this time? Think of it — strong as a man and gentle as a woman, and ready to work day and night to make it safe and sure. Do you believe a dozen cases in the city, with plenty of folks at hand, can balance that?"

Amsden's pulse responded to the picture. "It is magnificent," he said; then Ruth's laugh from the road ahead reminded him. "Still, I can't help feeling that it could be done nearly as well by a coarser instrument," he objected; "by some one whose training had not prepared him — and his family — for a different sort of life. Why should not Gallop have an honest, sober doctor, sufficiently skilful and reliable, but not — too good for his job?"

"And so it will have, if I'm spared."

"You? Are you going to be a doctor?"

"Well, sir, I am one now, so far as having a certificate goes; I went down last spring and took the examinations. I had been working towards it ever since my voice broke down and I had to give up my church, five years ago."

"But you are not practising?"

"Oh, there's time, there's time. I'm not sure as .there's quite room here yet for two of us, but if she does want to go, she'll feel easier." There was a simplicity of devotion in the words that moved Amsden to a keen desire for a better understanding.

"Then you do it for her as well as for the people?"

"I do it, sir, because it's needed."

The answer moved the younger man to impatient protest. "But — yourself!" he exclaimed. "Haven't you any personal life, any personal desires? Don't you want money or children or fame — something that isn't all for the good of others? Where is your human self in all this?" The little eyes rested on him indulgently for a moment.

"Well, sir, it's sort of this way. If you were hurrying down a street and saw a child get hurt — so that it screamed with pain — you'd forget for the moment that you had a car to ketch, wouldn't you?"

"I suppose so. Yes, of course."

"Well, that's what happens when you get to hearing the world's crying; you forget you wanted to ketch a car. And it don't feel like giving up what you call your personal life — it's more like finding it. That's what you *want*, don't you see? To ease that crying."

After a long silence, Amsden gave it up with a sigh and a shake of his head.

"I think you're splendid, you know," he said; "but I am a son of the world and the flesh — out for myself, I'm afraid."

"Well, sir, I suppose you're right happy and satisfied?"

Amsden laughed reluctantly. "No; neither happy nor satisfied, except when I am too busy to think."

"To think about yourself?"

They were nearly at the point where the trail branched off from the road, and the others were waiting for Amsden.

"Yes, myself, I suppose."

Mr. Gilfillan paused and held out his hand. "If you once got outside of yourself, sir — you'd never want to get in again!" The two men smiled at each other over their clasped hands.

"Good luck to you," said Amsden.

The others attacked him teasingly on his new friend as the ancient frock coat flapped out of sight.

"That is all right. He's a splendid old fellow," Amsden insisted. "I like his philosophy."

"Good. He'll make a man of you yet," said Wallace.

VIII

THE days drifted by very lazily and happily for Amsden. He was increasingly glad that he had come. Ruth expanded under his approval like a flower in the sun, and covert tilts with Ellen gave a subdued excitement to their meetings at meals. She said nothing about her professional troubles, though Amsden learned from Mr. Gilfillan how serious they were, and would have been sympathetic if she had given him a chance.

The idea that had occurred to him in the hollow on Lone Cedar — that Ruth might "do" — came back tentatively now and again under the influence of her brilliant sweetness. It would be frankly a compromise, but no doubt the element of compromise was as inescapable in marriage as in everything else. She was certainly a dear soul. The fact that a battle must be fought with Ellen first added an amused zest to the idea; he had already in hand the plain truths with which he should meet her unwillingness to let Ruth go. A grimly satisfying rehearsal of these, one evening, was broken in on by a plaintive, "Hello, central! *Can't* you get Mr. Amsden?" from Christine. He started and laughed.

"Please forgive me," he said, withdrawing his gaze

from the unconscious Ellen, who was herself lost in thought, a little apart from the rest. "Did you ask me something? I was wool-gathering."

"Looked more like scalp-gathering," commented Wallace from the hammock. The lamp was not yet lighted and they were lounging about the fire, Ruth and Christine curled on the hearthrug. "Who were you laying for, Amsden?"

"I think he was fighting for a principle," put in Ruth. "Have you heard anything at all for the past ten minutes?" He had to admit that he had not. "Then you don't know that we are thinking of going camping for a couple of days?" Ellen moved slightly, as if she too had only just heard the news.

"We'll sleep in bags and have a camp-fire," explained Christine, joyously. "And maybe we'll see — a bear!" Her mouth and eyes were rounded to a suitable awe. Ruth turned to her sister.

"Will you go, Ellen?" she asked, simply and sweetly. Ellen's face lit with a warmth almost maternal.

"Yes; I should love to," she said quickly. She moved a little closer to the hearthrug. "Don't you want a back?" she suggested. Ruth leaned against her knees and Ellen's hand touched almost timidly the soft mass of her hair. Amsden had to admit that in that moment Ellen was beautiful. The firelight brought out the blond shine in her heavy, straight hair, parted across a low forehead that was sunburned to a darker tone: steady strength looked out of her grey eyes, warmth lay about her unconscious mouth: the power of her wonderful arms and shoulders was as clearly expressed in repose as in work. Yes, she was beautiful, and in this moment of gentleness it was hard to think harsh things of her.

Christine seemed to find cause for irritation in the friendly tableau.

"I wish you'd pad your hearthrugs," she said with a restless movement. "Will, throw me a cushion — oh, not a turkey-red one, silly! Have a little respect for the colour of my hair."

"I thought it would just match," said Wallace, innocently; and received it back full in the face. "Wow! These red-headed tempers!" he exclaimed, blinking from the force of the blow. "And just when I was beginning to take a sentimental interest in you, Christine!"

"Oh, Willie!" Scrambling up, she flew to the hammock and fell on her knees beside it. "Are you, really?" He was holding both hands pressed to his cheek.

"I was, Christine," he said with dignity. "Now I am in pain and it's gone. If you cared to make the place well in the good old orthodox fashion —"

"Vinegar and brown paper?"

"Yes: that is exactly what I meant. 'Her mother, vex't, Did whip her next,'" he added dreamily. "I'll bet that did Jack more good than the vinegar cure."

"It didn't. Jack was a very nice boy."

"So'm I," asserted Wallace.

"Well, if you feel that sentimental interest coming

back again, will you tell me?" she urged with mock anxiety.

"What will you do?" he asked cautiously.

"Scream for help," was the unexpected reply, and they all laughed.

"When you come to a lull," suggested Ruth, "we will go on planning our excursion."

"A lull? What's a lull?" asked Wallace. "I never came to one yet. You people are too sophisticated for me."

"A lull," explained Christine, "is what happens when you are not around."

"Oh, then I suppose it's brushing your back hair and telling secrets. Girls always do when they're alone."

"No doubt men would, too, if they had any back hair to brush."

"Not much. Do you suppose you'd catch Ying at it? — and he has back hair to burn." The picture of Ying gossiping over the plaiting of his pigtail made the girls laugh.

"Oh, Willie, you're lovely," sighed Christine. "I almost think I might do worse."

"Well, think it over some more — don't decide in a hurry," he protested.

"Oh, I'll let you know in plenty of time," she assured him.

"What a shy, timid, reserved thing modern sentiment is," commented Ellen, who had been looking on amusedly.

"So'm I," returned Wallace. "I guess we'd better talk about the excursion."

"We will borrow Rory's spring wagon, and two can go in that with the outfit — the rest on horseback," Ruth explained, turning to Amsden. "We have a special place near the head of Juniper Creek, where we go every year. We might ask Rory to go — what do you say, Ellen?"

"By all means," Ellen assented with warm readiness. Ruth moved a little closer to her.

"We shall have to have more horses," she went on. "I wish we could get that little brown mare of Larsen's that Miss Finch drives; but it is engaged for the summer."

"So'm I," murmured Wallace with a heavy sigh.

Ellen usually excused herself or slipped away unnoticed early in the evening, but to-night Ruth's head against her knee seemed to hold her — seemed also to bring her into closer sympathy with them than usual, for certainly her presence proved no constraint. A tangible pleasantness pervaded the big, firelit room; they laughed easily, warmed with a grateful sense of human nearness. It was late when the men set out down the trail.

When Ellen had gone to lock up, Christine turned a significant glance on Ruth.

"That was a good idea to ask Rory; now we're an even six. Of course, we couldn't have gone without any chaperon," she added with a faint sigh.

Ruth yawned happily and openly. "Don't, Christine," she protested. "I'm good to-night; for heaven's sake let me see if I can't stay so!"

Rory consented drily to the expedition, and agreed to furnish a horse for the spring-wagon, on condition that no one but herself should touch the reins. They were not tempted to dispute that privilege with her when a gaunt, black beast with rakish hips, a hostile eye, and a lower lip evilly protruding, stood scowling and stamping before the door a few days later. They had just finished an early lunch and were giving a final look to the equipment of the four saddle horses.

"That's all right," said Rory, unmoved by their comments. "He'll get us there in three hours without turning a hair, which is more than those two thoroughbreds you've hired can do. I guess Dr. Ellen isn't afraid."

"She's afraid of Ying," confided Ruth in a whisper. "He doesn't approve of excursions, and he's been going about like the Wrath of God ever since this was broken to him." Ying stalked out at that moment and stowed the provisions into the wagon with a thud that made the horse start. Ellen followed him looking somewhat chastened.

"Good-by, Ying," she said with conciliatory friend-liness as she got in beside Rory.

A scornful "H'h!" was the only answer, and the door was slammed upon them. They did not dare smile at one another until they were beyond range of the windows.

Ruth, riding cross-saddle, her hair in a braided queue

tied with a black ribbon and the brim of her felt hat blown straight up in front, looked like a gallant young Continental. The costume was less becoming to Christine, who was slightly irritable in consequence. At Wallace's guileless comment that she "ought to train down a bit," she decided that she had a headache, and disliked riding in the hot sun, and that her saddle was not comfortable.

"She wouldn't mind the sun if she could see how enchanting her hair looks, would she, Will," said Ruth, generously eager to have everyone as happy as herself. "It's just like burnished copper."

"Too bad locks of hair have gone out, as keepsakes," assented Will. "Wouldn't one of those little corkscrews be a jolly thing to have found over the heart when one was dead!"

"Over the left — that's the only place you will ever wear one," returned Christine; but her headache seemed to be better. She was in high spirits by the time they reached the village, and did not share the impulse of the others to attract as little attention as possible. The surly looks they met served only to deepen her amusement over the funny little place, and she would have stopped at the store for candy but for the sudden appearance of Ned Spaulding, gaunt and scowling, in the doorway. Her laugh as she rode on sounded insolently loud in the silence that had fallen on the street at their approach.

"The girl's a fool," muttered Rory, touching up her horse. Amsden glanced back at the turning, and saw

Spaulding with impassioned gestures holding forth to a gathering crowd.

For the first few miles their road was little more than an elongated dent in a sheer mountain side, with stations built out at infrequent intervals where teams might pass. At each of these Rory pulled up and sent her clear halloo echoing on ahead: the lack of an answering shout showed the road clear. The only shade here was given by occasional rocks that jutted menacingly over their heads. From the tangled growth of the sharp descent beneath came the aromatic scent of sunned herbs; jack-rabbits bounded down the road ahead of them, and once they saw a huge snake pouring like a jet of brown lava over the edge of the bank. It was a relief to turn into the cool freshness of a road that wound up the long ascent of a pine-clad ridge, and finally plunged abruptly down into the shallow cañon where Juniper Creek played among the rocks in eternal childhood, ignorant of the toil awaiting its lusty strength farther down.

When the outfit had been unpacked and wood gathered for the camp-fire, the two men were sent down stream while the girls bathed in a shallow granite basin, its waters gilded to a specious effect of warmth by the sun's final burst of glory, poured down over them through the western opening of the cañon. The men came back wet-haired and ruddy, to find the fire crackling, and Ellen setting out their supper. She would not allow anyone to help.

"You have all ridden or driven all the way, while I

have come in absolute idleness," she insisted. "I am going to do everything. All I ask is that Ruth puts on her sweater, whether she thinks she needs it or not."

Ruth laughed and obeyed. Her attitude towards Ellen had been wholly sweet all day, and Ellen showed a grateful happiness that struck Amsden as almost pathetic in one so strong and self-reliant — so superior, as Christine called it. Ruth turned to him to have her sleeves pushed in.

"It isn't really necessary, with this shirt, but it is such a pleasant custom," she confessed. "Don't you wish really big sleeves would come into fashion again so that you would always have to tuck them in?"

"Why do you like it?" he asked, smiling down on her. He felt an unexpected impulse to complete his work by buttoning the sweater under her lifted chin, but thrust his hands firmly into his pockets instead.

"It feels so kind and friendly and protective!" Ruth was leading the way up the brook, Wallace and Christine having taken the other direction; her rubber-soled canvas shoes gave to her natural poise a lightness and security that made her seem almost more than mortal in her flitting over the rocks. "And they do it so considerately — oh, I could cry with gratitude." She laughed at herself. "It makes me feel little and beloved," she confided. "Fashion ought always to arrange openings like that."

"Well, doesn't it? I notice that I have had to button my sister up the back occasionally, of late years." He followed to the top of the boulder where she had seated herself, and stood for a moment looking down through the cleft of the cañon to the western sky, barred with fading gold. The wonderful night smells of the mountains were flooding up to them from the dark, massed green beneath, where the chill had already fallen, though their sun-steeped rock was still warm. "But Aileen doesn't seem moved to cry with gratitude about it," he added, dropping down beside her.

"Oh, that is different;" but she was evidently thinking of something else. "Are you always nice to your sister?" she asked abruptly.

"I have to be. She wouldn't let me play with Nell and Poppy, otherwise."

"Ah, you probably want to be." She sighed. "You haven't any hateful feminine streaks in you. But I have been good as gold to-day," she added, her face clearing and lighting with its magic swiftness of transition. "I have discovered a great new truth. I am going to give it to the world presently, but you shall hear it first. It is, Be good and you will be happy."

Amsden, who was lying on his back, pulled out a note-book and, holding it up against the sky, wrote down the words and the date with her initials.

"When your great discovery has made you famous, I shall point to this and say, 'She told me first.' There is a secondary discovery, by the way, that you will probably make before long."

"What?"

"That that is a high price to pay merely to be happy."

"Oh, no! Oh, you mustn't put such thoughts into my head!" But she laughed delightedly. "You are so human," she said with a little movement towards him, as unconscious as the brimming light in her eyes.

"God knows I am!" he said half to himself, looking away from her with an effort.

The wonder if Ruth would not "do" had come back persistently all that day, and in the pause that followed it grew suddenly to a wonder that he had ever doubted. Surely life could hold nothing better for him. The conviction brought a relieved joy; some tiresome protest deep within was silenced at last, and he could set about his wooing like any other man, happy in the hope of success. He had been expecting too much of love, that was all. It was not a master passion, but a warm and cherishing kindness, inexplicably touched with pity. His revery was broken in on by her impetuous, "Mr. Amsden!"

"Miss Chantry," he returned mockingly. She looked disconcerted, and smiled at him helplessly. "If we had been cast six years ago on a desert island," he went on, "I suppose you would still be saying, 'Mr. Amsden, will you pass the breadfruit?' or, 'Mr. Amsden, do you see a sail?'"

To his surprise, she coloured vividly. "I can't help it," she protested.

"Philip is a very simple name; you would think

anyone could say it. However, as you please, Miss Chantry. You were saying — ?"

"But I don't want you to call me that! You said 'Ruth' this morning."

"It was a great liberty on my part, Miss Chantry. I apologize."

"Ah, now you are a thousand miles off!" She was genuinely distressed. "Please don't — do come back! I don't want to call you — that. I don't know why — I just can't! But I want you to call me Ruth. Oh, *please* be good to me!" Tears on her eyelashes startled a warm laugh from him.

"Ruth, you absurd Ruth —!"

"Supper!" called Ellen's voice from below. Ruth jumped up, vividly gay again, and Amsden followed her back with amused, kindly, possessive eyes. Most assuredly she would "do," for any man in his senses. That he had no lover's doubts of the issue should have been a warning to him; but he was in no mood to heed warnings.

Rory had gathered crimson fireweed to decorate the blue tablecloth spread on the pine needles, and as Ying's disapproval had not extended to his preparations, they supped luxuriously, contentedly quiet after the long day. By the time supper was cleared away black darkness lay like a wall outside their circle of firelit trunks. The fire was built on an embedded rock and safeguarded with a trench, so they piled it recklessly high and roasted alternate sides, doubling up their blanket sleeping bags for cushions. Amsden, lying on his back beneath a young hemlock, saw its feathery branches marvellously decorated with stars, like brilliant blossoms studding the stems and tipping the delicate points of the needles. The darkness had wiped out the distance between bough and sky. It was so enchanting, his tree full of stars, that he felt vaguely selfish in keeping it to himself.

"But Christine would find it funny," he reflected, "and Ruth would enjoy it only by sympathy — because someone else did; she doesn't care for natural beauty. And Dr. Ellen —" He paused, suddenly beyond his depths, and lifted his head to look across at Ellen. She had thrown herself back to stare up through the branches overhead, and there was a half smile on her face, a look of wonder and delight. Evidently she too had discovered a tree full of stars.

"And she doesn't want to share it, either," he decided.

Christine sat up with a bored yawn. "Why didn't we bring cards for bridge," she exclaimed.

"Oh, we couldn't see to play unless we sat too close to the fire," said Ruth, drowsily.

"Won't there be a moon, later?"

"Not till after midnight, I think. It's on its last quarter."

"So'm I," murmured Wallace.

"What can we do, then?" Christine persisted. "I think somebody might be amusing."

"Lie down and think about nice things," counselled Ruth. "A night like this is all full of the dearest little thoughts, if you give it a chance."

"So'm I," came again from Wallace's blanket.

"But I hear such queer noises when you're all quiet," Christine complained. "I know there is a whole circle of wild beasts out there watching us."

"Oh, nonsense. You hear the horses and the brook. There is nothing to be afraid of, is there, Ellen?"

Ellen, who had obviously heard only the last sentence, repeated, "Afraid of? Here?" with a frankness of surprise that Christine resented.

"I think people who consider themselves brave are often simply stupid or unsensitive — coarse-fibred," she said into the air. "If you are all going to sleep I will draw a picture of you and call it 'A sociable evening on Juniper Creek.' Have you a knife, Ruth? This pencil is dull."

"So'm I," said Wallace. Christine turned on him wrathfully.

"Willie Wallace, if you say that again, I shall strike you. You have kept it up for twenty-four hours, and I am so tired of it I could scream."

"So'm I," said Wallace, meekly, and she had to laugh.

"Rory, you amuse her," suggested Ruth.

"Tell her the story of your life," Wallace added. Rory, whose idea of lounging was to sit bolt upright on a very hard rock, shook her head.

"I doubt if Christine would be finding it amusing," she said, with a free-born disregard of prefixes that made that young lady lift her eyebrows.

"Why not?" asked Wallace.

"There's no men in it," was the dry answer. Even Christine had to join the general laugh.

"Did you never have even one tiny little flirtation, Rory?" she asked with good-humoured condescension.

"What's that?" asked Rory, coolly.

"Good for you, Rory — make her define it," applauded Will. "Just what do you mean by flirtation, Christine?"

"I never mean anything by it," was the triumphant answer.

"You score," Wallace admitted, sinking back dejectedly on his blankets. "There's no use trying to beat a red-headed girl. Say, did you mean that?" he added a moment later.

"Mean what?"

Even Wallace, for once, found explanation difficult. "Oh, well, nothing," he said with a sigh.

"I think," mused Christine, "that Willie Wallie is asking me my intentions."

"Well, they're honourable, aren't they?" asked Ruth. "I have been asleep three times," she added. "The night has a thousand eyes, but they seem to shut very easily."

Ellen rose. "Bed time," she announced.

The night outfit consisted of a thick flannel suit, woollen stockings and wrapper, a scarf for the head and a long bag of doubled grey blanket. There were also extra rugs to soften their beds of pine twigs, which Rory had prepared before supper. She had also insisted on chopping logs for the night fire, irritated at Amsden's willing but unprofessional strokes. Ellen tucked the girls up within the circle of the firelight, then retreated with her bag to a black solitude sown with stars, full of resinous scents and a marvellous silence. Christine, cowering under her wraps, obviously wished that their guardian men need not sleep on the other side of the circle, and might have been heard to mutter that "the proprieties were too silly in a forest full of wild beasts;" but Ruth in the bag beside hers had already gone to sleep and she soon followed. If wild beasts stole out later to peer at their fire, no one knew it.

Amsden thought at first it was daylight that had awakened him, but as his eyes cleared he found himself staring up into an ancient, jaded moon, looking flushed and decrepit as it sagged above the tree tops. The fire still showed red coals, so, slipping on his clothes, he softly built it up, then lit a cigarette and sat down with his back against a rugged trunk to revel in the solitary beauty of the hour. The night was not cold and he must have dozed, for suddenly he discovered that the fire had sunk to a glow and the moon was high over his head. His cold cigarette was still between his fingers. He threw it away and was about ' to return to his bed when a sound on the road below checked him. This road was little more than a trail and led only to an abandoned logging camp, yet he thought he heard wheels and the creak of a wagon. A horse whinnied and was answered. The wheel sounds ceased and seemed to be followed by stealthy movements, the scraping of a board, then slow footsteps.

"I'm crazy — I'm dreaming," he assured himself. "It is a woodpecker or a squirrel." Nevertheless he sat rigidly listening in the inky shadow. Complete silence seemed to have fallen; he was ready to smile at his startled nerves when close beside him came the muffled pad of cautious feet on pine needles, and four men marched past, suddenly revealed by the moonlight. He started up, then hesitated, watching with tense muscles. Wallace lay sleeping thirty feet away, his own empty blankets looking like another form at his side, but the men paid no attention to him, or to the shadow where the women slept. Then Amsden saw that they carried by its four corners some sort of a box, which they lowered with infinite caution and placed on the ground before the fire. That done, they stole away as softly as they had come, and a moment later he heard wheels again, going recklessly fast now.

He sprang up and went to investigate the present they had left, still assuring himself that there must be some simple and rational explanation of the whole scene. At first he saw only that it was an open black box; then, as a stick blazed up, a quick, outraged "Good God!" sprang to his lips. For it was a rough counterfeit of a child's coffin that confronted him, and within, cushioned with staring white, lay a horrible caricature of a dead child, a strangling cloth wound about its throat and on its breast a paper with "Murdered!" printed blackly across it.

"Oh, why didn't I kill them!" he muttered. He would have attacked them single-handed at that moment, with no weapon but his righteous rage. The one thing to do now was to destroy the hideous object before anyone else had seen it, and he gathered it up, then stood hesitating over the method. To break it with the axe would make too much noise in these silent woods, no matter how far he carried it, and the fire could not burn it whole. Ghastly as the idea was, burial seemed to be the only way to be rid of the thing. He set it down and, walking noiselessly in his rubber-soled shoes, went down to the wagon in the hope of finding some implement to dig with. A small shovel had been put in for roasting potatoes, and armed with this he hurried back.

He was too late. Before the coffin stood a motionless figure, looking tall and austere in her straight grey wrapper, her eyes fixed steadily on the effigy with its staring label.

"Oh, I wanted to spare you — I didn't want you to see it," broke from Amsden. She motioned caution. Her eyes as she lifted them seemed to him desolately sad, but her voice was quiet and natural.

"I saw them come and leave it," she said in a low tone. "I thought I recognized them — did you?"

"I have seen them hanging about the saloons; I don't know their names."

"Well, it does not matter. How shall we get rid of

it?" He told her reluctantly of his plan to bury it, but she nodded quiet approval. "I can lead you to the best place," she said, when he begged her not to come, and set out ahead of him along a winding trail, dimly lit by the moon.

The box was heavy, and his shoulder ached with its weight before she brought him to the edge of a marvellous little meadow no bigger than a room, walled with crowded pines and carpeted with thick, fine grass. Through the centre wound a baby stream, and the grass was starred with tiny white flowers, here and there a pale orchid rising slenderly above their heads. The ground was spongy with water, and, laying his burden in the shadow, Amsden silently set to work. She stood beside him in her straight grey gown like some priestess of a strange rite, and her very stillness seemed to give him a new knowledge of her. He felt her strength; her deep capacity for sorrow, and her power to put it by; her warmth and her sane readiness for happiness when it came; the touch of divine mystery that lies about those who wholly lack self-consciousness. When the hole was dug he looked up into her face, and his anger flamed again.

"I could kill them!" he said between his teeth.

"Ah, they don't know, they don't know!" she murmured. As he lifted the box she took one end from him and they lowered it together into its place. The moonlight showed with horrible plainness the caricatured child as she stood looking down on it; her heavy braid, hanging over her shoulder, shadowed her face, but Amsden saw her hands clench and heard her shuddered "Oh, God, God!"

He dropped his shovel, and putting his arm about her turned her away.

"Dear woman, don't, don't care so," he begged. Her knuckles were driven against her mouth.

"It isn't that — oh, it isn't that!" she said in a broken voice; and then Amsden remembered that she had borne and lost a child.

She sank down on a fallen trunk, and laid her forehead on her knees, her arms clasping them about. He felt her mute appeal to be left alone, and, turning helplessly from her, he spent his passion of sympathy in hiding the brutal thing. It was weirdly like a real burial as the earth covered the coffin, with the moon lighting the white orchids of the tiny meadow, and the bowed woman beside him, her braid falling to her feet. When the grave was filled he dragged a dead branch over the place, then sat down near her and waited. The mellow moonlight was fading before the clean, new white of dawn when she lifted her head. Whatever had passed, her face was clear and quiet again.

"You should have gone back," she said. "You must be cold and tired."

"No. Shall you do anything about this?" he added. "Or will you let me?"

She shook her head. "What is there to do? I can't believe that Spaulding had any hand in it. Those rough young fellows are always looking about for

99

mischief; they would champion a cause simply as an excuse for making trouble. No; I shall win in time without fighting back."

She rose and turned to the trail, and Amsden, following, believed that he was again forgotten. But at the camp she paused and held out her hand.

"I am more grateful than I show," she said with an effort. "You know it, don't you?"

"Yes. Good-night." He stole back to his blankets without arousing Wallace. Neither of them had seen a head sharply lifted, and two startled eyes staring at them from Christine's couch.

The morning was not a success. Wallace declared that he had not closed his eyes all night, and, as no one cared to dispute the statement, he was left to doze in peace over a magazine. Christine was mysterious and haughty, and avoided Ellen so pointedly that only Ellen herself failed to notice it. Ellen's eyes, on meeting Amsden's, had not shown the faintest memory of a secret held between them, and, after a momentary disappointment, he liked her for it, his brief engagement having taught him that the power to forget the night before would be a valuable morning trait in woman. She was absent-minded, however, and soon disappeared by herself. Rory, to whom idleness was a physical impossibility, went off with Ellen's two saddle horses, to give them a lesson in jumping, and Amsden showed a strong tendency to follow Wallace's example.

"I never saw such a stupid set," Ruth exclaimed at last. "This is a pleasure trip, not a rest cure! What you all need is a good tramp to wake you up. Come on!" She jumped up and dragged Christine to her feet. "Let's eat some lunch now and go over to old Tamarack. We can get nearly to the top if we start soon."

"Do you know the way?" asked Christine.

"Yes, of course. I have been dozens of times — I mean twice," she added with a laugh. "Come, everybody, and just eat; we won't spread the tablecloth."

Christine, still reserved, finally consented to go, and Wallace was dragged groaning from his retreat. They pinned a note for Ellen on a pine trunk, and presently set out, plodding in single file along a narrow trail. The sun was hot, and the distance proved greater than Ruth had remembered: they were still far from Tamarack's great flank when Christine planted herself on a bank and declared that she had had enough.

"Me, too," echoed Wallace, whose plump face was a deep, even pink. "The view may be all that you say, Ruth, but I'd rather see a bath tub and a whiskey and soda than the grandest vista ever — visited."

"You won't see those at the camp."

"Well, there is beer and the creek, Miss Literal."

Ruth turned to Amsden. "Suppose we go on without them? They are only cry-babies, anyway." He was willing enough to go on, though he wondered a little at Christine's dissatisfaction with the arrangement; she was usually more than willing to be left tête-à-tête with Wallace. She tried to make Ruth turn back, and still sat looking uneasily after her when she disappeared with Amsden.

"I don't like leaving her alone with That Man," she said, the corners of her mouth tightening. Wallace dropped the handkerchief with which he was patting his moist forehead.

"Oh, come off, Christine," he exclaimed. "What's got into you? Amsden is the straightest chap I know." Her eyebrows went up expressively, but she said nothing. "Now, see here!" She had never seen him so nearly indignant. "You had better tell me what you mean, for, whatever it is, you're dead wrong."

"Oh, no doubt. And I dare say Dr. Ellen is just as perfectly above suspicion in every way, isn't she?"

"You can bet your life on that," said Wallace, so gravely that she was piqued into plain speech.

"Well, then, what were they doing off together in the woods before daylight?" she demanded.

"Looking after the horses, no doubt; building up the fire; anything."

"As you please," she shrugged. "I only know that I had been awake an hour at the very least, when they suddenly appeared together out of the depths of the woods. He held her hand and they whispered a moment, then separated. I never was so upset in my life."

Wallace said nothing at first, and she thought him overwhelmed by her information until he turned to her; then she found in the boyishly good-natured face a sternness before which she secretly quailed.

"Christine, there are a few things in this world so sure that no human evidence can touch them," he began, "and one of these is Ellen Chantry. I don't care if she and Amsden went off together for a week — I should know it was all right, some way or other. Now you just take my word for it, and don't you ever think of what you saw again — much less speak of it."

"Well, I don't see what explanation there can be," she objected sulkily.

"What do you want an explanation for?" was the wrathful answer. "Don't you know Ellen? And isn't that enough for you?"

"Yes, quite enough for me!" said Christine, her chin in the air, and they marched nearly to the camp in cold silence. Then, seeing that he would not weaken, she put away her resentment and sent a plaintive, "Wil-lie!" after his uncompromising back.

"Well?" he said, without turning.

"Are you going to be cross at me all the rest of the day?"

"I am not cross at you, Christine."

"You just don't like me very well?"

He hesitated. "You did give me a jolt," he confessed.

She came closer and put her hand through his arm. "Christine is sorry," she murmured.

"But is Christine convinced?" he asked, not looking

at her. Her fingers slipped down to the hand in his coat pocket.

"Of course, only she hates to admit it!"

Wallace melted at once. "Then it is all right," he said, smiling on her. "By Jove, I wonder what this queer little thing in my pocket is?"

"In your pocket?" She was eager curiosity personified. "Take it out and let Christine see."

"No: she is too young. I shall keep it to myself."

"Oh, Willie, please show me what is in your pocket!" she begged. "What is it like?"

"Well, it's soft, and small, and warm — and a trifle sticky —"

She caught her hand away with an indignant laugh. "Horrid man! It isn't," she declared.

"It is. Come here to the brook and wash it."

They had reached the camp, but no one was in sight, so he took her by the shoulder and marched her to a gravelly pool. All the little girls in the world boiled into one could not have been so little-girlish as Christine, trotting meekly beside him. When her very pretty hands had been well rinsed, she offered them for his inspection, looking up with anxious gravity. He turned them over, then expressed his approval with a matter-of-course kiss on one cheek.

"Yes, that's a good girl," he said encouragingly. She sprang up, flushing.

"Will Wallace! How dare you!" she began in outraged tones: then laughter was too much for them and they frankly shouted.

"What is the joke?" asked Ellen, appearing from the woods across the brook.

"It couldn't be repeated," said Christine, making an effort at cordiality.

"I'm not so sure," commented Wallace, who was looking exceedingly pleased with himself. "I think the oftener it was repeated —"

"Will, be still!" commanded Christine. "We have had such a broiling walk, Dr. Ellen: you were lucky not to be with us." But, for all her friendliness, her narrowed eyes said, "I'd like to know what you were up to last night, just the same, my superior woman!"

IX

AMSDEN took little heed where Ruth led him, glad
of her contented silence. She was a pleasant fact in
his life, something he was going to think about presently; but just now he was struggling to reconcile the
Ellen with whom he had so just a quarrel with the
impression left on him by the Ellen of last night. It
was a hopeless business and ended by irritating him.
He turned back to Ruth with relief.

"How do you know the way?" he asked. "I can't
see any trail."

"Oh, as long as we are going up hill, we are bound
to reach the top," she explained light-heartedly. "We
got off the trail some time ago, but I knew we should
find it again up there, so I didn't bother."

She seemed so at home, leading the way up the
sharp ascent, that Amsden, knowing little of wood-
craft, left the matter comfortably to her. They
emerged presently above the timber line and, by
agreement, climbed to the bald, stony summit without
looking up, that the full glory of the view might burst
on them at once. When, at Ruth's "Now!" they
turned to face the prospect, Amsden was disappointed.
Instead of being poised on a solitary peak high above

a rolling sea of crests, they seemed to be on the end
of a long, bleak ridge, no higher than its neighbours.
and offering little outlook.

"Why, we can do better than this at the cabin door,"
he exclaimed.

Ruth, after a long, silent look in every direction, sat
down on a stone with her chin on her knuckles and
sent him a guilty, furtive, amused smile.

"The trouble is, you see," she confessed, "this isn't
Tamarack."

"What is it, then?"

"I'm sure I don't know."

"And where has Tamarack gone?"

"I don't know that either." They laughed at themselves, at their hot, steep climb for this puny result.
"I thought we were getting to the top remarkably
soon," she admitted. He looked at his watch.

"Not so very soon, either," he exclaimed. "Do
you know that it is after four?" She rose slowly and
stood studying the mountains to the west.

"Of course, we have come from over there somewhere; but it doesn't look so very familiar," she said,
showing for the first time a touch of uneasiness.

"But if we go down here where we came up, can't
we strike the trail we were following?"

"Yes, I hope so. We must try it, anyway." But
Ruth, who knew something of the ways of mountains,
still stood looking in vain for a familiar outline. "Well,
we know our general direction — we'll cling to that,"
she said anxiously, starting down.

This was not difficult so long as the western sunbeams slanted through every gap in the trees. When an opening gave them a glimpse of Tamarack, looming far behind them on the right, they went forward with new courage.

"We didn't lose the old mountain, we just mislaid it," Ruth explained, gay with relief. "Now I have some idea where we are."

"Aren't you very tired?" Amsden asked. She smiled at him with quick gratitude for the sympathy in his voice.

"No, really," she asserted.

A distant mountain shouldered between them and the sun, and presently even the glow was cut off as they plunged down and down, making an arduous short-cut in the hope of striking the lost trail. The sparse woods grew more dense; half an hour was spent in crossing a thorny ravine, and twilight was already upon them when they emerged, scratched and panting, on the other side. They were less sure of their direction now, but they did not say so.

The woods that closed about them took on a forbidding character; not a blade of grass, not a bush or a young shoot softened the austerity of the bare, hard ground, harsh with rocks or slippery with needles. The pine trunks were so close together that the lower branches had died for lack of sun and air, spreading a roof of death and decay above their heads. In the crevices of the rocks were holes before which lay sinister fragments — a whorl of desperate feathers or tiny, broken bones, showing that the dense silence was not untenanted, and adding a belittling touch of forlorn disorder. All the beauty and majesty of pines was lost; they appeared stark, dismal, blighted with degradation and death. Ruth came closer to Amsden and finally put her hand in his, and so they went on until the dusk was nearly darkness and their cheerful talk died out unnoticed.

"I *am* rather afraid," she said suddenly. He drew her closer.

"I don't wonder! But it must end sometime — no human forest could last much longer than this has."

"Unless we are going in circles."

That well-known possibility had been haunting Amsden and he had kept a sharp lookout for recurrent landmarks; but he answered lightly:

"Oh, we should have come across one of your combs by this time, or a handkerchief, if we were. They always do."

"But I haven't lost anything," she objected seriously.

"You seem to have lost your way."

"If you knew more about mountains, you wouldn't joke — you would be frightened, too."

"But we are not so very badly lost, after all. We can't be more than a few miles from the camp, whether we find it or not."

"Well, if a few miles from supper and bed satisfies you! It is getting so dark — I wish we could come out somewhere. I know now why they called the woods 'horridus' in Latin. This is the most horridus wood I ever saw "

"It is — a grubby, degraded slum of a wood." Amsden spoke quickly, keeping himself between her and a low-hanging rock on his left, from beneath which two flat discs of green fire were turned towards them. "I didn't suppose a forest could go down hill to such an extent; it is no fit place for a lady." The disks were too far apart to belong to a little animal; their position must mean some big head pressed on the ground, and he seemed to see a bristling outline about them in their black retreat. "We certainly haven't been here before, for the branches are getting lower and lower. We shall have to go on our hands and knees presently." They were safely past now; furtive glances backwards showed no green lamps tracking them, and he fell into relieved silence. Suddenly Ruth stopped short.

"If another branch jabs me in the head, I shall scream!" she whimpered. "I am so tired of being hurt. It's not fair to hurt me like that!" She was so like Poppy in her despair that Amsden could have laughed outright.

"It is outrageous," he sympathized. "Keep close behind me, that will break a way for you."

She obeyed and they went forward in Indian file. The character of the wood was changing; presently they were confronted with a dense wall of undergrowth. Amsden forced his way into it for a few feet, then came struggling back to where Ruth stood staring miserably after him.

"Oh, don't leave me again!" she exclaimed. "I would rather be lost forever than stay another minute by myself. Please don't."

He promised, but felt a touch of impatience in place of the typical male pride of protectiveness; and was not too absorbed to wonder at it a little as they followed the edge of the thicket. The world's old generalizations made courage and independence scarcely necessary to woman's charm; yet in that moment he had a warming vision of a figure in a straight grey gown, marked only by the shining line of her braid, leading him without word or look through the moonlit forest.

The ground under their feet sloped up and presently they were climbing with new hope, seeing a glimmer of light ahead. Fifteen minutes later they emerged on a clear hillside under the open sky. A film of cloud hid the stars that might have guided them, and the surrounding hills were only denser masses in the semi darkness, yet they had a rejoicing sense of being no longer lost. At the top Ruth dropped down in tired silence.

"Well, there is just one thing to be done," Amsden decided. "We are fairly high here; I shall build a fire and let them find us. It is ignominious, but practical."

"I will help," said Ruth, pulling herself up. He pushed her gently down again and, taking off his coat, wrapped it about her.

"You stay there," he ordered.

A shelf of rock just beside them jutted out from the hillside, and on this he piled brush and sticks. When he came back to get matches from his coat he found Ruth asleep. He tried to take them without disturbing her, but her eyes opened.

"Philip?" she said sleepily.

"Yes, Ruth. I want to get the matches." His hand touched hers in the darkness, and, finding them cold, he held them for a moment. Then he started up. "Come close to the fire; you have been so heated," he commanded abruptly. When the blaze was going he busied himself gathering more wood. It was half an hour before he sat down opposite her, his hands clasping his shirt-sleeved arms.

"You must have your coat," she said, sitting up and beginning to take it off.

"I don't want it, really."

"But you must. I shan't feel comfortable. Here!"

"Ruth, put that on again at once."

"I won't."

"Then I shall come and put it on you by force."

"I don't want your old coat. I'm roasting."

"It does not matter in the least what you want. Do you intend to put it on?"

"Please, Mr. Amsden, it would worry me so — I have on loads more clothes than you have. You wouldn't want to worry me, would you?"

"But, child, there is nothing to worry about. I never take cold — while if you should, your sister will pack me off to town by the next train." He came over and kneeling beside her held up the coat. "Here, now. No more nonsense." She looked up at him very much as Nell and Poppy did when it was advisable to see how far he was in earnest. He was rash enough to smile; whereupon she closed her eyes with a suppressed laugh and curled down tighter on the ground. "Very well, then." He took one arm and thrust it, unresisting but helplessly limp, into the sleeve, and lifted her, a wicked dead weight with eyes still screwed shut, to find the other arm. Then he buttoned the coat under her chin and laid her down with emphasis. Her eyes opened suddenly, laughing, gleaming with life, absolutely innocent of intention; he laughed with her, but abruptly rose to his feet and turned to pile more wood on the fire.

"Oh, for a beefsteak!" he exclaimed. "Were you ever so hungry in your life? See if there are any cigarettes in that coat." She felt in the pockets and gave a small shriek of delight as a package of chocolate was discovered.

"I am sure I never put it there," he exclaimed, falling on his half. "I always knew you were clever — feel again and see if you can't find some lamb chops or even a few baked apples."

"I gave it to you yesterday when we were starting out. Wasn't it beautiful that we forgot it! Yes, here are some cigarettes — only two, though. I think you ought to let me have one."

"Assuredly. I didn't know you used them."

"Well, I don't. Christine showed me how, but 1 thought them very nasty. She says all the nice girls do it now. Do they really?"

"I know one nice girl who evidently does not." It was pleasant to say such things to Ruth, she enjoyed them so frankly.

"But how do you feel about it?" she persisted.

"I am afraid I don't feel at all. I mean, if I like a girl, I like what she does; and if I don't like her she may take to a pipe for all I care."

"That seems to me rather unprincipled," commented Ruth. "I sometimes think you don't say to me the things you really mean," she added wistfully.

Her penetration startled Amsden, and even disconcerted him. He had scarcely acknowledged to himself how little part in this lazy summer intercourse his real self had taken, and just now, with Ruth sunning herself like a little lizard in the happiness of the hour, he did not want to remember it. He had tried once or twice when he first came to draw the talk away from the eternal personal, but she had no interest in anything else, so he had amusedly followed her lead, content to keep his real interests to himself and to let her flash back and forth undisturbed in the tiny walled garden of her desires. The fact that she did not fulfil his ideal of companionship had not troubled him then: now it brought a quick impatience with himself. There was a battle on to-night, a battle so active that he had forgotten their precarious position, the anxiety at the camp, everything but the warning knowledge that if he crossed over to where Ruth lay, he should be sealing up in eternal loneliness the self that had given hearth and home to the man all these years; and a sharp realization that if that tired little hand, flung on the ground palm up, were held out to him, loyalty to the secret self would not have the power of a straw to hold the man back. Yet he sat quiet and impenetrable behind his cigarette, his hands clasping his shirt-sleeved arms, letting the night decide the battle as it would. Ruth, as untroubled as he by their situation, since she was warm and happy, kept the issue at bay by her very unconsciousness.

"Do you say to me what you really mean?" she repeated.

"When I think it would amuse you," he replied quite honestly. She was satisfied with that.

"We always talk about nice things, you and I." she said. "Now Ellen likes to talk about things in the newspapers and general, abstract topics that nobody cares anything about, really. I suppose that is why I have so much more fun with Christine."

"What do you and she talk about?"

"Oh, clothes and men and good times — all the nice, human things. Men don't talk together when they're alone the way we do," she added.

"How do you know, since you aren't there?"

"Oh, I know! Now and then one says something and the other gives a little grunt; and presently *he* says something, and the first one gives a grunt; and at the end of an hour that is all that has happened, except their cigars."

He laughed. "You have been eaves-dropping," he accused her.

"I couldn't help it. You and Will were sitting under my window all the time I was dressing, the other day."

"We were being cautious. If your window had not been there, we should have been talking passionately about waistcoats and girls and 'all the nice human things,' instead of merely grunting."

"You are making fun of me, but I am so comfortable I don't care. Do you know," she added presently, curling down closer to the ground with her cheek pillowed on her arm, "I think we are both going to remember this evening all our lives. We were so lost and hungry and tired and frightened, and then we got out of all that horror and found something to eat and had the fire and gave up worrying — so that it will all stamp itself in a lovely little warm picture on our memories. Don't you think so?"

"Yes; I think we shall remember it," he said quietly.

"If it weren't for worrying them, I shouldn't mind very much if we had to stay here all night — should you?" she went on. "The ground is rather hard, but there is plenty of wood, and it's so nice being just our two selves — don't you think so?" She smiled drowsily at him. "Don't you like it here?"

He rose without answering, and plunged down into the darkness beneath them, returning some time later unnecessarily laden with sticks and brush.

"What time is it?" she asked, starting from a doze.

"I don't dare look." He threw an armful of brush on the fire, sending the blaze high above his head, as he stood outlined against it.

"Ah, I know you are cold!" Her voice had a troubled warmth. "Won't you take your coat now?"

"Truly, I don't need it."

"Please — Philip!" He looked down into her up-turned face, and forgot to answer. "We may have to stay here all night, you know," she went on, still with her firelit face lifted to his. "I couldn't sleep a moment, thinking of you over there all cold. Don't make me!" His back was to the fire, so that his face was in darkness, but the quality of his silence suddenly reached her, and though she did not understand, she was startled. "What is it? You hear something?" she asked breathlessly.

Truly, he heard things: heard the ancient call of the blood to take this child in his arms and keep her there: heard still above that cry the stubborn protest, "Not this, not yet! Wait!"

"Ruth!" he said desperately, as though she could help him. "Ruth!"

Then through the inner tumult came a sound from without, faint and distant yet unmistakable, a human call. It came again, Ellen's resonant voice with its contralto note. He whirled about, shouting his answer across the darkness to a pinhead of light that meant a waving torch, shouting it joyously in the glory of free-dom, of escape. For in a flash the battle was over, and the victory lay, clearly and forever, with the self that could wait and hope, but could not compromise. And Ruth, all unconscious, shouted happily beside him.

X

EVERYONE slept late in the morning, and after breakfast, Ruth, who was evidently over-tired, went back to her blankets and slept heavily through all their preparations for departure. Ellen put off starting till noon. She seemed worried and abstracted, and Amsden fancied she was thoroughly glad that their pleasure excursion was over. The trip back to the camp, the night before, had proved surprisingly simple with torches and shouts to guide them. No one had seemed seriously worried by their adventure except Christine, who welcomed Ruth solicitously and pointedly avoided speaking to Amsden at their late supper. By morning she had slept off her unexplained resentment, and would even, in Ruth's absence, have exchanged Wallace for Amsden had the latter shown any disposition to be monopolized. He obviously preferred grooming the horses under Rory's patronizing instructions, and so presently she went for a walk with Wallace, a walk evidently destined to end at the first spot that invited lounging.

Rory, after rubbing up the harness, backed the wagon into the creek and began washing its wheels.

"Why not do that when you get home?" Amsden

asked, giving the brush a professional scrape on the currycomb and approaching with some caution the rakish hind quarters of the black.

"And Dr. Ellen ride home in it looking like that? I guess not."

Her scorn of the idea gave him an amused suspicion. "Would you clean it up for Miss O'Hara?" he asked.

"Naw," said Rory.

"For Miss Chantry, then?"

"Oh, go 'long; you do ask questions." He laughed.

"I was just wondering," he began, but a nervous jerk on the part of the black clipped the sentence.

"He'll put a hole through you if you go wondering too much," Rory warned him. "You'd best let me finish him. Here, you can go on with this." She held out the dripping sponge and he meekly made the change, balancing himself on two stones in mid-stream.

"Well, this is energy!" said Ellen's voice from the bank above where she had paused, a book under her arm. "Why are we putting on so much grandeur?"

"Well, Rory thinks the wagon wouldn't be good enough for you unless it was washed," Amsden explained mischievously. Rory shot him a vengeful look and the black horse winced, lifting a threatening hind leg.

"Rory knows what a crank I am about dirt," said Ellen, with a smile at the scowling little face. "However, I think Ruth will have to take my place going back, she is so tired; and she would never notice the difference. So don't do any more than you want to."

Rory's eyes had clouded. As Ellen turned away she finished her grooming with a careless rub and picked up the shafts of the wagon.

"It's clean enough; don't stand there swabbing all the morning," she commanded.

"Clean enough for Miss Chantry," Amsden assented. Rory turned her back.

"You're that foolish," she muttered.

Towards noon Ellen reluctantly aroused Ruth, who complained of a headache and ate her luncheon in deep dejection. Ellen looked at her uneasily, but said nothing until Wallace opened up the subject with his usual frankness.

"You look like a boiled owl, Ruth. Why on earth do you try to ride home? You won't enjoy it."

"Oh, yes, I will. Riding always does me good," she said hastily.

"I'm afraid it won't to-day in this bright sun," put in Ellen. "I really think you had better give it up and drive, Ruth." Her tone was apologetic, but Ruth was not to be conciliated.

"You would like me to give up everything," she said petulantly.

"Suppose we don't go at all," suggested Wallace. "We can stay over another night just as well, can't we?"

"I am going whether you do or not," said Ruth, and finished her meal in heavy silence.

Ellen looked depressed, but it occurred to Amsden that she also looked firm. When they rose to start, she turned to Ruth, who was pinning on her hat.

"Ruth, your doctor gives positive orders that you are not to ride; so you might just as well submit gracefully." Her friendly voice offered every chance for graceful submission, but Ruth would not follow her lead. She flung her hat on the ground and turned away.

"You spoil everything. You never want me to have any fun," she said with a sob.

Ellen broke the uncomfortable pause that followed her disappearance. "Ruth's headaches always upset her nerves," she apologized.

"Suppose we don't go," said Wallace.

"I think we had better," Ellen decided. "We all need home comforts. And, besides, Ying would worry; he expects us to supper."

"Then by all means don't let's disappoint him. I suppose you will ride with us."

"I suppose so," she assented reluctantly. She evidently hated to take the pleasure she was denying Ruth.

The little scene left Amsden musing. "It would be like marrying Nell and Poppy," he realized. Relief at his escape did not lessen his sense of warm affection and presently he went in search of her. He found her sitting on a boulder over the creek, her eyes heavy but her lips tranquil and smiling. She was watching a trout in the pool beneath, and motioned him to come cautiously. She was as free from embarrassment as

Poppy herself, ten minutes after her small tempests.

"How is your headache?" he asked when the trout had flashed out of sight.

"Much better," she assured him. "I cried some of it off. Wasn't I horrid," she added.

He smiled. "Very horrid."

"Well, I told you I was petty and unreasonable and all that, the first time I met you," she protested. "You thought it was funny then."

"Perhaps I do still."

She shook her head. "I know. It's only funny when you hear about it, not when you see it happen. Don't be cross at me — don't disapprove of me, will you!"

"Not if you are a good girl."

"And polite to my teacher," she added ironically. "Are you going to ride with Ellen?"

"And with you, too. Can't we ride beside the wagon?"

"Oh, will you, truly?"

He laughed at the naïve joy of her voice. "If Rory will let us. You must come now: the other two have already started."

The attempt to ride beside the wagon did not work very well. The excitement of companionship was too much for the black horse with his head turned towards home and a two days' rest animating his gaunt bones. He persistently travelled in leaps until Rory ordered the two riders to fall behind out of earshot. Ruth looked wistfully back as the winding road gave her a last glimpse of them, sitting silent on their horses, apparently oblivious of each other.

"You could have held him, Rory," she objected.

"Maybe I could and then maybe I couldn't," was the tranquil answer. "Anyway, there's no sense in wearing out the harness before its time."

"He wouldn't be so nervous and jumpy if you fattened him up a little;" Ruth was frankly peevish.

"Haven't I been fattening him these three months? You may think he's poor now, but when I first got him, I give you my word I had to tie a knot in his tail or he'd slip through the collar."

Ruth laughed in spite of herself. "What did you buy such an ugly beast for?" she asked.

"Ten dollars," was the concise answer. "I'll get eighty for him in a few weeks more — you'll see. Maybe a hundred. All he needed was proper handling, poor brute."

"Dear me, I wish I could make money like that."

"What do you want it for?"

"What for! Clothes, and the city, and people — freedom to do what I like!"

"Gewgaws and men," was the dry interpretation. "I'd not turn my hand for them."

"But what do you want, then, Rory?"

"Want? What's the good of wanting anything? I'd not waste my time that way."

"That is perfect nonsense! You want your horses, don't you? You want to succeed in breaking them?"

"I'm willing to make a living that way, and I have a kindness for the poor beasts. I'll not say I spend any emotion over them."

"Don't you spend any emotion over anything or anybody?" Ruth asked incredulously.

"Why should I?"

"Well, I don't believe you, that's all. Even Ellen, for all she's so calm and independent — well, she doesn't care to live alone, you notice! That is why I am chained up here year after year." Ruth's voice had grown resentful. Rory shot a side glance at her, wondering and a little scornful.

"You won't find anyone better than Dr. Ellen to live with, search the world over," she said impatiently. "Why don't you thank heaven on your knees that you were born her sister, instead of blatting about parties?"

Ruth was too astonished to take offence. "I didn't know you were such an admirer of Ellen," she said.

"Who wouldn't be, given a grain of common sense? She's as far above the common ruck of us as Lou Dillon is above this ten-dollar bargain beast of mine. It needs only an eye in your head to see that."

Ruth laughed triumphantly. "And you don't spend any emotion over anybody! Oh, Rory!"

A dull red rose in the girl's scowling face. "Aw, now, don't be foolish!"

"You don't know emotion when you get it: that's all that is the matter with you," Ruth teased her. "You think Ellen is a wonder, don't you?"

"I happen to know it, that's all."

"You wouldn't believe anything against her?"

"Why should I? It wouldn't be true."

"And you would adore to do something for her, wouldn't you? Something awfully hard and unpleasant?"

"You're too foolish, Ruth Chantry. I'll not talk with you." But the red in her cheeks had deepened.

Ruth crowed happily. "That's affection! That's love! Oh, Rory, you're just as bad as the rest of us. We shall come to your wedding yet!"

"Naw, naw! I saw enough of marriage to last me my life before my dear father was mercifully relieved of his earthly cares by the kick of a horse. I told you I had a kindness for horses," she added with wicked pensiveness.

"You dreadful girl!" laughed Ruth.

"That's all right," said Rory, and her mouth looked grim. "There's a lot of things you don't know, Ruth Chantry."

"Tell me some of them."

She shook her head. "Keep canaries in their cages, say I. I've been sparrowing around in the dirt all my days, and I'm none the better for it."

"I'm no canary!" A quick contraction of her arms showed a flash of some obscure feeling. "Sometimes I feel more like a tiger," she exclaimed, frowning.

"You're fire in the straw," was the sober answer.

"Quick and hot and then all over?" she interpreted without much interest.

"Just that."

"Sometimes I feel like an eagle in the air," chanted Ruth, remembering with delight an old darkey song of her childhood. She sang it exultingly:

> "Sometimes I feel like an eagle in the air,
>   Feel like an eagle in the air!
>
> Sometimes I feel like a mournin' dove:"

her sweet, high voice, suddenly plaintive, came back from the hill above to the silent riders following:

> "Sometimes I feel like a mournin' dove,
> Sometimes I feel like a mournin' dove,
>   Feel like a mournin' dove:
>
> Sometimes I feel like a motherless chile:"

she crooned it over and over:

> "Feel like a motherless chile,
> Feel like a motherless chile!"

Amsden, glancing at Ellen, saw that her lips were set in a sorrowful line. "Poor little Ruth," came from his heart, but before it was spoken her laugh, fresh and joyous, followed the haunting notes. After all, why poor Ruth? She was probably happier than any of them. Why did he persistently find her pathetic?

The prospect of a three hours' ride with Ellen interested Amsden more than he thought best to betray in the face of her obvious indifference. This was so complete that he wondered presently if the true name for it were not hostility; surely thorough indifference would have made more effort to be friendly. After two or three topics had been killed with courteous commonplace, he gave up and rode beside her in an abstraction that was presently as deep as her own. He knew why he was down on her, or had been before that mock burial in the woods had blurred his impressions and his judgment; was she down on him merely because she had felt the unspoken ciritcism, or for himself? His revery led him to the eternal mystery of human attractions and antagonisms, out of which he finally made one more attempt at conversation.

"Rory is a strange little person," he began. "Do you really believe she is as detached as she seems? I think she might be capable of a big devotion — kept very secret, of course."

The long silence seemed to have tempered Ellen's mood; she answered with a note of interest.

"I don't know. I don't pretend to understand her. She has a certain dry kindness, but I doubt if she has much — what people call heart."

"I am not so sure. Poor child, how she must have been batted about. I always have a sense of dreadful, devastating experiences in her past. She is a good hater. I would give something really to find her out."

"Why?" It was an aggressive monosyllable, but he ignored the tone.

"Because I have a passionate curiosity about my fellow creatures," he answered placidly. "Haven't you? Don't you long to listen at their moral keyholes?"

"I don't think I am analytical;" Ellen's voice implied that she was thankful for it. "I have a strong interest in my fellow creatures' lives and problems; I doubt if that is the sort of interest you mean, though."

"I don't see how you can understand their lives and problems if you ignore their psychology." Amsden's friendly patience was rather irritating, a fact of which he was fully aware.

"What do you do with all this deep understanding after you have got it?" she asked impatiently.

"Why, I sit and think about it. It is vastly interesting."

"And then?"

"Then I go out and get some more to think about." He knew that he was caricaturing himself, but her scorn of the dilettante drove him to a perverse assumption of the attitude.

"Ah, yes. No doubt that is amusing." Her profile showed that she was ready to drop the subject, and him as well, but he persisted.

"It is deeply exciting. And I think I may get a new science out of it some day — the science of human chemistry."

She evidently did not want to show interest, but as he relapsed into meditation, she presently brought out an unwilling, "And what would that be?"

"It would begin with a table of human elements. Every person, of course, is made up of a combination of these, and, by referring to the table, you could give him his formula. Then suppose I wanted to go into partnership with a person; I would take his formula and mine and in a few moments work out the chemical effect of these elements on each other — fusion, explosion, whatever it might be. And so we could shake hands on it and give it up, or go ahead and prosper, according to what we discovered. Think of the hopeless attempts at combination it would save." She was actually smiling.

"I suppose one would go to have one's formula taken or corrected every few years, just as one is vaccinated," she suggested.

"Of course. And the formulas would all be registered. No one could conceal his; the word 'dupe' would disappear from the language."

"But there would be an end to drama," she objected. "The heroine would look up the villain's formula in the first act, and then where would your play be?"

"Oh, we should have a new order of play, and I am sure it is time. I am tired of the duped lady, myself."

For some reason, the interest that had lighted her face was abruptly withdrawn. She turned away.

"I doubt if even formulas would save her," she said from a long distance. An impatient challenge, a demand to know why she met him this way, was on Amsden's lips; but a turn of the road revealed Mr. Gilfillan riding to meet them, and the change in Ellen showed him and his subject forgotten. She rode forward with alert interest and her eyes searched the homely, earnest face.

"Well?" she greeted him.

"Nothing wrong here, M'z Roderick. Mr. Amsden, how do you do, sir? I thought you might have something for me to do, so I rode this way on the chance." His compassionate little eyes met Ellen's for a moment, and Amsden divined that he had heard of that night visit to the camp. Ellen evidently saw it too.

"I am glad you came," she said with quiet warmth. "There are several things I want to talk over with you."

"Then suppose I ride on ahead out of your way," Amsden suggested, though he would have given much to stay and hear.

"It would not interest you," Ellen assented, and he went on feeling rather lonely and left out, and not a little irritated. It would not "interest" him; she would have spoken just so to Christine. She knew better, but she wanted to be rid of him.

He forgot his irritation presently in the pleasure of the ride; even the hot side-hill stretch that followed the cool beauty of the wood road had its charm, the charm of savagery. He found Wallace in the village, where he had returned to leave his horse, so he left his own and the two walked on together whistling light opera, thoroughly content with life.

At the turning where the road to the cabin branched off, they came suddenly upon a very pale young woman seated against the bank. A wagon with a broken shaft held the centre of the road, while a nervous, panting horse was fastened to a tree near by. Rory's left arm was carefully supported in her right hand.

The light opera ceased abruptly.

"Well, what on earth!" exclaimed Wallace as they scrambled down from the bank, startling the horse to fresh plunging. Rory managed a dim smile.

"He didn't get away from me, anyhow," she said. "Ruth is all right — I had left her up at the house."

"But what happened? Automobile?"

"'Twas my own fault. I was mooney and he climbed the bank on me — I spilled out."

"And you're hurt?"

"Oh, I lit on my feet all right, but he kicked my arm while I was untangling him and I guess it's broke. Could you help me get him home?"

"We'll get you home first," exclaimed Wallace. "He can jolly well wait." They insisted on putting her into the wagon and drew her to the Dorn cottage. Her mother came running out, tearful and excited.

"Now, Rory, didn't I know you'd kill yourself some day! What is it, child? If you will drive wild beasts! Can you lift her down, Mr. Wallace, dear? Let me take her feet. Oh, Rory, I ought never to have let you. I'll run for Dr. Pocock myself." Rory had grown very white, and Wallace and Amsden would have carried her to her room, but she insisted on walking. She stopped abruptly.

"I'll not have that windbag of a Pocock," she said with spirit. "Get Dr. Ellen — she's good enough for me. Don't run, now," she added as Amsden started away. Then her eyes closed, and she let Wallace lift her on to her bed without protest. He stood beside her, patting her hand in helpless kindliness, while Mrs. Dorn fluttered about, bringing haphazard offerings for the patient's comfort. In a very short time they heard Ellen's firm step on the porch. Rory looked up with her usual grin.

"Well, Doctor, here I am, you see. Now, Mama, you go sit by the window and concentrate. And if you don't mind, just concentrate on the other arm — this one's got trouble enough. Thank you, Mr. Wallace."

"Oh, I'll stay and see you through it," said Wallace, taking her right hand in a comfortable grip.

"Well, if 'twould interest you. I'll not holler," she promised humorously. And she kept her word, though the sympathetic Wallace looked limp by the time the work was finished.

"Gee! You've got sand," he exclaimed, when her fingers finally relaxed their grip. "I should have made the welkin ring." Rory's spirit was still unconquered.

"Ah, well, you're only a man," she murmured.

Amsden brought back the uneasy horse, fed and bedded him, not without difficulty. He enjoyed the struggle, enjoyed the dominion of his will and voice over the powerful brute. The superiority of man to all created beings was pleasantly upon him as he sat on the steps half an hour later, awaiting Ellen's reappearance. Perhaps a touch of this consciousness showed in his outlines, for Ellen's face changed a little at sight of him, the serenely humane gravity of work well done giving place to a slightly ironical smile.

"Rory is worried about the horse," she said. "Do you think you could —" her glance passed over his fresh linen, smooth hair, and generally neat aspect — "get someone to bring him back?" she finished.

"Someone did," said Amsden, reading the look perfectly; "and I believe he has been watered and fed and tucked up for the night. How is she?"

"A broken arm isn't pleasant. Still, it is a simple break. She won't be laid up long." Her eyes turned to the dusty, unkempt yard, trodden hard and bare, littered with bits of rusty harness, stray cart wheels, horseshoes and divers old bones, at one of which a half-grown cur was gnawing with arched back and clamped tail. "What a looking place," she commented. "I should really enjoy taking hold and clearing it up."

"Suppose we do," said Amsden. He surprised an incredulous laugh out of her.

"It would not hurt me," she said with an expressive glance from him to her shabby denim skirt.

"That is easily fixed — if you are not too tired?"

"Tired? Why should I be? I ride as much as that every day."

"Very well. Find something to collect rubbish in: I will be back in two minutes."

He hurried into the house, laughing silently at her astonished expression. A glance from the window showed her obediently comparing the efficacy of two broken fruit baskets. He shook his head at her from the shelter of the curtain.

"I've found the treatment you need, my good Ellen," he murmured. "You will be friends with me yet." But there was only businesslike alertness in his face when he came back to her, in clothes that had seen service.

They established a pile of rubbish that would burn, and Amsden dug a hole behind the barn where the rest might be buried; tools and properties worth saving were stored in a shed. A subdued gaiety crept into their voices. The joy of sheer bodily work set smiling curves about Ellen's mouth; her eyes were cleared of their hostile reserve. Amsden wondered at her strength, and was exhilarated with a boyish desire to prove his own. When all the rubbish had been cleared away, he set her to sweeping and raking while he pumped up water to sprinkle.

Wallace, plump and pink and clean, appeared on the doorstep, and his amazed voice made them both laugh.

"Well, what in hell! Excuse me, Ellen, but what do you think you're doing?"

"These are professional services," explained Amsden. "There's another bucket, if you want to help."

"Thank you, no. I will hold Rory's hand in this emergency, but I'm darned if I'll wash her back yard. I think you're both crazy! Stop raising that dust till I get by — I am going up the hill after refined society." He paused to look back at them in mild disgust. "You are *sights*," he commented.

They looked at each other and laughed acknowledgment: they undeniably were "sights." Amsden threw a final pail of water, then perched on the well-curb and took out a cigarette.

"Suppose we contemplate our labours," he suggested. She evidently was not sorry to sit down. The last sunbeams, coming in long lances between the western peaks, lingered on their finished work.

"Aren't order and cleanness the most beautiful things in the world!" she exclaimed.

"But I don't like brand newness," Amsden objected.

"Oh, no: I should choose a dusted and well-ordered antiquity." They smiled at having found a common meeting-ground. "I don't suppose Rory will appreciate it, but it will be a daily pleasure to me."

"Did she tell you how the accident came about? It seems incredible that Rory should be spilled out, and on a good road."

"I know it. She would only say that she was 'mooney,' and that the horse cut off the corner, sending the wagon up the bank. She is an impenetrable little thing: we shall not know any more than she wants us to."

"I was fortunate in meeting you so soon: I was afraid you might have stopped somewhere with Gilfillan." He meant to stop there, but the latent antagonism that was always impelling him to force issues with Ellen, to break through conventional surfaces and demand frankness from her, made him go on: "I hope he had no more trouble to report."

"Trouble?" her quick look was a question.

"Yes: I suppose Spaulding is making it very hard for you."

"Oh, not very," was the defensive answer. He felt the door shut in his face and waited in dignified silence, intending that she should repent. It came quicker than he had expected. "Yes; he is making it very hard indeed," she amended gravely. "The people here are ignorant, and the new doctor has been adroit in making capital out of this."

"They haven't all gone back on you?"

"Some have stayed loyal, but the majority have gone over to him."

"Well, doesn't that rather set you free?" he asked after a pause.

"Free?"

He turned and faced her. "Don't you ever want to go back to the city? To your friends and some life of your own? How can a woman like you expect to be satisfied here, year after year?"

"Satisfied! I don't expect it. If I can just keep myself quiet —" She broke off, but there was unmistakable longing in her eyes, lifted to the western horizon. "I stay because I must," she added in a low voice. "Don't make it harder for me."

The last lance of sunlight was cut off and instantly a chill seemed to pour out of the shadows. She rose.

"You must not sit there without a coat," she said. They were back at plain, matter-of-fact surfaces as she turned away. Amsden went in pondering. "If I can just keep myself quiet —" Someway, that had not sounded like missionary zeal.

XI

WHY Rory should have had an accident, with a tired horse, on an open road — Rory, whose skill with half-broken colts and unmanageable bronchos had made her famous throughout the region — remained a mystery. On their arrival from the camp, Ruth had gone straight up to bed, leaving Christine to help take the things out of the wagon. She had seen no signs of "mooniness" on the long drive, nor could Christine throw any light, though she held herself somewhat aloof from the subject and answered impatiently when appealed to.

"Of course, I talked with her when I took out the things, just as I should with anybody," she exclaimed. "She seemed to me rather rude and snappy, but no more so than she always is. I am not at all surprised that she had a smash-up with that beast; I'm only thankful that Ruth got home alive."

"That seems to settle it," murmured Wallace, and the discussion dropped.

Mrs. Dorn, who was a reed to every wind of gossip, worried persistently that Dr. Pocock had not at least had an eye on the setting of Rory's arm.

"You mark my words, Rory Dorn, you'll have one

arm shorter than the other, or crooked, or something,"
Amsden heard her holding forth as he came down
stairs the morning after the accident. "I've nothing
against Dr. Ellen — I don't for a minute believe she
meant to let that little Spaulding girl die. But it
stands to reason that a smart man like Dr. Pocock —"

"Oh, Mama, let up! I wouldn't trust Pocock with
a sick chicken," was the emphatic interruption. "This
town has gone silly over him. Just concentrate on the
young gentlemen's breakfast now, or they'll be holler-
ing for it. Pocock — huh!"

The utter contempt of her tone made Amsden smile
to himself. The man had impressed him unpleasantly
in their casual meetings, and it interested him that
Rory had escaped the glamour cast over the neighbourhood. There were brains behind that shrewd little
face. After breakfast he turned to the dingy and
airless coop known as the parlour, where she was established on a four-foot sofa, never intended for ease.
Her eyes were closed, and he paused in the doorway,
startled by the expression of her small, brown face.
It was never a genial face, but usually it carried a look
of dry cheerfulness, as though its possessor found a
measure of amusement in this arid business of living.
To-day, seen off guard, it looked wholly, desolately
sad. Amsden tried to think it was physical pain he
saw; but the bitter line about the mouth came from no
ill of the body.

The look vanished as she opened her eyes and greeted
him with an ironical grin.

"Visiting the sick and afflicted — that's good of you," she said. "Where's your jelly? They took jelly to the invalid in the only book I ever read."

"Do you mean that literally, Rory — that you have read only one book?" he asked, sitting down beside her.

"One story book: 'twas more than enough. Mama's daft over them, and I had to read it to her one time when her eyes were bad. I should think anyone's eyes would go bad over such rot."

"What was the name?"

"How should I know? I never looked to see. 'Twas in paper covers, and there was a picture of two young fools eloping on the outside. Not for me! The *Horse Record* gives me all the literature I need."

"I am afraid it won't, now that you are laid up. Suppose I bring you down some good stories — not rot — from the cabin: will you try them? It will be better than lying here thinking of dismal things."

She sent him a quick, suspicious glance. "And why? If there's dismal things happening — and I don't see much else — why not think about 'em? I'm no hand for dope, myself: I take my bad times the way they come."

"I thought you had more sense. You might as well refuse mattress and pillow because the ground is hard."

"It's no harder than this sofa, let me tell you! I'd as soon have the ground as any pillow that comes my way. No; this world's a bad, ugly place, Mr. Amsden, and I take no pleasure in seeing it dressed up in stories to please young ladies."

"How can you call it wholly bad and ugly, when it holds such people as Dr. Ellen, for instance?"

It might have been a pang from her arm that made Rory's eyes close and her mouth contract.

"Oh, yes, she's good. Nothing — no one could ever make me think Dr. Ellen wasn't good," she said hotly.

"And Gilfillan?"

"And Gilfillan — that's right." She opened her eyes again with a faint smile. "And Mama's good in her way, poor little goose! She'd 've sat up all night concentrating on me if I hadn't told her the pain was all gone. She felt lots worse about it than I did."

"It is a living mystery, Rory, how you came to spill out."

She scowled. "Everybody's a fool once in a while, ain't they? I should think I was paying hard enough without being pestered to death with questions. The black has got to be turned out this morning: there's no knowing when I'll touch reins again."

"I will see to it."

"Well, thank you. You might go do it now," was the ungracious answer; and Rory turned her face to the back of the sofa as though weary of entertainment. Her visitor felt amazingly young and snubbed as he went out.

The broken arm brought Ellen frequently to the house, and her brief meetings there with Amsden gradually took on a character of their own — an intimacy half unwilling on her part, and of which their

meetings at the cabin gave no sign. He frankly
watched for her, but hid the satisfaction with which
day after day he saw her linger — her hand on the
saddle, her face often turned from him in the intention
of mounting, and yet held minute after minute by those
abrupt plunges into intercourse.

Christine and Ruth visited the invalid with cheerful
assiduousness. They usually found her on a shaky
little porch, so narrow that they had to sit in a row as
on a street car, or perch on the slim railing at the risk
of a tumble into the yard beneath. It was an attrac-
tively tidy yard now, and Rory frequently looked from
its severe orderliness to Amsden's neat and scholarly
outlines with an expression of wonder on her sardonic
little face. "Well, I never!" seemed to be the daily
sum of her meditations. After the first ten minutes
Christine was apt to forget the invalid, turning her
back to carry on gaily with Wallace, in spite of Ruth's
gentle attempts to keep Rory included. Rory's face
at such times was worth watching; it suggested the
serene contempt of a tiger dozing with eyes half
closed.

To the general amusement, Ying jogged down the
trail nearly every day with some offering, which he
put down by Rory with a stern, "You eat 'im — do
you good." His admiration for Rory was equalled
only by his withering contempt for her mother. He
arrived one afternoon just as the latter was bringing
Rory her early supper and stood staring at the tray
with a yellow scorn that made Mrs. Dorn fidget ner-

vously and tip over a glass of water. Rory serenely plunged a fork into the pale grey stew, but Ying could not stand it.

"Here! You let 'im alone!" he snorted, and sweeping up the tray, disappeared into the house. Mrs. Dorn fluttered distressfully after him, but did not dare go into the kitchen, where he could be heard striding between pantry and stove and slamming pots about with an occasional "H'h!" of disgust that nearly drove her into hysterics.

"Rory, whatever will I do?" she gasped for the seventh time. "That heathen is —"

The kitchen door opened and she scuttled out of the way as Ying reappeared bearing high in front of him a supper such as that house had never seen before, though it was made up of such familiar elements as eggs, toast, and hot chocolate.

"Your Mama, she cook for the chickens!" he muttered, and strode away, still outraged.

"Food's food," said Rory, philosophically. "Better have some, Mama."

"Not I. Every egg in the house, and that's the cream for the young gentlemen's coffee you're using up, Rory Dorn. Whatever they'll say —"

"'But leave a kiss within the cup, and I'll not ask for cream,'" chanted Wallace's voice as he came round the corner of the house. "Rory, I've come to entertain you," he announced. "What will you take? Conversation? Circus? Charades?"

"Well, if you feel that energetic, you might see if

there is an egg or two for your breakfast in the barn,"
Rory suggested.

"That's too easy. Give me something really hard,"
he said hastily, seating himself on the steps and using
his hat as a fan. "Something so hard you have to
do it sitting down."

"Well, I dare say gassing here with me, and the
others off somewheres else, is hard enough in its way,"
she commented.

"Oh, they're coming," was the ingenuous answer.
"They're all down in the village buying things. Miss
O'Hara was not quite ready to leave, so I strolled on
ahead." His tone had unconsciously become urban,
formal.

"Had a scrap?" said Rory.

An unwilling smile grew to an acknowledging
chuckle. "You're too sharp for me, Rory," he confessed. "We did."

"What was the trouble?"

"Hanged if I know. I guess it was just for the fun
of making up again; but I fooled her by walking off.
The next move is up to her."

"She'll be equal to it, I'm thinking."

"Trust her." He laughed comfortably. "She's a
great girl, Rory."

"I've no doubt," was the expressionless answer.

"It's funny about girls," he went on. "You can
know one for years, like her a lot and all that, and
then, all of a sudden — well, there you are!" he concluded confidentially.

"So they tell me."

He turned to her with unwonted seriousness. "Now, Rory, you listen to Uncle Willie," he began. "Men may be a bad lot, but they happen to be the best there is going in that line; and you'd better realize it before it is too late. Hang it, there isn't anything better than marriage in the long run; you're going to want a home of your own and some kids, and you'll be a darned sour old woman if you don't get them. What you need is to get busy and corner some decent chap and make the best of him, instead of slinging rocks whenever a man is mentioned. You believe your uncle!"

Rory's attentive gravity had a mischievous cast, and Wallace closed his oration with a hasty glance over his shoulder, to find Christine standing at the foot of the steps with clasped hands and rapt eyes uplifted, while Ruth and Amsden, seated on a box, listened with equal fervour.

"Oh, Willie, those inspired words will stay in my heart forever," breathed Christine. Wallace was chuckling, wholly unabashed.

. "Well, it's straight goods. I am glad you heard it — old rubber-soled sneakers!"

"'Man is the best thing there is going,'" repeated Christine, mounting slowly, a step at a time. "How simple, yet how complete."

"Oh, come off!"

"'You need to get busy and corner some decent chap —'" She made a sudden dart at him, both arms out. Wallace scrambled to his feet and dodged

146

behind Rory's chair with a shrill howl of, "Help!" The little porch rocked with the excitement that followed, and Rory sat patiently in the centre of the chase, her eyes half closed, her mouth twisted wearily down at one corner.

Amsden and Ruth exchanged small, mischievous glances that deepened into smiles of understanding. Moving very quietly, they left their box and stole away. Two minutes later they were established in a small hay-field, pleasantly shut in by a stunted oak tree overhead and the sharp upward slope of the land. In this region of grand views, it was a relief now and then to see nothing bigger than haycocks.

"Not but that I should be very happy to stay and amuse Rory," Amsden said, scooping out a hollow for her in the hay; "only I have my doubts of our succeeding on just those lines."

"She thinks we are awful idiots, most of the time," Ruth assented, settling herself with a little wiggle of satisfaction. "To tell the truth, I don't think she likes Christine very much."

"Well, not as much as Wallace does," he suggested, and they both laughed, though Ruth sighed a moment later.

"Do you suppose it is the real thing?" she asked wistfully.

"Oh, real enough for practical purposes."

Amsden instinctively took a cheerfully matter-of-fact tone before questions of sentiment, with Ruth. There were times when she gave him the uneasy impression of a person carrying a full cup which the slightest touch would cause to spill over, with disastrous results. Then she would laugh whole-heartedly, throw herself headlong into some plan of amusement, and he would be ashamed of his momentary suspicions. She bloomed under his approval, and the little-girl quality of her happiness made it hard for him not to show her open affection; but a dawning recognition of an emotional nature full grown and reckless kept him scrupulously practical. She was sensitive to his tone, wholly docile in her desire to please him.

"Christine and I have a perfectly beautiful secret," she said, with a prompt change of subject. "It will be the nicest thing that ever happened. Will you cross your heart not to tell? Well, then. When she leaves here she is going down to Del Monte for a week, and — I — am — to go with her!"

"Good for you! How did you persuade your sister?"

"Didn't. Ellen has nothing to do with this party. Christine has — has invited me for the whole trip and everything." She looked at him anxiously. "Do you think it is dreadful of me to take it? She truly wants me."

"Of course not — I think it is splendid. You would be foolish to refuse."

She brightened happily. "And it is the best time for Del Monte. Christine is going to lend me some of her summer clothes; she has loads, and it doesn't matter if thin things are a little big. We have been trying them on, and I did look so nice. There is an embroidered blue linen — but you won't be there."

"I might come down over Sunday."

"Oh, will you? Will you, truly?"

He smiled. "If I can, my dear."

"You are making fun of me; but I am so happy, I don't care."

"What does your sister think of it?"

Her face clouded. "She doesn't know yet, and you are not to tell her — you promised. When the time comes, I shall just say to her that I am going. I don't see why I should ask her permission, as if I were a child. Do you?"

"Of course not. And I really don't see why she should object." But he had a premonition that Ellen would object. Ruth evidently shared it.

"She always objects to my getting any fun out of life," she said impatiently. "And the worst of it is, if she makes a fuss, it will dampen my fun. I shall go just the same, but I'll feel horrid. It worries me to death."

"Why don't you sound her about it? Perhaps you are worrying for nothing."

"I can't sound people. I always look so guilty."

"Shall I?"

"Oh, will you — without letting her know?"

"Yes; I think I can."

"You are so good and kind." Her eyes were lifted to his with an intensity that troubled him. "What should I do without you! You're always so — thought-

ful — and dear — and — careful of me. I can't tell
you —" She caught his hand in both of hers and
held it for a moment against her blouse. "What shall
I do without you?" He could feel the soft little
beating of her heart. Amsden was human; but he
gave the hands a frank and friendly shake, then drew
his own away.

"You're a nice girl," he said, smiling at her.

"I thought I heard voices." Ellen was looking
down on them from the other side of the haycock.
"Do you realize that it is supper time? Rory and I
have been waiting hours — she said you were all
calling on her somewhere."

Amsden, realizing only the temptation resisted,
thanked his good angel as he rose. "We thought the
other two callers would be entertainment enough," he
said, brushing the hay from the back of his coat.

"But they had vanished, too. I have just discovered
them sitting in the hay-loft. They said they were
looking for eggs."

They strolled back together and Ellen showed herself
unconcernedly friendly; yet Amsden was conscious that
the barrier was up again between them, the barrier of
reserve, half resentful, half anxious, that their afternoon of hard bodily labour had seemed partly to over-
come. Obviously, then, she had seen just enough
over the haycock to misunderstand, and was nursing
her unwillingness that he should fall in love with
Ruth. In his irritation he almost wished that he had
done that very thing.

"You can't run the universe, my tryannical young friend," he thought, with a cool eye on her slightly flushed face; she was unmistakably the Viking figure-head now, and aimed towards battle. She looked up and, catching the glance, returned it steadily. It was a silent declaration of war.

Wallace, somewhat sheepish, was explaining to Rory the difficulties of finding eggs in a loft, Christine beside him smiling consciously under demure eyelids. Rory on the porch above listened grimly, assenting with a dry, "That's so!" when he paused. After they had all gone she rose with a bored sigh.

"Poor fool of a man!" she muttered.

XII

THAT evening proved unusually warm. For once the sun seemed to have left enough of its quality in the rocks and pines to defeat the mountain chill, and a windless moon, peering over the peaks, filled the valley with its calm and lonely light.

Ellen was silent, almost severe, during supper, and Amsden found her grave eyes on him more than once. As soon as the meal was over she left the room, and, looking out of the window, he saw her pacing up and down the road beneath. He stepped out and joined her.

"May I come?" he began. "It is far too good a night for the house."

She assented with something of an effort, and they walked on in silence, broken by an occasional perfunctory comment on the blackness of the shadows, or the aromatic odours that seemed to lie across the road in warm currents as they wound slowly down towards the town.

"I should like to see some of the really wild country back of here," Amsden commented presently, feeling curiously tense, as though a struggle lay just ahead. "Who would be a good guide?"

"Ned Spaulding is really the best; he has hunted all over this region. But I doubt if he would be a very good companion now."

He welcomed the chance for a personal opening.

"Is he still making trouble for you?" He half expected a snub, but she answered frankly.

"More or less. But I shall beat in the long run. You see, Dr. Pocock really is ignorant; he will make some bad blunder."

"I don't know but that a few days in the wilds would do Spaulding good," Amsden suggested. "It might straighten him out."

"Yes," she assented. "He has wholly neglected his work. He really needs exercise."

They turned and went slowly back. The lights of the cabin reminded Amsden of Ruth and her new project.

"Miss O'Hara says that she is going to Del Monte after leaving here," he began boldly.

"Yes." Her tone was guarded, as though she suspected where he was leading, but he went on intrepidly.

"I wish your little sister could be transported there; she would get such solid happiness out of it.

"No doubt," said Ellen, drily. "But I am afraid it is not practicable this year."

"I wish it might be," he persisted, with a gentleness that apologized for the persistence. "It would be such delirious joy to her."

"Mr. Amsden," said Ellen, stopping abruptly in the

road, "it is your opinion that I don't care enough for my sister's happiness, isn't it?" Amsden met her eyes with a tightening of his hands in his coat pockets, but no other sign of disturbance.

"I don't think you always realize in what her happiness consists," he answered honestly.

"And you think that you do care about her happiness?"

"I know that I do." They stood facing each other like combatants, the slope of the road putting their eyes on a level. Ellen spoke very quietly:

"Then why do you go on making her care for you, when you know that you don't care for her, and never will? Is that your idea of increasing her happiness?"

The shock of the charge sent the colour to Amsden's face. His first impulse was to angry denial, but he waited till he could speak with her own calmness.

"I think you are unfair to her and to me," he said finally. "I have not made love to your sister."

She shrugged impatiently. "Oh, not in words, perhaps! I dare say you have been careful to avoid incriminating phrases. I have no patience with that kind of masculine honour!"

"You are absolutely mistaken."

"I wish I could think so! But what I saw this afternoon — well, there is no use going into explanations. But when you talk about making her happy, it is a little more than I can stand!"

She turned away and walked swiftly up the hill, leaving Amsden as thoroughly angry as he had ever been in his life. He knew that the charge was an unjust one; that he had taken care of Ruth to the very best of his ability, guarded her scrupulously from herself as well as from his human response to her charm. If she cared — and a memory of the sweet, eager face lifted to his made him wince — that was beyond his control. No doubt any man who had come into her life just at that time would have been the object of her overwhelming need to love. Only another man might have had the good fortune — the good sense, he called it — to care in return. A mood of bitter self-contempt followed his anger as he paced up and down in the moonlight. The girl was most lovable; surely it was some dire lack in him that he could not love her.

The night was very still. Christine and Wallace had disappeared up the trail behind the cabin half an hour before. He had passed and repassed the porch several times before he saw a figure huddled down in a steamer chair. Ellen had gone inside — he had heard the sharp closing of the cabin door after her; it must be Ruth. As he hesitated, she lifted her head from her arm and the moonlight fell on a pale and desolate face. She looked at him silently.

"Dozing?" he asked with an effort at lightness, as he mounted the steps. She turned her eyes away.

"Ellen went in there, if you are looking for her," she said sullenly, with a jerk of her head towards the open window behind her.

"But I am not looking for anybody," he declared, longing to run away, yet held by the transparent misery in every line of her aspect.

"No, you are not looking for anybody," she repeated recklessly. "That is just it. There has not been a moment when you have not made that — perfectly clear to me."

"I don't see why I am being scolded," Amsden protested, trying to keep her to lightness; but Ruth would not be checked.

"It isn't scolding, it is admiration. I have to admire you for the way you have conducted yourself. And that makes it all the worse, don't you see? For I have no right to be angry. I can't hurl reproaches." Her attempt at a laugh ended in a gasp. "I have to compliment you on your strength and your discretion," she added bitterly.

Amsden stood before her sick at heart, but outwardly unmoved.

"Ruth, don't let a mood run away with you," he said gravely. "You didn't feel this way this afternoon, and you won't to-morrow. Go to bed, like a good girl, and see how different everything will seem when it is the sun instead of this abominable moon. It is enough to upset anyone's nerves. Your sister and I fought horribly."

"But you stayed with her — all the evening!" Then the colour rushed into her face and she sat up, smoothing her hair with her hands. "I told you I had all the petty feminine vices," she said with an attempt at an amused tone that wrung his heart. "What you are seeing now is hurt vanity."

"I suspected as much." They smiled at each other, relieved at this remnant of covering for the naked truth between them. "Good-night, spoilt child." They shook hands almost gaily. He turned to the trail, realizing, not without impatience, that now it would be impossible for him to take the next day's stage, as he had determined after Ellen left him; that would magnify this last interview out of all proportion in Ruth's memory. He must wait a few days and let her prove to him how entirely a matter of transient mood the scene had been. Ellen would probably misunderstand his staying. Well, let her! He squared his shoulders and threw back his head; then halted abruptly as a turn of the trail showed him the figure of a man seated in the shadow of a towering boulder just beneath. For an instant it was not easy to go on down this solitude of silver-white crags and ink-black pines, casting ominous shadows; then he stepped unconcernedly into the moonlight, and let himself down a pitch in the path with a hand on a projecting rock and wary eyes ahead.

"Good evening, Mr. Amsden, sir. Don't let me startle you;" it was the welcome voice of Mr. Gilfillan, who rose to meet him.

"But what are you doing here?" Amsden demanded, with a laugh for his momentary apprehension. Mr. Gilfillan stood gently clasping his little beard, his elbow resting on the back of his hand.

"Well, you see, sir, Ned Spaulding is down in the town this evening, and when it's moonlight, he sometimes takes the trail home, up by yonder;" he nodded towards the cabin above them. "I reckoned I would just — well, fall in with him for a mile or so."

"You don't mean —" Amsden's eyes were turned anxiously to the lights of the cabin — "that he would *do* anything?"

"Oh, no, sir; surely not. But he's mighty unsettled, poor fellow, and I thought I would just — well, fall in with him."

"If there is any real danger, the man ought to be shut up," Amsden said sharply.

"Oh, I think not — I think not. I'm doing all I can, Mr. Amsden. I mean to spare M'z Roderick any — trouble, but I want to straighten the poor fellow out at the same time. He's worth saving."

"And so you are sitting here on guard all the evening!" Amsden stared thoughtfully down the whiteness of the valley to the blue-black wall of jagged peaks as the deferred chill of night seemed to rise and roll about them like a vapour. "How you do carry your fellow-beings on your shoulders!"

"I reckon we're all part of one whole, Mr. Amsden. You just try thinking of yourself as part of one big effort, rather than a little separate effort not hitched to any other, and see if it don't —" his arm made a wide sweep — "carry you along; make you feel the motion of the earth. It's a mighty good thing to feel, that motion." He was a strange figure on the gaunt mountainside, with his floating hair and homely, likeable face, the little eyes lifted, for once, with the earnestness of his conviction. Amsden felt suddenly crude and young and limited. He said nothing, and they stood in silence until a sound on the trail made them glance significantly at each other, then saunter down to meet the shadow mounting.

Long hours passed before Amsden could get to sleep that night, but he had forgotten Ruth. His thoughts were all of Ellen — angry, troubled thoughts, crossed with persistent anxiety at the memory of Ned Spaulding's sullen face, sharply black and white in the moonlight. The preacher's simple tact at the encounter roused his wonder, stirred in him new thoughts that seemed to have been coming to him out of the bigness of the mountains.

"I am glad I didn't die without knowing Gilfillan," was his conclusion. A floating vision of a Viking ship finally bore him off to sleep.

XIII

AMSDEN awoke the next morning with a strong sense of depression, a sense of pleasant things spoiled and the holiday ended. It was a soft grey day that would have been charming to him ordinarily, but that seemed only dull and dejected like everything else in his reluctance at mounting to the cabin — a reluctance he was ashamed of in the face of the gay serenity Ruth presented. Her eyes met his clearly, without self-consciousness or defiance, her laughter was unmistakably spontaneous. Evidently she had thrown off the mood of the night before as lightly as she did her other moods, whose swift changes from black to brilliant had always been an amazement to him. She and Christine were seated on the floor in a chaos of paper patterns and sewing materials, cutting out garments of blue and white calico with feverish absorption.

"We have decided to make the world better and happier, and it's great fun," she explained, displaying the front of a child's frock. "This is for the little fat Flannery, so I'm allowing — that is what you call it when you make a thing bigger than the pattern."

"And this is for the little thin Flannery," echoed Christine, holding up her creation. Wallace, seated

160

on the piano stool, looked down on them disapprovingly.

"Well, I never thought I should see the missionary spirit coming out in you, Christine! It just shows. Are you going to do this all the morning?"

"All day and all to-morrow."

"Amsden, I guess we'd better go back to Rory. This is no place for us." But Amsden was interested.

"What started you towards good works so suddenly?" he asked Ruth.

"A poem in the Gallop Weekly Gazette. It said,

> "'When you're feeling somewhat blue,
> Something for someone else go do.'

Don't you think it's a nice poem? We cut it out at once."

"I'll bet Ellen wrote it," said Wallace. "Well, I suppose it is a good training for a poor man's wife."

"What a horrid thought," objected Christine. "Don't ever marry a poor man, Ruth; you would have to watch for him at the window every night. They always do."

"I think that would be fun," said Ruth, pinning up the fat Flannery sleeves with a capable air.

"You have a bourgeois soul. How should you like to dine at six? I suppose they do that because they can't afford much lunch and they are too hungry to wait till a decent hour."

"Not at all; it is because they keep one girl, and she has to get through *some* time." Ruth's tone of practical experience made them laugh, it was so little congruous with her personality. "I shouldn't mind anything if it was a nice poor man."

"Good for you, Ruth," declared Wallace. "You're the right stuff; you will get your reward. We'll let Christine keep her old millionnaire."

"But we will go and visit her," amended Ruth. "Oh, bother that telephone! I wish Ellen would stay home and answer it." She scrambled up and they filled her absence with the usual perfunctory talk of people too near a telephone conversation to ignore it and too courteous to listen. Presently she broke in on them through the open door with a reproving, "*Who* has taken the telephone pad?" No one would plead guilty, so after a brief search she came back to' her work with a careless, "Oh, well, I shall remember. Christine, I am going to featherstitch my tucks," she added.

"Oh, Ruth! If I try that, the thin Flannery will be a grown woman before she gets her gown."

"But think how dear it would look, done in blue cotton. Besides, I shall have to go off and stitch on the machine if I don't and I can't bear to leave. Let's make Mr. Amsden read to us."

"For pity's sake, do," sighed Wallace.

Amsden picked up the imperishably funny "Rudder Grange," and a contented half-hour followed, marred only by Christine's incessant whispering about her work. He had laughed himself partly out of the depression with which the day had started when the door opened and Dr. Ellen came in. His rising to his feet was as much an instinct of self-defence as of courtesy.

"I must interrupt you a moment," she said, and, to Amsden's surprise, her eyes went straight to his with quiet friendliness, a quality they had never expressed before. "Ruth, I don't know when I shall be back; I am going over to Bald Mountain to visit a little with Mrs. Garcia. I have my lunch with me."

"But it is thirty miles, there and back," Ruth exclaimed.

"I know. I shall probably be home late; Ying can save me some supper. Good by, everybody." Again Amsden found her eyes turned to his, and now he was certain that they conveyed an intentional message. He felt curiously elated. All his just anger against her was wiped out by this subtle intimation that, for some unknown reason, he was forgiven. He read on mechanically with little attention for the story. Ellen was not capricious, nor had she Ruth's volatility; if she had put away her antagonism, it meant that in some mysterious way he had been exonerated.

The girls had to be dragged from their work at luncheon time, and Christine insisted on featherstitching in the intervals. She and Ruth chanted in chorus,

> "When you're feeling somewhat blue,
> Something for someone else go do,"

at every pause.

"Amsden, we've got to get in line," Wallace exclaimed finally. "Everybody is making the world happier except us. There's Ellen gone off —" He was interrupted by an anguished exclamation from Ruth.

"Oh, I forgot! I forgot Ellen's message!"

"Was it very important?" asked Amsden.

"Yes; it was old Mr. Balch. Oh, she will be simply wild!"

"Wouldn't they have telephoned again if they had needed her so very much?"

"But they are miles from a telephone." Ruth looked ready to cry. "I shan't dare tell her."

Amsden consulted his watch. "She has been gone less than an hour and a half; I don't see why I couldn't overtake her." He rose, buttoning his coat for action. "Ying can saddle while you point out the road to me. Don't let's lose a minute."

Ruth, for once, was eager to have him go. Ellen had taken the sedate Adam, so that the fleet little chestnut Eve was left for him, and she would certainly ride slowly, the first few miles of so long a trip; the prospect of overtaking her was not too discouraging. Less than five minutes later he was mounting.

"If a girl and a half rides a mile and a half in an hour and a half," Wallace began, "how long will it take a man and a half on a —" But Amsden had ridden off without waiting for the rest of the problem.

The chance for active effort with some end in view beyond the effort itself was exhilarating. Within the past few days Amsden's refreshed mind and body had begun to chafe at the aimlessness that had at first proved so delicious, at the perpetual "hanging round," as he expressed it. He was not quite ready for the city and his work there; but he was beginning to be impatient for a more grown-up manner of life and for achievement of some sort. The consciousness of an important errand, combined with the amazing prospect of a friendly welcome in its execution, strung him to a tensity of elation that he had not felt in years. The chestnut mare was in wild spirits herself and flew along the road with ears set for mischief, greeting familiar landmarks with snorting affectations of terror that delighted them both and that cost them nothing in speed. They were enjoying themselves so thoroughly that they might have passed a sober brown horse tied before a cottage where the Bald Mountain road branched off from the stage route, if a loud whinny had not startled Eve to a shrill response. Recognizing Adam, Amsden pulled up, frankly disappointed that his pursuit should have ended at three miles. Ellen evidently saw him, for she came out at once.

"Am I wanted? I have finished here," she said.

"I thought I was to have a ten-mile chase at least," he complained, dismounting and feeling in his pockets for the message Ruth had written.

"They called me in here to set a sprained thumb, and I had to take dinner with them or else hurt feelings," she explained. The shadow of unwillingness that had hung over any previous friendliness she had shown was wholly gone; her smile was that of a comrade as she took the message and let him strap her medical bag in place.

"It came over two hours ago and we are horribly apologetic for forgetting to give it to you," he said. Her face clouded as she read.

"Oh, thunder!" she exclaimed. The expression was so unexpected, and so unlike her, that a laugh broke from Amsden. She echoed it ruefully as she mounted.

"But it is my best patient, my bulwark, my last stand!" she said in humorous desperation. "Pocock has seduced the son and the daughter-in-law, but the old man has stayed by me. And he is the prize patient of Gallop. He pays! Pays well, too. Ruth ought to be —!"

"Pays! Do you mean to say you ever give that a thought?" She had turned her horse down the side road and he accompanied her as a matter of course.

"Don't you in your work?"

"Oh, yes — rather. But I thought you were too high-minded. I have a terribly exalted idea of your public character," he confessed.

"I am not too exalted to pay my bills, thank you. Besides, I want to protect the old fellow — Pocock will make so much more out of him than I do. He shan't have him!" she added, touching up her horse, who grunted dismally but obeyed.

"There, I knew it was something more public-spirited than your own profit;" and Amsden sighed.

"You can call it vanity if that will make you feel

any easier. My pride will be in a white rage if he gets away from me. That wretched Ruth! The telephone pad was right there on a chair, and as there was nothing written on it I didn't think to ask her."

"Do you suppose he is very ill?"

"Oh, no. He has attacks of indigestion now and then and gets frightened half to death. And this time, you see, when I didn't come — there is Pocock's chance at last. The only hope is that he was away. Now we must do a little climbing; I am taking a short cut."

They passed through a gate and straight up the side of a bald and stony ridge, a few lank cattle staring at them with stupid amazement, then floundering out of their way. The horses mounted with the ease of goats, choosing their own footing, and Ellen, as unconcerned as though in a chair at home, talked to him for the first time in their acquaintance with her face turned fully towards him.

"The Balch family has been nearly rent in two between Dr. Pocock and me," she explained. "Old Peter is a fine, sturdy, pious old German — he is the big lumber man, up here; and young Peter is a gentle, sentimental, pious young German who would probably have been a minor poet in another sphere of life. For lack of that outlet he is rapidly becoming a hypochondriac."

"How did Pocock get hold of him?"

"Oh, easily. It needed only a little solemn interest in his symptoms, a little talking aside with his wife about his delicately balanced constitution, and they

were both ready to swear by him. Ah! How I hate
the tricks of the trade!" she ended with a blow of her
fist on her high pommel as they scrambled up the last
steep pitch, and paused on the top of the ridge. Below
them lay a deep cañon, wide at this point but narrowing sharply to the northwest. The slope on their side
was thick with yellow pine and tremulous aspen, but
the opposite ridge was fairly open and showed the cut
of a road along its flank. From the hidden bottom of
the gorge the sound of a creek came faintly.

"There is the proper road where we should be,"
Ellen explained, nodding towards the opposite slope.
"But you can't cross the cañon: we should have had
to go six miles round at least from where we were.
There is an old road on this side that is good enough
for horseback, and it brings us out on the real road in
about four miles."

Amsden was looking intently at a cart and horse
moving swiftly along the opposite hillside. His first
thought had been how oddly minute it looked, like a
sidewalk toy, with no other gauge of distance to accent
the width of the valley. Then an unpleasant thought
struck him.

"Does that cart look familiar to you?" he demanded.
Ellen needed only one glance.

"Pocock!" she exclaimed.

"Can't we get there first?" Their eyes met over
the idea, dismay yielding to the light of adventure.

"We can try it," she said with a note of laughter in
her voice, plunging forward. A three minutes' scramble

down the steep descent, their horses squatting and sliding, brought them to a rough road, stony and uneven, ploughed with gulleys, but at least clear of trees and fairly level.

"Shall we change horses?" He was ready to spring off at her word, but she shook her head.

"I can get more out of Adam in a real emergency. We mustn't start off too furiously." she added. "It is five miles to the house."

The horses cantered easily side by side, avoiding or scrambling over obstacles with a capable air of knowing their business. The soft grey day had not sensibly changed colour or tone since early morning: it seemed as though they might continue to take from it as many hours as they pleased without leaving it any more spent, as one might take coins from a magic purse that was always full. Through an occasional opening in the trees they could see the little trotting horse on the opposite slope a quarter of a mile ahead of them, moving with mechanical evenness. Pocock had a better and a much shorter road as well as a swift steed. Their work was cut out for them, and they bent to it with rising excitement.

So long as the enemy was not aware of them, they gained on him rapidly. Soon they were abreast, and as the cañon walls came nearer together they darted out ahead across a hundred yards of open ground. It was then that they were discovered: the roads were near enough now for them to see the quick turn of the doctor's head in their direction, and the momentary pause of his horse, as though sharply pulled up. Ellen on her cavalry saddle was an unmistakable figure in that region. The doctor went evenly ahead again with no sign of having seen them, but a moment later, when a group of pines gave him shelter, they heard his horse break into a wild gallop. He emerged at a calm trot; but there were other sheltering groves ahead for him and a steep gravelly hill for them. Ellen's eyes were shining with laughter. For the first time Amsden saw the strong, unbroken youth that underlay the maturity life had thrust upon her. She was still his Viking figurehead, but gloriously at play.

The hill put Pocock ahead of them, but they plunged away from him on the down slope. The cañon walls were now so near together that, but for the trees, they could not have kept up the farce of not seeing each other.

"Whoever gets to the gate first, wins," said Ellen. "We can't race openly, you know!" The gallop of the other horse was close behind them.

"Then we get there first," returned Amsden, bending down jockey fashion with a touch of the heel that sent Eve scudding ahead. Adam dashed after her, and the rocking canter changed suddenly to the smoothness of a run. The grey air streamed over them, cool and milky soft, as they skimmed into the last thicket between them and victory. Then defeat loomed before them in the trunk of a fallen pine, lying stark and straight across their path. Amsden shot a glance into the tangled growth on either side, and his eyes met Ellen's.

"Can they jump it?"

"They've got to!"

They flew on with speed unchecked, whips ready. He felt the falter of astonishment in the mare's gait, but Adam was plunging sturdily ahead, and the whip brought her up snorting beside him. There was a quick lurch, the striking of a hoof, the jar of alighting: three minutes later he had flung himself down and opened the gate to victory. Pocock was not even within earshot.

Ellen was flushed, radiant, splendid with life and satisfaction, but Amsden's spirits were suddenly drowned in a wave of cold fright, not for himself.

"Had you ever jumped either of them before?" he demanded.

"Never," she laughed.

"How could I have let you do it!"

She still laughed. "Wasn't it glorious! You must walk them up and down after I have gone in. Poor Pocock — isn't he in a rage, though!"

"Will he turn back?"

"Not he! But he can't get my old man while I am on the field." She dropped the reins and stretched her arms out wide, lifting her heated face to the cool air. "Oh, isn't it good to ride, and to beat!" she cried, curling her fingers tightly into her upturned palms. Amsden shivered: "*If she had fallen!*" was his dominant thought.

The road mounted past the rough shanties and barracks of a logging camp to the more substantial house of Peter Balch, set in a waste of stumps, but showing glimpses of the ancestral taste in fantastic rock-work, and an arbour guarded by two little painted iron gnomes. A woman looked out eagerly from an upper window as they halted, and they could hear her running down the stairs.

"Poor Minnie, with her hopes all set on Pocock," Ellen murmured as she dismounted. Then the smile vanished before a look of alert concern as another sound came to them from the open window above, a sound of hoarse, difficult breathing. Race and rivalry were forgotten: she caught her bag from the saddle, and ran up the steps just as a young woman with a frightened face threw open the door for her. Amsden could hear her quick step on the bare stairs within, the quiet strength of her voice speaking in the room above: then there was silence, but for the distressed breathing, an active silence in which he seemed to see her taking all this fright and suffering up into her steady hands and quieting it. He was humbly grateful that he could do something for her as he led the steaming horses away.

He had had time to walk them until they were fairly cool, and to rub them down with handfuls of grass before Dr. Pocock came jogging peacefully up the road, his horse as cool and composed as himself, but for a telltale ridge of foam that had been overlooked on the breeching.

"So my colleague is already here — that's good, that's good," was his genial greeting as he pulled up beside Amsden and held out a patronizing hand over the wheel.

"Yes, she is here," Amsden assented, taking the hand as briefly as possible, but amusedly interested in the doctor's tactics.

"She is fortunate to have a companion in her rides," Pocock went on. "It's a lonely business, this travelling about the mountains, Mr. Amsden: she does well to take time for pleasure jaunts. I only wish I could. But the suffering, the suffering —!" And he shook his head with eyes solemnly reminiscent of painful scenes. Amsden resented the implication of his words, and was still more irritated by the impossibility of any direct reply. He could not quite let it pass.

"I never have known anyone whose devotion to work was so whole-souled," he said, his tone successfully casual.

"Ah, surely, yes! No young lady could be more in earnest," was the equivocal answer, given warmly, but with a slight smile that made Amsden's right hand automatically clench. "Ah, here comes my special patient," he added, as a melancholy young man, with a three days' growth of blond beard on his chin, appeared from the house. The doctor drove forward to meet him, and Amsden, the two bridles over his arm, seated himself on a stump and watched the interview that followed with an echoing of Ellen's sharp disgust for the "tricks of the trade." He had no need to hear the words: the adroit game was clearly pantomimed. A bottle was produced, with earnest directions: young

Peter placed it reverently on the porch, then got into the cart, and they drove off together, the doctor favouring Amsden with a florid wave of his hat.

"Fat hypocrite!" was Amsden's impatient thought as he nodded coolly in response.

An hour had passed before Ellen came out, followed by the young woman she had called Minnie. As Amsden brought the horses up to the door, he noticed with poignant relief that the harsh breathing upstairs had ceased. It had been hard to get the sound out of his ears.

"Now, Minnie, you understand everything?" she was saying as she drew on her gloves. "I don't expect any more trouble this time, but I will be up in a few days. What is this?" she added, picking up Peter's bottle, and examining the label. "Dr. Pocock's Prescription, — cough, inflammation, nervous disorders — it seems to cover a good many diseases, Minnie."

"Oh, it's a wonderful remedy, Dr. Ellen," Minnie assured her. "Peter has had two bottles, and, my, he's another person. Lots of the folks are taking it, and they keep it at the store now. You see, it isn't a patent medicine, it's a regular prescription."

Ellen appeared thoughtfully interested. "I see!" she commented. "Well, I must have a look at it. Good-night: call me any moment if your father feels he wants me."

"You just try a bottle of the Prescription," Minnie called after her, evidently hopeful of making a convert.

"Oh, won't I try it!" said Ellen, with meaning as

they rode away. "This very night, if there is a bottle left in Gallop."

"Not on yourself, I hope?" Amsden suggested.

"That won't be necessary: I have a better way in my laboratory. I found my poor old man very ill," she added.

"It was not indigestion, then?"

"No: a serious heart attack. It is over for this time, but —" She fell into musing silence. Amsden, remembering her covert hostility on their last ride together, accepted her mood contentedly, wondering if he should ever know why he had been so suddenly taken into friendship. Perhaps she felt his thought; or perhaps the words that came like an answer had been in her mind all day.

"Mr. Amsden, I owe you an apology." Her face flushed a little, but her voice was direct and earnest. "I think I was very unjust last night. I hope you will forget what I said."

"What makes you think otherwise now?" he asked after a pause.

"When I left you and went in, I threw myself down on the couch by the window. I did not know Ruth was on the porch until you spoke to her."

"And you heard —?"

"I went away as quickly as I could when she — but I inevitably heard what she was saying. It put you in a very different light. I can't forgive not playing fair in anyone, man or woman!"

"But you believe now that I have played fair?"

"Yes. I ought to have known that you would, but I was troubled, and rather ready to be unjust. I think I wanted a grievance against you. But you met her so — so beautifully, I was ashamed." She held out her hand. "Is it all right?"

"It is very much all right! I have so wanted to be friends with you," he added impulsively.

"Yes, I think we could have been good friends," she admitted.

"It isn't too late, is it?"

"I don't believe it will be — practicable." The thought of Ruth rose between them, and they turned hurriedly from it. "Besides, you have been criticising me," she added. "You do still."

"You are so strong, one has to! It is an instinctive effort to keep you in your place."

"What is my place?"

"I suppose I was referring to the good old idea that the man shall be the head of the woman."

"It is a very bad old idea!"

"So it is. And yet the primitive impulse towards headship isn't all civilized out of us, I'm afraid. We shall have a big fight yet, you and I, and the better man will win." They smiled at each other, and the curves of her mouth were femininely sweet. He could not keep away from the dangerous topic. "Do you really mean that we can't be friends, that you won't let me ride with you now and then?" The shadow came back to her face and she hesitated.

"Mr. Amsden," she said finally, her eyes on the

road ahead, "I care more for Ruth's friendship and affection than I do for anything on earth. Isn't that — answer enough?"

He knew that it was and accepted it without protest. "Only you must not take what you heard last night too seriously," he said presently, with an effort, "or think that I do. A momentary mood, with her —"

"Yes, I understand. And she forgets things. Oh, it will be all right. She has to take what comes to her, poor baby!"

"Do you want me to go away?"

"I don't believe it would make any difference. No, stay as long as you had intended, and we will give her all the good time we can." She threw back her head with an impatient movement. "There, that is finished. Now let's get home."

She put her horse to a canter, and they left the topic behind them in the cañon. At the edge of the town they separated, Amsden to find a bottle of the Prescription and bring it up to her at supper time. Eve objected violently to being torn from Adam and the home road, and her petulant impishness was so devious in its ways of expression that Amsden felt mildly thankful when he and the Prescription arrived at the Dorn cottage intact.

"I won't keep you half an hour, old girl," he assured her with an apologetic hand on her soft muzzle as he left her securely fastened.

Wallace, who was dressing with his door frankly thrown back, greeted him with a loud:

"You're a nice one!" as he came upstairs.

"What have I done?" he asked in all unconscious-ness.

"Well, you haven't made the world any better and happier, clearing out for the whole day, let me tell you."

"Oh, nonsense. Wasn't I sent?"

"When the little boy is sent to the grocery, he isn't supposed to take in the circus on the way home. You will have some making up to do, if I'm any judge of the signs. Girls are the deuce," Wallace added sympa-thetically.

Amsden turned to his own room with an expressive shrug. He was hungry and tired, and the prospect of having to deal with feminine complexities irritated him. He would have stayed away but for the thought that Ellen might be paying in some way for his defec-tion.

He found Ruth alone in the living-room, sitting dejectedly on the rug before the fire. If she had met him with coldness or reproach, she would have found him coolly impenitent. But she only looked up at him with a little wavering smile, just as he had so often seen Nell and Poppy look when denied something and trying to be good about it; and he melted at once.

"How did the Flannery dresses get on without me?" he asked, bringing a pile of cushions for her, and a chair for himself.

"We didn't do much more on them. Christine and Will went for a walk."

"And what did you do?"

"I don't know — just *sat*," she said forlornly; then she seemed ashamed of her answer, for she smiled up at him, and added quickly, "Did you have a nice time?"

"Very: though I, too, just sat a good deal of the time, holding the horses. Did your sister tell you about our adventures?"

Her lips stiffened at the mention of Ellen. "No: I haven't seen her. I wish I ever had any adventures! A girl's life is so hideously tame." She moved restlessly among her cushions. "Don't you sometimes feel that you'll die if you can't have a good time this minute?"

"Suppose we have one to-night," Amsden suggested with creditable enthusiasm. She caught fire at once, sitting up eagerly.

"Oh, let's! What shall it be?"

"Why not a dance?"

"Beautiful! We will clear the room — and Christine and I will put on low neck! Christine! Hurry down!"

Christine dashed down the stairs with feverish excitement. "What is it? What is happening?"

"We are going to have a dance to-night — low necks and everything!" Wallace, who had just arrived, waved his hat, but Christine looked dubious.

"But I am the only one of you that plays dance music," she objected. "Much fun it would be for me, Ruth Chantry!" The light vanished from Ruth's face.

"Oh, dear, I didn't think of that," she sighed.

179

"Why can't I be the musician?" Ellen was standing in the doorway behind them. "I am a little rusty, but —"

"Bully for you," exclaimed Wallace, and even Christine was moved to graciousness. Ruth looked away with a frown, but she made no objection.

Food enforced Amsden's determination that Ruth should have as good a time as possible. After supper, when she and Christine ran upstairs to dress, he pushed back the furniture and rugs, while Wallace strewed the floor with candle shavings. Ying, grinning approval, brought in a big bowl of lemonade.

"Ying knows the size of a thirst," Wallace commented. "Hello, here they come — my eye!"

The girls paused above them, laughing, for their approval. They had piled all the finery they possessed on their thin white frocks — lace, scarfs, jewels, and chains, and then, not satisfied, had powdered their hair and added courtplaster patches. They made a radiant picture as they stood outlined against the rosy panels of redwood, with their bare arms about each other, frankly revelling in the sensation they caused. Wallace put himself at the foot of the stairs with arms outspread.

"You ducks!" he cried. "Come down and let Uncle Willie show his appreciation in the only true way." They came down slowly, then darted past him like swallows, one under each arm.

"Ingrates," he commented. "Well, then, let's dance. Where is the orchestra?" And he went in search of Ellen, who had retreated to her laboratory with the bottle of Pocock's Prescription.

"She will think we are perfect idiots to dress up like this," Ruth said petulantly to Amsden. "I do wish we had someone else to play for us."

Ellen did not seem to think them idiots. "Oh, how pretty you look!" she exclaimed, so spontaneously that Ruth was a little ashamed.

"But nothing could hire her to do it herself," she persisted as they began to waltz.

"Well, she does not ask that you take to her pursuits, does she?" he demanded with a touch of severity.

"She makes me live here," sighed Ruth. Then, sensitive to his disapproval, she looked up anxiously. "Don't think me horrid! I know I am, but please don't you think so," she begged. "I do want a good time to-night — ah, please think I'm nice!"

He laughed. "I think you are very nice. And you dance like a little white puff of smoke. I don't believe you move your feet at all — you are simply floating here."

"I was so afraid I had grown stiff and awkward," she said happily. "Ellen plays well, doesn't she? No one can be a wall-flower to-night: it's really a perfect party!"

Ellen played tirelessly, glancing over her shoulder, to smile at them now and then, but for the most part with eyes fixed absently on the keys, her real attention very far from them. Amsden, conscious of her aloofness, found his end of the gaiety hard to maintain, but it served to free the others from constraint. The dancing grew fast and furious: an absurd quadrille was organized, then a Virginia reel. Ruth was fairly iridescent with joy: Christine romped, but she seemed to dart about with the compact grace of a humming bird. Amsden, watching the brimming light in her face, realized with fresh kneeness that Ruth must be set free. He knew now what it would mean to Ellen to let her go, he felt with new understanding the value of Ellen's work: and yet he could not believe that either her deep affection or the needs of her mission gave her a right to cut this flaming little soul off from everything it craved. Christine had said that Ellen was not poor; but if want of money should prove an obstacle, then in some way it must be supplied. Ruth must have the rights of her youth. He glanced across at Ellen's bent head and rhythmically moving hands with quiet readiness for the struggle, rejoicing that the new friendship between them would force her to meet him frankly instead of with cold evasion. She had admitted him too far now to shut the gate of convention in his face. And she was a just woman: he had no doubt of the issue, once he had made her listen.

Consciousness of the joy ahead for Ruth warmed him to benignity. He whirled her up to the lemonade bowl, and poured her out a glass — "to all the good times coming!" They stood looking on and laughing while Wallace and Christine organized and led a cotillion, dashing up to imaginary partners with imaginary favours, taking them out on the floor and performing intricate figures, then leading a grand march with so convincing an air that the brilliant ranks behind them seemed almost visible. Ellen, watching them over her shoulder with amused eyes, suddenly broke into the unmistakable opening chords of the wedding march.

"That seems to be a nice tune, Willie," commented Christine with massive innocence. Will's face was one large fatuous smile.

"I kind of like it," he admitted; then both broke down and giggled helplessly. With a final chord Ellen rose.

"Christine, come and play a waltz," she exclaimed. "I haven't danced in years — Will, are you afraid to try it with me?"

Some of the vivid youngness that Amsden had seen on their ride up the cañon lighted her face as she waltzed with increasing ease. Intangibly disturbed and depressed, he slipped out through the open window, glad of a moment's quiet.

The sky was dark, with only a dim blur to show that the moon was up. As he stood in the shadow of the porch drawing deep breaths of the clean night, he became presently aware of a step coming slowly up the trail. A moment later he could make out the stooping form of Ned Spaulding plodding wearily past, his head sunk forward, his arms hanging despondently. He was evidently unaware of the lighted windows and the music until a laugh from Ruth seemed to check him like a blow. As he threw back his head and stood to stare in, Ellen waltzed past the window in Will's arms, flushed and clear-eyed and wholly happy in the moment. The light, falling on Spaulding's face, showed a dark spasm of anger: his hand slowly lifted and clenched to an accusing fist. Amsden stepped quickly forward, but before he could speak the other turned away and strode swiftly on up the trail.

The quiet darkness, after he had gone, seemed to cover unnamed dangers. Amsden lingered wondering uneasily what he ought to do, and how far Gilfillan was capable of holding the man in check while he worked through to a sane acceptance of his sorrow. Presently, Ellen called to him from the window.

"There is to be another entertainment, a very brief one, in my laboratory," she explained, lighting a candle. "I want to show you all something. Will you come?"

"We probably shan't understand it if it is scientific," Ruth objected.

"Oh, yes, you will," said Ellen, good-humouredly. "Put wraps on, both of you. It won't take five minutes."

Amsden had never seen her laboratory, a rough little room built off the kitchen, with shelves full of medical appliances and books. The girls balanced together on the only chair, and she faced them with the bottle of Pocock's Prescription, now half empty, held up to view.

"This," she began, "is a great cure-all put on the market by my rival, Dr. Pocock. It sells at the store for a dollar a bottle, and sells well. They are all taking it — men and women and children. To a certain extent, with the help of the magazines, I have broken them up here of the patent medicine habit: they know all about the percentage of alcohol in their old favourites, or it isn't my fault if they don't! I have worked harder over that than over any one thing since I have been here. I thought I was succeeding. But this, you see, is not a patent medicine: it is a universal prescription from their well-known and respected Dr. Pocock. It is not simply strong drink in disguise, it's a genuine cure for most human ailments. Well, now, we shall see."

She poured some of the Prescription into a bottle, and set a Wellsbach burner in its neck, then placed it on a bracket over a lamp. This she lighted, and presently the liquid began to seethe and bubble.

"If you blow us up, Ellen —!" Ruth remonstrated.

"I won't," she promised. As a vapour began to ascend into the burner, she held a lighted match over its top. The muffled explosion, as it lighted, startled the girls into small shrieks. "It is perfectly safe," she assured them. "Now you see how it is burning, a large, clear, generous flame? That is fed entirely by alcohol fumes from the famous cure-all. Whiskey, beside it, is a tame and harmless beverage. This is the medicine that is being spread through this community, where drink is the worst evil we have to fight. Isn't it outrageous?"

"What can you do?" Amsden asked.

"So far I have not fought Pocock," she said thoughtfully. "I have felt so sure he would undo himself in some way that it seemed wiser — as well as more dignified — just to wait. Now I have got to do something active: I won't stand his dragging these poor people down. It has come to an open fight between us." She looked fully equal to it: she was "the Cause" personified in the flickering light of the burner. The beauty of her strength and her devotion brought a quick, swelling warmth to Amsden's spirit, big out of all proportion to the occasion. He had felt so at sight of a torn, stained battle-flag.

"Ellen, if you get Pocock down on us, he will come and burn the barn up or something," Ruth objected.

"Nothing I should like better if I caught him at it! But he won't: he will simply slander and insinuate, and always keep himself just clear of anything actionable — I know him!"

"I'll go punch his head if you like," Wallace offered as the girls rose.

"Thank you, Will. I wish it were as simple as that."

"Well, we enjoyed this very much," said Christine civilly.

"And you were a brick to play for us all the evening," Wallace added. As they went out, Amsden turned back to her.

"Do let me help if you can," he urged, holding out his hand. She took it gratefully.

"I will," she promised.

XIV

ELLEN breakfasted early the next morning, saddled
her horse and went down to the village. Her intention was to find Mr. Gilfillan and map out her course
of action under his advice; but Dr. Pocock's sign and
a glimpse of his bristling pompadour through the
window appealed irresistibly to her native directness
of action. Perhaps the knowledge that Gilfillan would
inevitably counsel patience and prudence had its influence in deciding her to see her rival first.

The doctor was alone in his office, and sprang to his
feet with effusive cordiality at her appearance. The
close little room had a professional air, a result of
massive furniture, medical works, and an odour of
drugs, and the ragged magazines on its mission table
showed that many patients waited here. Ellen took
the proffered chair, and waited unsmilingly until his
light flow of conversation dwindled and paused. He
crossed his knees and managed to swing his seat so
that its back was to the light.

"And now what may I do for my distinguished
colleague?" he asked with florid ease, leaning back to
clap his hands on the arm of his chair.

"Dr. Pocock, I have been working here for three or

four years, and I know this community fairly well," she began slowly. "And so I know what you have perhaps not realized as yet — that drink is the worst evil here, the hardest thing to fight, the strongest agent in dragging the men down and bringing misery on the women and children. I have worked against it day and night, and others with me; and we have made enough headway to know that the fight is worth going on with, whatever it costs."

"Ah, so — certainly," he agreed, looking puzzled. "Yes, rum is the curse of the poor man: I heartily agree with you."

"It is alcohol that is the curse," said Ellen, and she caught a flicker of understanding in his eyes before he could avert them. "For that reason I have steadily opposed the patent medicines; and more or less successfully, for the women were against them when they understood. And that is why I have come to you to urge you very earnestly not to spread among them this Prescription of yours."

He met it blandly. "And what connection, my dear young lady, do you make between my Prescription — a result of nine years' patient study — and these so-called patent medicines?"

"Alcohol," was the direct answer. "I am not speaking in ignorance, Dr. Pocock. I have tested it, and I know as well as you do how much of its success it owes to that. You don't deny the alcohol, of course?"

He smiled. "You cannot expect me to hand over to my rival the formula of my remedy! Very adroit, my dear Doctor; but working in so limited a field, we surely are justified in keeping our discoveries to ourselves."

Ellen rose with a mounting sense that the room was too small to hold them both much longer; but her voice was quiet.

"So far I have not tried to counteract your influence here," she said. "I have felt very sure that it would be temporary and I preferred to wait. But I will not sit by and see you wilfully hurting these ignorant people and undoing my work." He kept his seat, looking up at her with covert impertinence.

"'When doctors disagree—'" he quoted gently. "Of course, I understand that your practice has suffered by my coming; but we have to take these things as they happen. Believe me, you would have to encounter rivalry in any field. You must not get discouraged." His intention of enraging her was too obvious to be effective. Her eyes showed only grave contempt.

"I simply want you to understand," she said, "that hereafter I shall fight your influence and your medicine in every possible fair and open way. If I can get your patients away from you, I shall do it. There is no question of professional etiquette in dealing with a man like you. Good morning."

"Good luck!" he returned with a laugh as the door closed after her.

Ellen's plan of action had flashed into her head ready made before she untied her horse. She had always kept a bi-weekly office hour down in the village, hiring the use of a room on a side street for the purpose and not even troubling to hang out a sign. The need for keeping it had grown painfully less of late: the last two or three times no one at all had come. With the alert cheerfulness that always showed in her carriage when she had a vast amount of work before her, she now turned to the main street and dismounted in front of a saffron-yellow house that seemed to have got in by mistake among the stores and saloons. Its bay-window, jutting to the sidewalk, displayed on a shabby, discouraged looking card the word, "Dressmaking." The woman who answered her knock was also shabby and discouraged looking.

"I declare, it's a comfort to open the door to somebody, even if it ain't a customer," she said, sighing.

"But it is, Miss Gowdy," said Ellen, entering. "Only I don't want clothes this time: I want your parlour and dining-room."

"Well, for the land's sake!" said Miss Gowdy, sitting down to the topic.

An hour later the dressmaking sign had been trans-ferred to the pillar of the little porch, and plain scrim curtains were being whirled through the machine to take the place of the grimy and rotting lace draperies that Ellen herself had thrown down. A boy, sum-moned haphazard through the window, had taken up the carpets, reaping a small fortune in pins, and a smell of soap and wet boards began to drive out the ancient mustiness. By noon two clean, bare rooms

with shining windows were in Ellen's possession, and
the boy was tacking down Gallop's staple article, dark
blue denim, for a floor covering. She would have
preferred fresh paint, yet was not sorry that the boards
were too soft and warped, for waiting for it to dry
would have been a sore trial to her active spirit. Of
the Gowdy furniture she reserved only a table and a
chair or two, having no use for fringed patent rockers
and "what-nots" bearing hand-painted shells. A few
plain necessities were found in the village, then she
borrowed a horse and wagon and drove home, leaving
Adam temporarily stabled.

Ruth and her guests were already at the hearty
luncheon that was their compromise for the prevalent
noon dinner, and looked up in amazement as Ellen
came in, dusty, dishevelled and radiant.

"Well, whose back yard have you been washing
now?" Wallace demanded. Her joyous energy ran
over in laughter.

"Don't get up," she said. "I must go and make
myself tidy. Have something kept hot, Ruth — I am
starved."

When she came back she explained about her new
office. "I do love a good, big, dirty piece of work,"
she confessed, "and I've had it!"

"You didn't do the scrubbing!" Ruth exclaimed.

"I did — half of it, anyway. Miss Gowdy finished
after she had done the curtains. I am going to see
what furniture I can steal from the house: Pocock's
mission-table is worth a dozen diplomas to him."

"Why didn't you let us come and help?" Wallace asked.

"You can all help me with the furniture. And I want a picture or two; the walls happen to be very fresh and decent."

"There's that beast of a 'Nydia' on my closet shelf," said Ruth. "And the grateful-patient rug is about somewhere. I wonder why it is that grateful patients always have horrible taste," she added.

"Because the really knowing people get so spoiled that they aren't grateful," Wallace explained. "Look at Amsden here — you could bet your last cent on his taste, but save his life and would he be grateful? Not at all. He'd be civil about it, and privately he'd think it was no more than you ought to have done. While you take an ordinary chap like me, who doesn't know a Corot landscape from a blue plush thermometer, and any little kindness turns him into a mush of gratitude. And he's more apt to give you the thermometer than the landscape, somehow."

"Well, I shall take care never to rouse your gratitude, Willie," said Christine.

"I think that is perfect nonsense," broke in Ruth, whose sense of humour could never quite weather any attack on Amsden, no matter how much he enjoyed it. "Mr. Amsden might not spill over about things, but he would remember years after you had forgotten, Will Wallace."

"Wow!" murmured Will.

"Well, who volunteers to help me?" interposed

Ellen. "I must be in order by night, and I begin to realize that I am tired."

"I think it would be fun," said Christine, who had been markedly cordial to Ellen since the little episode of the wedding march the night before. "It will give us a chance to see this wonderful taste of Mr. Amsden's."

"*And* his gratitude," added Amsden with a smile at his hostesses.

They found various pieces of furniture that could be spared, and Ellen put in the wagon a few properties from her laboratory, including the Wellsbach burner and the lamp.

"I think they may be useful," she said significantly.

When she arrived driving the load, the others following on foot, great was the excitement in the town of Gallop. Not that it showed itself openly. The friendly questions and offers of help that would have met her a few weeks ago were wanting, and, with a sudden drooping of her spirits, Ellen wondered how Pocock had spent the morning. Actively and calumniously, no doubt: she could not look for an easy victory.

Signs of his activity came to her unexpectedly soon. While the others, with somewhat noisy enthusiasm, were transforming the dining-room into an impressive waiting-room for patients, she dropped down for a moment's rest in the front room, leaning her head against the wall. Miss Gowdy was talking to a neighbour outside, and the nasal voices came to her with merciless clearness through the open window.

"Rent's rent, of course," the neighbour was saying, "but I don't know as I should want her in my house. Somehow, a woman that could go off jauntin' with a young city feller, and leave a little child to choke to death — and those pore people had waited thirteen years for that child — well, she ought to be made to feel it, I say."

"Well, Miss Murray, I don't know much about the doctorin' part of it," said Miss Gowdy, reasonably. "I ain't needed a doctor for the past twenty years, and I don't lay out to need one for some time to come. But ever since that Madam McGuire come here with her modes and fashions and her coloured pictures, and took most of my trade away from me — and it's no use pretendin' she ain't, for you'd know better — I tell you, I've had a real feeling for Dr. Ellen. I know just what she's goin' through every time she sees that other doctor's sign, and the folks crowdin' after him; and I declare, rent or no rent, I'm right glad of a chance to do her a good turn. She's a real nice woman, anyhow."

"Oh, I guess she means well," Miss Murray admitted. "She ain't so sympathetic as Dr. Pocock, though. You tell him the least little thing, and, my, he's so concerned and interested! He's real kind about Dr. Ellen, too. He was speakin' of that Spaulding child this morning in the post-office and when someone blazed out, he says, 'Oh, well, you can't expect a young lady to be as steady and reliable as us old fogies.' It was pretty magnanimous, for young

Peter Balch says she don't speak any too well of him."

"And I ain't goin' to speak any too well of Madam McGuire," said Miss Gowdy, emphatically. "She may have more style to her than I got, but I don't feel any call to go around mentioning it. I'm with Dr. Ellen, whether or no. If you know anyone as wants a skirt turned, Miss Murray, I ain't above doin' it."

"All right, I'll remember;" and Miss Murray moved on.

Ellen had listened wearily, with closed eyes. She did not open them until she heard the voice of Mr. Gilfillan at the door.

"I am in here," she called to him, and rose with fresh courage. "So you have heard already," she said, holding out her hand. "I meant to get your advice first, but I was swept away by my own energy. It is war now between Pocock and me — I went to him and declared it!"

"You've got a right handsome office," he conceded. "I don't know but what it's time to sort of assert yourself, M'z Roderick. I reckon you're right. Did you see anything of Ned Spaulding last night?" he added after a moment's hesitation.

"Last night? Why, no." Her tone was a question, but Mr. Gilfillan left it unanswered, seemingly lost in thought.

"I'm afraid I'm kind of losing my influence with that poor soul," he said finally. "He has turned against me, somehow. I wouldn't say Dr. Pocock had done

it, but they're pretty thick. And last night when I
started to fall in with him, like I often do — well, the
poor fellow turned on me. I had to let him go alone.
He's mighty unsettled, M'z Roderick!"

"Oh, I am not afraid, personally," she said, answering his unspoken thought. "He hurts me professionally, of course. Mr. Gilfillan," she added suddenly,
"why don't you begin practising your profession?
You are a doctor now by right — why not put out your
sign? I don't undervalue the work you are doing;
you give yourself day and night. But why not take
your title and place as a doctor, too?"

"Oh, there's no hurry, no hurry! I reckon there's
doctors enough here for the present." He would have
turned away from the topic, but she brought him back.

"Look here," she commanded. "My sign will be
ready to-morrow morning: 'Dr. Ellen Roderick,
Office Hours, 10 to 12.' You go over to Jensen this
moment and tell him to do another sign just like it, for
the other side of the window: 'Dr. Gilfillan, Office
Hours —' whenever you please. You are always my
partner in fact — I never go through a hard case without you: why not formally as well? We shall be two
against one, then." Her eyes were shining. "Oh, I
think it will be splendid!" He was touched, sorely
tempted, yet he hesitated.

"I didn't allow I'd practice much so long as you
were here and equal to everything," he confessed at
last. "Somehow, when it comes to cutting into your
practice, M'z Roderick —"

"But you will be helping it, bringing it back to me," she interrupted. "They all love you; they will get in the way of coming here, and so I shall profit. Why, you will be doing me the biggest possible service. Hurry, now, or Jensen will say he can't have the sign done in time for to-morrow morning."

His face cleared and lighted under her enthusiasm. When she had silenced his last scruple, he hurried off, and she watched him from the window with eyes warmed by new hope and a deep appreciation of his devotion. She had not realized how great his desire to take his place as a doctor had been until she encountered his firm determination not to so long as the field was hers.

"Dear soul — dear, big, selfless soul!" she murmured.

The two signs were in the window at seven the next morning. By eight nearly every able-bodied citizen in Gallop had seen them, and the news was well on its way to the outlying regions. When Ellen arrived, at ten, half a dozen loyal supporters were waiting to congratulate and wish her success: one had even mustered a lame side for the occasion. Ellen concluded the exhibition of her rooms with an informal lecture, illustrated, on the Prescription, and all unconsciously they went out her emissaries as well as her supporters. When she had disposed of the lame side, she found Rory, wearing her bandages as conspicuously as possible, in the waiting-room.

"I thought you'd better attend to my arm down

197

here, Dr. Ellen," she announced humorously. "It will need attention as many days a week as you think best."

"Did you walk?" Ellen asked, glad to see a glimmer of fun in the shrewd little face. Rory had seemed to her more depressed than was justified since her accident.

"Did I walk! And have nothing to tie outside while I was in being treated? I'm a better friend to you than that. I borrowed the most conspicuous piece of calico in the region."

"But you mustn't ride yet, child!"

"Oh, you couldn't call it riding: he's warranted never to go out of a walk. There's no one else in Gallop for whom I'd mount such a beast," she added disgustedly. "Take a look at him if you doubt his powers of drawing attention."

Ellen glanced out at a stout old piebald, glaringly red and white, and laughed her appreciation.

"You are a good friend, Rory," she said. "Now, let me see your arm."

"Oh, it's all right. You just looked at it two days ago." Rory moved restlessly about the room, talking disjointedly, and Ellen gradually realized that she was trying to say something: a glance at her face showed it absent and troubled.

"Sit down here, Rory," she commanded, and when the girl had reluctantly obeyed, she laid a hand on her shoulder. "What is troubling you?"

"Pocock," said Rory, instantly, with face averted.

"In what way?"

"I met him this morning when I went to borrow the piebald. I've no love for him, as you know, but I had to wait while they caught the beast, and I couldn't stop him from pulling up beside me."

"Well?"

"Well, after some palaver he got round to — our first night in camp up by Juniper Creek." She drew a hurried breath, and would have started to her feet, but Ellen pressed her back.

"Go on: tell me exactly what he said."

Rory bent her face down over her bandaged arm. "He didn't say much: I guess he was trying to get something out of me. He began about the strange doings up to our camp that night; 'you must have been a good deal startled,' he says. 'I don't know what you're talking about,' says I. 'You didn't notice anything unusual in the night?' he says. 'I've only just been informed of it,' he says, 'and I deplore exceedingly that it should have happened' — fat old hypocrite! 'Dr. Ellen is of course young and thoughtless,' he says, 'but I'm sure she never meant —' Well, there I blazed out at him and I told him to shut his head, and that nothing had happened, and then my horse came, and I left. And Dr. Ellen, dear," she thrust a cold, shaking hand into Ellen's, "I don't know what he was talking about, and I don't never want to know, only he's a dangerous man, and you must look out for him. So I had to tell you." And, to Ellen's amazement, she plunged her face into her well arm with a gasp.

Ellen waited a few moments, knowing that Rory would hate any sympathy that made it harder for her to get back her self-control.

"I think you had better know just what happened, Rory," she said presently. "Some roughs made a dummy of a dead child in a coffin, and left it by the fire that night, to remind me that I had — lost Spaulding's little girl. Mz. Amsden and I saw them, so we carried it a long way off and buried it while you were all asleep. It was a cruel, barbarous thing to do; but I don't believe Pocock can make any special use of it."

Rory lifted a face transfigured and shining. "Was that all?" she cried. "Oh, Dr. Ellen, dear, was that all he was driving at?"

"Of course. Nothing else happened."

"Oh, my glory!" She had to dry her eyes again. "I ask pardon for being such an old fool — 'tisn't like me. Do Ruth and Christine know this?" she added suddenly.

"About the dummy? No, I hope not."

"Tell them, doctor!" Rory had become very earnest. "Tell them right away — you never can know what things people will be hearing. Pocock didn't get nothing out of me, but Christine has an evil tongue when you give her a chance;" her face darkened vindictively. "Let 'em know what he'll be driving at if he questions them — for he's got the nerve to. Promise me you'll tell them this very day."

"Rory, you are nervous: that arm is keeping you too quiet."

"Just so; but I'm the happiest soul in Gallop." She certainly looked it. Colour was burning in her cheeks, and though she was smiling ironically at herself, her eyes had a warmth of feeling that Ellen had never seen in them before. "Oh, I'm a bad lot," she burst out. "I've been round in the mud all my days, and it sticks. I'd go to the stake for a friend I believed in, no matter what he was accused of; but all the time, down at the bottom of my good faith in him, I'd be saying, 'Well, probably he's just like all the rest, and no doubt he done it.' It's a dirty mind that's my worst trouble. Get a medicine to cure that, now, and you won't need the piebald out in front for long!"

"I am going to give you some medicine, and overhaul you generally this very minute," said Ellen, emphatically. "You are getting as hysterical as any other shut-up woman, Rory Dorn. I'm disgusted with you. Put this thermomenter under your tongue, and don't say another word." Rory accepted it with an unresentful chuckle. Her eyes were shining, but it was evidently not with fever. She met Ellen's questions with a dry humour impossible to resist, but when she was finally dismissed she became grave again.

"You'll remember to tell Christine?" she urged, looking back from the door.

"Yes, I'll remember," Ellen assented absently.

A few moments later the first deserter from the enemy appeared in the form of a young woman newly come to Gallop. She carried a heavy child in her arms. Dr. Pocock might be a wonder, she said, but she didn't think he knew much about babies: Montrose had colic all the time. That she herself knew pitifully little about babies was evident after Ellen had mastered the appalling details of Montrose's diet. She was not unintelligent, and Ellen, sitting beside her on the sofa, gave her a simple talk on infant hygiene that roused a real enthusiasm of interest. She wished her married cousin could have heard it.

"Go and get her," suggested Ellen.

Less than half an hour later two baby carriages were blocking the front steps, and Ellen was again holding forth on the diet and care of children.

"And here is something you can do," she concluded. "A baby has many enemies to fight — teeth and cold and disease and neglect; but its worst enemy is the mother who feeds it with bananas and sausages at eighteen months, and gives it sips of beer to see the funny face it makes, and puts a cooky into its hand whenever it is restless. Haven't most of the babies you know got crumbs on their cheeks all day long? Now, I have told you generally how a child's diet should be regulated, and I want you to help me spread this knowledge. Just explain it to your friends as you would a new dress pattern, whenever the chance comes up. Help me to make the mothers realize how important this is — and you may bring your families to me whenever they need a doctor. I shall consider myself in your debt."

They went away full of zeal, and evidently began their mission work at once, for the next morning an irate follower of Pocock was waiting to ask belligerently if Ellen had said that no child could grow up who ate cookies. She had brought up five boys on them, and she guessed she knew. Ellen met her with mildness and hygiene, and ten minutes later parted from her with a friendly handshake. The outcome of this, and of two other calls from young mothers that followed, was a notice pinned up in the post-office to the effect that there would be a lecture on the care of babies at her office the next day at eleven o'clock, to which everyone was welcome to come. She knew that it was soon for so bold a move, but patient waiting was not natural to her, and the past weeks had been an exasperating experience.

She arranged the chairs the next day in amused trepidation, not knowing whether anyone would respond; but it was a drawing subject, and ten women, some of them sitting skeptically on the edges of their seats, faced her when the hour came. After she had given her talk on food and care, seeing that she still held them, she slipped quietly into the subject of children's diseases. They did not see where she was tending until she mentioned diphtheria: then there was a subdued movement, a hostile lifting of heads and exchange of meaning or startled glances. With quiet earnestness she told them about the discovery of the serum and the wonders that the new treatment had accomplished; and she explained the sudden dangers of the disease, against which human skill could not guard. Though no specific case was mentioned, it

was her first word in her own defence, and they could
not but be moved at her sincerity, and the evident
feeling under her words. Two or three went away
afterwards with mouths set to express that that was all
very fine, but they weren't so sure: the majority, however, lingered to ask questions and to shake hands with
her. She galloped home at lunch time in splendid
satisfaction, a Viking figurehead on the eve of victory.
She had wholly forgotten her promise to Rory that she
would "tell Christine."

XV

THE tale of Ellen's lecture and her incidental self-defence went through the town like wind out of a cloud. That same afternoon a committee of three citizens, sober, grizzled men, who had held back from taking sides in the town's quarrel over its doctors, called to ask her to repeat it in the town hall the following evening.

"You can leave out the baby food part," they suggested, smiling under their beards. "We believe in fair play, that's all. If you got something to say, let's hear it."

Ellen consented, and the self-appointed committee put up the notice in the post-office over their own impressive signatures. Dr. Pocock was called that afternoon to the sawmill where Spaulding had just gone back to work, and the news went with him, told temperately, considerately, as one of the further wrongs a much-wronged man must expect so long as irresponsible people held responsible positions. No doubt, Dr. Ellen would easily induce people to trust her again with their lives and their children's. Spaulding had better drop in at the lecture: he might be convinced himself. Spaulding muttered that he would see the woman thoroughly condemned before he would go and listen to her lies, and the doctor held his hand in a sympathetic grasp.

"You're a strong man, Ned, strong for the right," he said. His expression was one of peace and prosperity so long as he was in the public view, but it dulled to sour anxiety when he had turned his horse into the lonely road that climbed to the log cabin of the Flannerys. An hour later, as he wound slowly down again, he came upon a dismayed group. Christine sat on the bank by the road holding her foot in both hands, her face expressing extreme anguish, while Ruth patted her shoulder, and Wallace, a picture of wretchedness and guilt, made confused sounds of contrition and apology. Amsden was looking on with an obvious effort not to appear as skeptical as he felt.

"Well, if you will go jumping up and down every bank, Will, of course you are going to dislodge stones, and they are bound to hurt somebody," Christine was complaining. "I don't *think* you have broken any bones, but when a great stone comes with all its weight on your foot, it is apt to do some damage. Of course you didn't meant to — I never supposed you did. But you ought to be more careful."

"Say, I'm awfully sorry," Wallace pleaded. "I was a brute beast. I'll go and get a horse to take you home — I'll carry you myself if you say so."

Dr. Pocock pulled up beside them.

"An accident?" he queried. "I am so very sorry.

Do let me have the pleasure of driving Miss O'Hara home."

"Oh, there is no need of troubling you," said Ruth, hastily. Little as she sympathized with Ellen's work, she had enough family loyalty to shrink from obligations to the rival. But Christine, to whom any male being was a man, revived at the suggestion, and accepted with a gratitude designed to make Wallace still more unhappy. In spite of Ruth's worried reluctance, she had herself helped into the cart by Amsden, wincing and breathing heavily with pain.

"Tell the little thin Flannery how sorry I was not to bring her the dress myself," she said as she was driven away.

"Confound the little Flannerys and all their works," muttered Will, with a kick at the bundle that held the finished frocks.

Christine's foot grew better at once, though her cheerful face became decorously expressive of controlled suffering when Dr. Pocock interrupted his opening commentary on the weather to say:

"But I fear you are suffering intensely. Don't be too stoical — I sometimes think you women are really too brave in suffering. The nervous system needs the relief of letting go a little. If you would make one tenth the fuss that the average man does under pain your delicate organizations would feel less strain."

"But one hates so to give in to it," said Christine, earnestly. "I am just like a sick animal when I am ill: I want to crawl into a hole and not let anyone see me."

"I know, I know! I tell you, you are all stoics. One can't help reverencing you for it." The cart jolted over a stone, and he pulled up with a sharp "Ah!" of dismay. "How brutally careless of me," he exclaimed. "That must have given you a twinge of anguish; but of course you won't admit it."

"It was nothing," said Christine, faintly, but he insisted on stopping the horse and pouring her out a spoonful of whiskey in the cup of his flask.

"Ah, now we begin to look more like a normal being," he congratulated her, and she felt free to revive.

"I don't wonder all Gallop swears by you," she said as they drew near the town, and his hat flew off in answer to friendly greetings.

"They are dear souls, very appreciative of a faithful effort to help them," he said, carefully driving round a bump in the road. "You know, of course, that my professional skill would be entirely at your service if you had not a doctor in your family. Do beg her to attend to your foot at once — not to let it go neglected on any account."

"I have never happened to consult a woman doctor," said Christine, looking dubious at the prospect. "One has more faith in a man, someway."

"That is very natural. But there are things for which a woman is quite as competent — yes, really. Of course, too young a woman is not equal to a very grave responsibility: she is emotional, she wants the pleasures of youth."

"Yes, I think that is true;" and Christine's lips compressed significantly.

"She wants her pleasure excursions. I fear your last one up Juniper Creek must have been very seriously marred," he went on, lowering his voice to confidential sympathy. "I have heard what occurred there, that night, and I felt for you very much. It must have been a horrible shock."

Christine had turned wide, startled eyes on him. "How did you know?" she demanded.

"Such things always get about, don't they?"

"I haven't told anyone, not a soul," she protested excitedly. "I haven't known what I ought to do — I can't tell you how distressed and worried I have been, Dr. Pocock."

"Of course, of course," he murmured, looking puzzled.

"I had been persuading myself that it wasn't true, that there was some explanation," she plunged on. "But if you have heard it, too — I suppose I ought not to go on staying in her house. But it's too dreadful!" Dr. Pocock was listening with the intense stillness of a cat at a hole.

"No one could possibly — implicate you," he ventured softly.

"I know; but one can't afford to be mixed up with — such things. Though it seems dreadful to desert poor Ruth. She doesn't suspect a thing: she thinks

Mr. Amsden is as perfect as Dr. Ellen." The mouse had evidently come out: the quick gleam in Dr. Pocock's eyes was like a silent pounce.

"Perhaps we can do something to meet this rumour and stop it," he suggested after a pause. "No doubt what I have heard is exaggerated. How much did you see?"

"Why, I only saw them come out of the woods: it was just dawn. I had been awake hours and hours, and — well, I hadn't heard them go."

"It was dawn? You are sure of that?"

"Certain. I didn't go to sleep again."

"Naturally;" in his averted eyes shone a hard gleam of triumph. "I can't tell you how I regret it, Miss O'Hara. You see, I owe a duty to the community; and yet, a woman's good name!"

"Please don't quote me in any way," said Christine, hastily. "I am sure I don't know anything."

"No, indeed. You must be kept well out of it," was the reassuring answer. "But you will let me see you again some day, won't you? I may come to you for advice?"

"Well, I dare say I shall stay a few days longer," Christine conceded.

"Oh, Doctor! Doctor! Just a minute!" Miss Finch was calling from her cottage door. She ran down to the gate as he drew up. "Couldn't you come in and look at Benjy? I've been trying to get you all day. He's been poorly all the week, and now all at once —"

"I *am* sorry. As soon as I take this young lady home, Miss Finch —"

"Let me wait here while you go in," interrupted Christine. "I will hold the horse."

"If you are sure it won't be too hard on you —"

Christine was sure, and settled back comfortably as he followed Miss Finch. She was having a very nice time, and did not care to see it curtailed by professional hurry. It was annoying that Ellen should suddenly appear on horseback: she would find a reason for disapproving. Christine nodded in a manner indicating that she knew her own business, but Ellen drew up with a frown for explanations. The tale of acute suffering and Dr. Pocock's kind assistance did not abate her displeased gravity. She insisted that Christine should ride her horse home.

"I have urgent reasons for not wishing anyone in my house to be under obligations to Dr. Pocock, as I should think you would know," she said with a touch of sternness.

"When one is suffering, one can't bother about professional rivalries," said Christine. "Besides, I can't take your horse; I haven't my riding skirt on."

"We can change in my office;" Ellen forced her voice to friendliness. "I can look at your foot there, too. Here comes a wagon: they will give you a lift." She fastened the doctor's horse, and Christine sulkily dismounted, declining her assistance, but wincing pitifully with pain. She would have given much to decline Ellen's services altogether, but there seemed

to be no way out of them: Ellen had a terrible directness of action that swept other people along, protest
as they might.

When the mild bruise on her instep had been attended
to, Christine found herself riding home alone without
even a chance to thank Dr. Pocock, whose cart was
still standing in front of the Finch cottage. Her
seeming ingratitude troubled her so much that presently she stopped the horse and investigated Ellen's
buttoned pocket in the hope of finding materials for
a note. There was a note-book with a pencil attached,
and, tearing out a blank leaf, she wrote:

"So sorry to desert you in this fashion, but your
rival insists on packing me home on her horse. I am
very grateful just the same. I hope we can have
another visit before I go. "C. O'H."

She folded this, scrawled his name on the outside and
galloped back, a wary eye out for Ellen and an excuse
ready. Luck seemed to be with her, and she pinned
the note to the cloth back of the cart seat, then hurried
off unseen. That Ellen might pass before the doctor
came out did not occur to her; but that was what
happened not five minutes later, and it was an Ellen
still simmering with indignation. The note addressed
in Christine's unmistakable sprawl might have been
flung in her face, for the instantaneous effect it produced. Prudence, dignity, the rights of correspondence
were drowned in the sudden boiling over of her wrath.

Taking the missive from the cart, she tore it into little pieces.

"I'll tell her what I have done, and, please God, it will make her so angry that she goes home," she muttered as she threw the bits into the air. It was not till then that she saw Dr. Pocock coming down the path.

A chill reaction brought her very close to dismay as it showed her how hopelessly she had put herself in the wrong. She stood her ground, her hands thrust into her belt and her head thrown back, waiting for him to do his worst, but it was a moment before she could lift her eyes to meet the insolent smile so hatefully familiar to her.

Pocock, for once, was not smiling: his face was pale, and he stared at her blankly without a sign of having seen her. It seemed to Ellen that his eyes had a look of fear, of cowardly, selfish fear, and she forgot her own position in her wonder. He untied his horse with a nervous jerk, and drove hurriedly away without a word. She glanced curiously towards the cottage, but Miss Finch, appearing at that moment to shake a rug out of the window, presented an unconcerned face that denied anything unusual within. She must have misread the signs; and yet the man's expression haunted her as she walked on. Had he really not seen her? Or was it a ruse to make some better use of what she had done than a mere row with her?

"Well, I did it," she admitted with a sigh. "For once he will be in the right. I can't even explain it without calling my guest — the fool she is! He will probably hire a boy to stay with the cart now and tell everyone — regretfully — why he is forced to do so." Tired and irritated as she was, she laughed at the idea of herself as a menace to private property. "Well, I did do it," she repeated as she mounted the steps of the cabin. "Now for Christine."

The chilliest possible "Come in," answered her knock on Christine's door. A white silk kimono over a lace petticoat, a bottle of aromatic salts, and a novel, gave the proper air of distinguished invalidism, and the burnished curls shone delightfully against the white pillow. Though she was lying on her bed, Christine managed to give the impression that she was looking down on Ellen from a height that really called for the help of a lorgnon.

"Christine, you don't understand the situation here — you can't be expected to," Ellen began with not unfriendly seriousness. "Dr. Pocock is an unscrupulous man who has been working for weeks to hurt me, professionally, personally, every way. It is too long a tale to go into: you must just take my word for it that there can be no intercourse between him and my household. This is so important that I took the liberty of destroying your note to him — I happened to pass his cart before he came out."

Christine raised herself on one elbow, her face flushing.

"You took my note, a private note, written to some-one else?"

"Yes. It was contraband of war, and I seized it."

"May I ask if you have been opening or holding up any other letters of mine? It is rather important that I should know." She was furious, yet her eyes could not quite hold their own against Ellen's steady look.

"Oh, come, Christine, you know I haven't," she said tolerantly. "I admit that, from a conventional point of view, I behaved very badly: I apologize all you like. But you had not behaved well as my guest — didn't Ruth object? I am sure she would. So suppose we call it square."

"I am sorry if I can't see it as you do," was the frigid answer. "A man very kindly helped me when I was suffering, and I merely wrote to thank him — as you probably saw. The relation between that and stealing other people's letters — well, it is too much for me!" And she returned pointedly to her novel.

"Very well: we will make it a quarrel if you prefer." Ellen spoke with sudden sternness. "But please remember this: no one who stays in my house can have any intercourse with Dr. Pocock." And she went out, leaving Christine to reflections that evidently had their importance, for when Ruth came in, an hour later, all signs of anger had gone and she said nothing about her grievance. Christine was not quite ready to go home yet.

Ruth brought an offering of candy from Wallace.

"You must be nice to him to-night," she urged, sitting down by the bed. "The poor boy was so blue and cross all the afternoon. He really felt dreadfully, Christine."

"Oh, yes, I'll relent to-night," said Christine, complacently. "He is a nice boy, isn't he?"

"A perfect dear. And he adores the ground you walk on. Dear me, we oughtn't to eat this now and spoil our supper," she added, making careful selection from the paper bag.

"How did the Flannerys like their dresses?"

"I don't know. Mrs. Flannery didn't seem very pleased, someway. The children looked bigger than I remembered; I was so afraid they couldn't get into them that I flew off before she could try them on. She said we were 'rale kind,' and all that, but I don't believe it pays to make the world better and happier, myself."

"Well, we had the fun of doing them; I don't care whether they can wear them or not," said Christine, comfortably. "Is Will coming to supper?"

"Oh, yes. And you must cheer him up. He really is a love, Christine. I don't believe you would find anyone nicer."

"He hasn't very much money, as yet," objected Christine. "Still, I have heard that he is a good business man. Those silly, boyish men often are."

"And then you have your own," Ruth reminded her.

"Oh, of course: nothing would be possible without that. He is going to be too fat, later."

"Well, so are you."

"Brute! I am not. There's a doctor in London who can reduce you thirty pounds in five weeks. Betty

Hall has got his directions, and she is going to lend them to me."

"You know you would never follow them for more than a week. I will love you just the same, Christine, no matter how much you weigh."

"Thanks. Here, you are taking all the wintergreen. The nicest thing about Will is that is he always so fresh and clean. I really don't think I could care seriously for a man who didn't shave every day."

"Mr. Amsden is always beautifully fresh, too," said Ruth. Christine's eyes narrowed.

"I don't altogether — make that man out," she ventured. "There are things — I don't know that I would trust him too far, Ruth."

"I would trust him farther than anyone I ever knew," said Ruth with a flash of anger. "I don't know what you are thinking of, Christine!"

"Oh, of course he is all right," she amended hastily. "He just isn't my kind, that is all. Will adores him — thinks him the 'straightest chap he knows,' and all that."

"I should think he might," said Ruth, subsiding. "Now we must dress or we shall be late for supper."

"I wish I could go down like this," said Christine, limping to the mirror to look regretfully at the loose becomingness of her luxurious negligée.

"Well, you can't," said Ruth, who was not wholly appeased.

XVI

ELLEN was evidently relieved that the girls showed no disposition to attend her lecture the next night. Amsden had quietly made up his mind to go, but did not say so until the cart was at the door. Ellen objected at first, and only consented when he promised to take as remote a position as possible in the back of the hall. Ruth looked grieved as they drove off, and Christine's eyebrows were at a significant angle.

These days of Ellen's activity had been inexplicably oppressive to Amsden. He had resolved every night that he would leave by the morning stage, yet every morning found him mounting to the cabin and doggedly playing his part in the everlasting "good times" that the girls never wearied of planning. Ellen's radiant energy, her complete independence of them, kept him in a state of smouldering irritation. He was savagely pleased to-night that she seemed to have collapsed from the goddess of victory who galloped home every noon to a silent and rather depressed human woman.

"Are you afraid?" he asked as he helped her down at the hall.

"Oh, no. I was thinking of other things," she said, with a smile for Mr. Gilfillan, who was watching for her.

DR. ELLEN

The crowded hall was in giggling darkness as they entered, the electric lights having abruptly winked out, as they usually did on public occasions. Several youths had sprung to the rescue with matches and were mounting chairs to light the lamps set on brackets about the walls, and prudentially kept ready for service. The humorists — and Gallop had many — were making the most of the occasion: several empty kisses rent the air, and the sound of a tingling slap coming from a shadowed corner roused a roar of laughter. The growing light showed the elders grinning appreciatively, some of them with a sheepish embarrassment not noticeable in the younger generation. They were all in genial mood when Ellen appeared, and as she stepped up on the platform there was a murmur of applause, conspicuously led by Dr. Pocock. He had settled himself in the middle of the front row, and his expression was calmly tolerant.

She faced them with a grave serenity that brought instant quiet. The lamplight, falling on her straight, heavy hair, gave it the shine of stubble where it parted over her low, sunburned forehead, and touched with unreality the sheer whiteness of her gown, outlining her wonderful shoulders and arms. It seemed to Amsden at that moment that she was the strongest creature he had ever seen, and also, in a very big sense, the most beautiful. His heart beat heavily as he waited for her to begin.

Ellen was not frightened. After a glance at Dr.

Pocock, she looked calmly past him, and his varying expressions of amusement or remonstrance, the slow, dubious shakes of his head, did not reach her, however they affected the crowd about him. She spoke quietly and distinctly, the contralto note in her voice deepening with her earnestness, her meaning as clear as a child's primer. When she had finished the indirect self-defence that underlay her explanations of antitoxins, there was a burst of hearty applause; only Dr. Pocock sat with folded arms, frowning more in sorrow than in anger.

He was not prepared for the next step; for Ellen, without a glance in his direction, went on to the subject of patent medicines. Her war upon them had been so persistent that the crowd laughed a little when Mr. Gilfillan brought her two well-known bottles, but the laugh hushed uncomfortably as the familiar Prescription was set on the table with the others. Shy glances at Dr. Pocock showed him smiling with a somewhat rigid blandness. Ellen had never applied the test for alcohol in public before, and the crowd watched intently as Mr. Gilfillan arranged the apparatus. The formality of the lecture was at an end: she talked to them as she would have in their own homes. The mellow lamplight and shadow on the rough, upturned faces gave them a beauty that the electric glare would have wiped out, and Amsden carried the picture for long afterwards, though at the time an indefinable nervousness for Ellen clouded his appreciation. One by one the medicines sent up their alcoholic blaze, and the Prescription blazed the highest of all.

"If you really must have alcohol, you know, whiskey is a good deal cheaper," said Ellen, casually, and the lecture ended in a laugh.

Dr. Pocock rose, and his eyes, hard and angry, looked straight into Ellen's.

"I ask the privilege of speaking a few words," he said, with ironical courtesy.

Ellen consented with a slight bow, and seated herself in the platform chair as he mounted. Some instinct told her that she must stay face to face with the house while he spoke. For all his controlled voice, she divined in him a rage that would stop at nothing. Silence spread quickly through the hall, but he waited a minute before he began.

"My good friends, I am not here to defend my professional reputation," he said, with a widening of the lips meant for a smile. "My methods speak for themselves. Do I cure you? Do you feel better after I have prescribed for you? If you do, that is all the testimonial I want — slander can't hurt me, nor mock trials with doctored drugs." His smothered fury flamed up for an instant, but he drove it back and his voice became ominously smooth. "We doctors stand or fall by what we do — have any of your little ones died under my care? — and by what we are — has my character as a man given you any right to distrust me?"

The significance he threw into the last words made Amsden's hands involuntarily clench. He tried to move nearer the front, but he was hopelessly wedged in by the crowd, and was roughly bidden to be still.

"I am not here to offer excuses or explanations," Pocock repeated. "If my skill fails you, do not employ me; if my moral conduct is open to question —" his narrowed eyes searched their faces, then his fist came down sharply on the table at his side — "do not admit me freely to your homes!"

Accusation flashed unmistakably through the thunder of his reckless anger. The crowd stared in bewildered silence from him to Ellen. He would have stepped down from the platform, but she rose and checked him.

"Dr. Pocock, you have gone too far not to go a little farther," she said with perfect serenity. "If you are referring to my conduct, where has it fallen below — your standard?"

This was evidently unexpected: his bearing lost a shade of its pompous dignity.

"I make no charges," he said curtly. "I advise you not to press such questions."

"But I insist on pressing that question," was the clear answer. "You may put aside all scruples, all your natural chivalry;" she smiled faintly, and to Amsden, sick with rage, came the astounding consciousness that she was enjoying herself; "charge me with any crime in the catalogue of which you honestly believe me guilty."

There was an echo of approval from the house. "Fair play!" they called. "Say it out — that's right!"

He saw how he was losing ground with them, and the last shreds of his prudence parted before a gust of rage.

"As you will!" he burst out. "Ask her what happened one night not long ago in a camp on Juniper Creek!"

The elation of battle was momentarily dimmed in Ellen's eyes. "Don't you all know what happened?" she asked, turning to the tense crowd, and she read in their faces that they did. "Some of you saw fit to leave the effigy of a dead child by our camp-fire. We carried it away at once and buried it in the woods."

"You and — one of your guests?" suggested the doctor, suddenly suave.

"Yes," she assented.

"You carried it away at once," he repeated. "And I am told that it was left there at about two in the morning. Well, then —" it was the pause of the enraged animal before he plunges straight at his victim, head down —"how did it happen that you and this man did not get back to the camp until dawn?"

The shock of the charge paled many of the uplifted faces. They looked to see her grow white or crimson, to storm or break down: no one was prepared for what did happen — for Ellen laughed. It was not a laugh of scorn or of defiance; merely a little impulsive note of amused relief.

"Oh, Dr. Pocock, these people know me better than you do," she said. "On that head, I don't need to explain myself to them!"

She might have spoken just so to an outrageous child, and her smile of perfect confidence fell on their strained nerves like a sign from the heaven of all righteousness. There was a storm of applause. A moment later, the entire hall was trying to shake Ellen's hand.

As soon as he could extricate himself from the jam, Amsden started with quiet singleness of purpose after Pocock; but the doctor had disappeared. After a brief search he made his way to Ellen.

"Shall you object if I get someone else to go home with you?" he asked.

"Yes," she said with a keen glance. "I prefer you. I am all ready now." And she smiled at his disappointed face. "I want you to promise me not to go back to the village to-night," she said later, as they were driving home.

"Must I?"

"Yes, please."

He promised with an expressive cut of the whip. Rage was still boiling within, and he rejoiced grimly that she extracted no promise for the morrow. Neither spoke again on the drive.

Everyone had gone to bed at the cabin. He put up the horse while Ellen brought out mild refreshments, then dropped into a deep chair to wait for him. Her eyes studied his set, angry face, when he came in, with a glimmer of amusement.

"You must not take it so hard," she protested. He softened a little as he stood in front of her.

"You wonderful woman!" he said impulsively.

"You were great — magnificent! But how can I help raging when mud is thrown at you?"

"But you would not be offended if you were accused of — well, say of murdering your grandmother," she argued reasonably. "It meant no more to me than that; it was too remote. Pocock has hurt himself — badly. He won't need any further punishment," she added, and there was mischievous understanding in her smile.

He threw himself into a chair. "Oh, let me go and lick him!" he pleaded boyishly.

"Not on any account. Remember, I won't have it. Now, come and eat, for it is late. One thing puzzles me," she added suddenly, looking startled. "How did he know that it was dawn when we came back?"

He had not thought of that. "Do you suppose they followed us and watched?" he wondered.

"No. Someone must have — perhaps Rory saw us and unconsciously let it out. Of course she saw us! That is why —". She fell into a thoughtful silence that presently led her away from Rory, for she looked up to say, rather despondently, "Do you know, some of Pocock's success has been my fault, a failure in me." Amsden looked skeptical, but poured himself out a glass of milk and waited for her to go on. "I never realized it until I overheard Miss Murray talking to Miss Gowdy one day. She said that Dr. Pocock was more sympathetic than I was: that the least little thing roused his interest and concern. Of course, Pocock is a sham; but it is true that I haven't been sympa-

thetic enough about small matters. When I think
them peevish and cowardly — I am afraid I show
it."

"But why shouldn't you? Surely your influence
ought to be tonic, bracing."

"But not antagonizing! If you could see Mr. Gilfillan with a sick person, you would understand. He
is so warm, so intensely *with* them, that nothing is too
small or mean to rouse his concern. In his inmost
heart it never occurs to him that anyone is peevish or
cowardly; he sees the great courage and the great suffering of mountain life, and for him it reflects back a
glory on each least little member. I have done something here — oh, yes, I have done a great deal: if you
knew the needless suffering in these far-off places for
lack of proper treatment! But the big work will be
his. My best contribution will be that I helped him
find his way to it."

Amsden slowly set down his glass of milk, and pushed
his plate away. He had felt pain in his life, mental
and physical, but never anything like this sudden
grinding, crushing misery. It had no name; but in
its glare he seemed at last to see truly, to see himself,
selfish, limited, a thing of unillumined clay, unfit for
even the friendship of such men and women as Gilfillan and Ellen. His forehead dropped on his hands,
and he stared down a vista of empty, arid years to
come, years in which those two grew and blossomed,
while he stood a dry stalk rattling in the wind. Then
it passed, as a wave of sickness might, and hope came

in its place. He lifted his head, and put out one hand to her across the table.

"Ellen, I want to belong. I want to pull myself up till I am fit to be your friend and Gilfillan's. Don't give me up — wait and see. You have been to me, you two, like sudden green things in a desert. I had almost accepted the desert as all that could be hoped for. Now I know better — and I shall find the water. Dear woman, I am going to be grateful to you all my life."

Her hands were clasped on her knees, and her averted face was troubled. "Oh, no — not to me! I always fail," she murmured. "Be grateful to him if you like."

"To you both. Good-night." He lifted her hands and held them for a moment between his palms, then turned to go; but halted abruptly with a warning finger held up, and a nod towards the window. The tall form of Ned Spaulding stood beneath them in bold outline, his gloomy face lifted to the stream of light, his attitude suggesting insolent waiting. Ellen threw back her head.

"Oh, this is too much!" she exclaimed angrily. "I shall go and have it out with him, once for all!" Amsden laid a detaining hand on her arm.

"No; let me go. It is not wise for you. I can send him away." Some of her anger turned on him.

"I prefer to go myself. You will please not interfere."

Ancient New England was clear in his quiet face.

"I must interfere. You will be insulted — perhaps hurt. I cannot allow it."

"I don't see what right —"

Amsden's muscles suddenly tightened. "Never mind my right. I ask you to go upstairs and leave this to me."

"And I decline. Please take your hand away." Their eyes met in a long encounter.

"I cannot bear to have you run a foolish risk," he urged. "I want you to go away and let me deal with him."

"And I refuse. We will not discuss it any longer."

A quick rage swept through Amsden like a flame, leaving him white. He drew his hand away and faced her over folded arms.

"Ellen, you will do as I say!"

The anger in her eyes died to amazement before the sternness in his. Her breath came quickly between her parted lips, but she said nothing. Her hands rose in exasperated protest, then fell helplessly. The pathos of her bewilderment smote him sharply, afterwards. Now he realized only that she was turning away and going slowly up the stairs. He waited a moment for the tumult within to subside. His pulses were still throbbing as though he had just run a victorious race when he went out to face Spaulding.

"Well?" he began shortly.

Spaulding stared at him with sullen insolence, then turned and resumed his waiting attitude. He was the taller by half a head, but Amsden was strung with a sense of power beside which physique seemed a child's weapon.

"You cannot see Dr. Roderick to-night," he went on. "If you have a message for her, give it to me. Otherwise, clear out."

Spaulding's eyes came slowly back to him.

"Message for her! Oh, yes, I got a message for her!" He laughed to himself. "I guess she'll hev' to come and get it herself — you ain't big enough to carry it."

"Don't be a fool, Spaulding. You will only get yourself into trouble." Amsden spoke temperately over a mounting desire to fling policy aside and meet the man with uncivilized methods. "You can't see her, and you might as well go peaceably."

"H'm! Afraid, is she? Guess she better be. Guess she —"

Amsden took a quick step forward.

"You crazy bully!" he said between his teeth. "I'll give you just one minute to get up that trail." Spaulding had fallen back a pace.

"And what if I won't?" he demanded.

"By God, you will!"

The primitive impulse surged, broke through the decorous years of restraint; before he knew he had struck, Amsden felt with savage satisfaction the shock of hard flesh against his clenched knuckles. An instant later the two men went down together in the dust of the road.

Shame followed swiftly on the first half dozen blows.

Amsden pulled himself away and got up, Spaulding making no effort to keep him.

"That's enough for to-night," he said quietly, though his muscles still swelled in challenge under his coat. Spaulding picked himself up and turned to the trail without a word or a glance; whether he went in weakness or in strength, to give up or to come back for vengeance, his unhurried step gave no sign.

Amsden shook the dust from his coat, and seated himself on the steps. The air was keen, but he was unconscious of it. Over his whirling thoughts one stood out clear and triumphant; it was good to be a man! The cords of his arms tightened, and he laughed silently, excitedly, with the magnitude of this consciousness. His alert eyes were blind to the silvered splendour of the mountains or the inky silhouettes of the pines; he saw only shadows that might give forth dangers for him to conquer. This household was his to defend, and its enemies were his enemies, and the battle was to the strong!

Late that night, when the cabin lights were out and Wallace in the next room was sound asleep, Amsden took his grey blankets, and, stealing out of the house, climbed the trail to a ledge just below the cabin. All that marvellous night, while the blazing stars gave place to the late moon and coyotes yelped from distant hillsides and the cold poured over him in a tide of primeval purity, he felt no need of sleep. He did not analyze, he would have laughed at anyone who told him that he was in love; this arrow flight of the triumphant spirit through bright space was the normal state of the young and living man.

The first whiteness of dawn found the peace undisturbed. He rose and turned to the trail, stopping to shrink into the shadow of a boulder as his foot dislodged a stone, setting it bounding noisily down the slope. The blind windows above gave no sign, so presently he took his way down, and, letting himself into the cottage, was soon asleep.

He awoke early, as refreshed as though he had done away with his usual bodily needs. Breakfast seemed as superfluous as sleep; he looked with wonder at Wallace's placid enjoyment of it, and presently left him to go for the mail, eager for movement and morning air. It was a sunny, kindly day, full of children who smiled at him, and nice dogs with a friendly wag of the tail for an acquaintance, and spirited horses with gallant riders. The air was alive with promise of good things to happen, and they all came true when he met Ellen at the door of the post-office.

"Oh, it is a good world!" he said, holding out his hand. She smiled with a trace of shyness deliciously unexpected. They walked on aimlessly, not noticing whither. Her hand was full of letters, but when he wanted to take them for her, she absently shook her head, as though she had no attention to spare for material trivialities. Her face was lifted to the glistening splendour of the morning as they crossed the bridge over foaming, cold breathing Juniper, and climbed in silence up the broken end of its cañon wall till they stood on the summit of a narrow ridge, green darkness and sheer granite cliffs on one side, and on the other a savage waste of chaperral and harsh rock, broken only by the cut of a road along the hot flank far beneath.

"That is the road we took to the camp," said Ellen, still with absent eyes.

"And where I rode back all alone," said Amsden. Her mood thrilled him unaccountably, and yet his doubting mind forced him to break through it to make sure that her silence was not merely forgetfulness of him. She came out of her dream with a little laugh.

"Ah, yes, I was hateful," she admitted.

"How could you help it, dear woman, believing what you did!" The note in his voice startled him as well as her: they both flushed, and she turned from the wide view to follow the rough top of the ridge. When she faced him again her every-day practicality had taken possession, and checked his mood like a hand laid on a ringing bell. The resonant joy of the morning was quenched.

"I must not forget that I have an office hour at ten," she said with desolating cheerfulness.

"But it is not nine yet," he urged. "Sit here under this old pine."

"Well, for a few moments. I don't want to be late; there may be results from my lecture."

"A stream of patients?" he asked listlessly, more interested in watching the smooth shine of her hair in the sun as he lay on the ground beside her.

"That, or a visit from Pocock. I don't suppose he will retire without expressing himself. Oh, he will fight; but just the same, I prophesy that in two months he will have vanished."

"Oh, are you never coming back? Is this life really everything to you?" broke from him. Her face clouded.

"I may come back some day — I don't know," she said, turning away. "I don't want to talk about it."

"You don't want to talk about anything but your infernal doctoring," he declared irritably.

"I will talk on any impersonal subject you like," she said with a grave frankness that made him ashamed of his petulance. He dropped his forehead on his arm.

"It must be impersonal?"

"It must not be about you and me. Oh, tell me what you said to Spaulding last night," she added. "Was he hard to deal with?"

"I didn't say much;" Amsden smiled to himself. "My argument seemed to work, however. All my arguments seemed to be effective last night," he ventured with a quick, amused glance up at her. She smiled in spite of herself.

"Well, you warned me that we should have a fight some day, and that the better man would win," she reminded him, rising. Her attitude said that since he would not be good, they must go.

"But that was not our fight," he protested. "That was merely a trial of tempers, in which mine was proved the worse. No: our fight is still to come, and it is for a principle. It has nothing to do with me," he added.

She seemed to flush easily to-day. "Then what is it about?"

"I can't tell you unless you sit down." She hesitated, then took a provisional seat on a jutting rock. "You will probably hate me for it, and, conventionally, it is none of my business," he went on with a seriousness that reassured her. "But you are too big to take things conventionally: if I am in the wrong you will prove it to me. It is about Ruth."

A frightened look came into her eyes. "Ruth?"

"Yes. About making her live up here, when she is so rebellious against it." She bent down her face over her folded arms, and said nothing: he had to look away from her to go on in the same quiet impersonal tone. "When I came up here I saw only her side. Every day since has been showing me your side — how fine and selfless your work is, how much you care for her, how much it ought to mean for her good just to live with a woman like you. And yet here she is, bitter, resentful, every inch of her demanding her freedom. And I cannot convince myself that she hasn't a right to her own life. I felt it so that night we danced — she is so passionately alive. Surely, surely, it isn't right to keep her cut off from everything her nature demands."

"But she has not always been like this;" there was a desolate note in Ellen's voice that wrung him. "Until this spring she seemed fairly contented, a good deal of the time. And it is only since she went down to the tennis tournament that she has been so — so bitter. You must believe that."

"Of course I do. But now she is awake and you can't put her to sleep again."

"You don't think — she might find some interests —?" Ellen spoke hopelessly, still with her head bent down so that he could not see her face.

"No. I think you have got to let her go." But he hated himself for saying it. "If money is a difficulty," he began presently as she did not speak.

"Oh, no. It isn't that. Oh, if that were all!" She rose abruptly, and all Ruth's passionate crying out had never hurt him like the sight of tears on her cheeks. Their battle was on, but she was not fighting, and all at once he did not want to win. He started to his feet.

"Ellen, forgive me — I am a fool!"

"You don't know, you don't understand," she said brokenly. "I will tell you, some day. Now I want to go."

He followed her down in silence, too heavy-hearted for her to care whether or not he had liberated Ruth. If she had only argued or protested, he could have fought even tears; but this stricken silence left him helpless.

The streets of the town were unusually empty, and finally they spoke of it, but with no room in their minds for any real wonder until a turn of the road brought them in sight of an excited crowd clustered along the sidewalk opposite the trim white cottage of the Finches.

A woman ran by them, crying, and instantly the crowd gathered about her. Her tale was borne back towards them in angry exclamations. Mothers clutched their children and drew them away, and the groups shrank back to either side as the woman, her tale ended, ran up the walk and into the Finch cottage. Ellen caught a hurrying mother.

"What is it? I must know."

"It's smallpox," was the breathless answer; "and my Johnny, he played with Benjy the last day he was out. Oh, my, my!"

"And Dr. Pocock won't come," volunteered another woman. "Miss Murray, she saw Benjy this morning, and she says, 'My God, Carrie Finch, that ain't no chicken-pox — it's smallpox, sure's you live!' She seen it before, and she run to the doctor. And he says, yes, he knowed day before yesterday 'twas smallpox, and he won't come. She's been again to beg him."

"Says it wouldn't be fair to his other cases," broke in a man. "Scared!"

"Mean little skunk," added another. "I never did set much store by him."

. Amsden heard with a terrible dismay, knowing what would come. Ellen handed him her letters and left him without a word or a glance.

"There goes Dr. Ellen — she ain't afraid!" exclaimed a voice. It ran through the crowd like a quick wind as Ellen crossed the road. "She ain't afraid. She never held back from nothing! She'll pull him through." Ellen, wholly unconscious of everything but her purpose, had almost reached the gate when Ned Spaulding broke from the crowd and confronted her with uplifted arms.

"No! Don't let her kill any more children!" he cried. "Let him die the Lord's own way, if he must. Don't let's have no more doctor murder in our homes!"

The crowd stared, too bewildered for the moment to take sides. Amsden started forward, but Ellen checked him with a gesture.

"Ned Spaulding," she said clearly, "no child and no grown person has ever died in this place through my neglect or my indolence or my wilful ignorance. I have given you — all of you — my human best, and I demand that you recognize it."

They moved restlessly before her accusing eyes. Spaulding laughed contemptuously, then his face darkened as no one echoed him or rallied to his side. Striding swiftly across her path, he stood blocking the way like an ancient prophet, gaunt and gloomy, his black eyes glowering at her, his great, bony hands resting on the gate posts.

"You'll not go in to that child!" he shouted. Ellen went towards him like an outraged Victory.

"Let me pass!" she said with a sternness before which his eyes faltered; his hands dropped to his sides. Then a flush of rage mounted to his face as though at his own wavering. He threw back his head, and one hand made a quick movement towards his hip pocket. Instantly, before Amsden could stir, the crowd was upon him, women as well as men. He was seized, hustled, dragged aside, shrill voices rose at him in bitter denunciation. "We've had enough of you, Ned Spaulding!" the cry swept after him as they rushed him down the street. A man might commit many crimes in Gallop, but he might not put hand to his gun against a woman, and by that movement Spaulding had hurled himself from his high position as martyr. His face was bewildered, stricken, when they let him go. There was no fight left in him.

Amsden, sick at heart, waited with the rest for a terrible twenty minutes. The air was filled with threats of what would happen if Ellen were interfered with, mingled with defiant praises of her, tardy recollections of her skill and devotion. What her simple courage the night before had begun, Spaulding's gesture had completed; she was theirs wholly once more. At last an excited woman opened the cottage door, and ran down to the gate.

"'Tain't smallpox at all," she announced joyfully. "Old Pocock was wrong. It's just chicken-pox — she says so. I'm going to stay and help; Miss Finch is just about done up."

"Good for you, Miss Murray," called several voices after her, as she hurried back. The crowd began to move away.

"He don't even know smallpox from chicken-pox!" was the universal comment. Everyone seemed suddenly to remember some mistake Dr. Pocock had made. The men laughed derisively. "Had his scare for nothing!" they jeered. "Guess we've had about enough of *him!*"

The street was deserted, except for Amsden, when Ellen came out. Miss Finch followed her, and they shook hands warmly at the door. Ellen was buoyant, smiling, filled with the satisfaction of her work, a mood that oppressed Amsden with a sense of the distance between them, and the completeness of her individual life. He repeated to her what he had overheard in the crowd.

"Pocock has ended his career here, I imagine," he added. "The blunder coming on top of the cowardice was too much."

She laughed. "It is queer that he should fall by this particular mistake; for, twenty-four hours ago, I could not have told myself that it was not smallpox — no doctor could. There is often a stage where they look precisely alike. He has made plenty of real blunders, but this time it wasn't one at all."

"But the scare was; he falls righteously by that." A shudder betrayed itself. "Oh, it was horrible, seeing you go in there," he exclaimed. "And I couldn't do it for you, I was utterly helpless."

"You couldn't even send me upstairs," she suggested with a repressed smile. He laughed.

"Please forgive that. I have been amazed ever since that you went, though I admit I expected it at the time."

"You seemed to."

"Oh, Doctor, dear!" Mrs. Larsen was balancing

239

nervously in front of them. "The poor man, he don't get well at all — he's suffering something awful. And you said, dear, that you'd come back —"

"Of course I will," said Ellen, laying a reassuring hand on the meek little shoulder.

"And, Doctor, would you take a look at my sister?" broke in a woman who had hurried after them. "Oh, you're just fine," she added. "You're the doctor for us."

Any group that paused in the town of Gallop instantly became the centre of a crowd. Men, women, children, and dogs quickly gathered about Ellen; hands were offered, shy apologies, hearty assurances of loyalty. Amsden, crowded out, saw her face brighten and soften, her eyes grow misty with kindness. Yes, her work was splendidly worth while; he had to acknowledge that without reservations. He had never admired her so deeply, or felt so far apart from her. She went away to look at the sister without a word or a glance for him.

The town seemed suddenly hot and dusty and squalid, and he turned away from it to the cañon that opened like a giant cleft in the mountains above, narrowing until it looked no more than a sharp knife-thrust between granite walls. The tumult of the creek compressed between its sides, the gold of the sun-touched cliffs and the cold violet of the wall in shadow, had been a delight to him before; but now the glory had gone off the world, his early morning elation seemed a piece of childishness, his exultant night ꝛatch a pompous and empty proceeding. Ellen obviously had no real interest in him.

"God knows why she should have," he admitted in bitter humility. The dense hopelessness that only lack of food and sleep can give in its perfection clung like a wet cloak to his shoulders. And yet he still would not have believed that he loved Ellen Chantry.

Half an hour's hard climbing softened the edges of his gloom. He was beginning to wonder a little at the acuteness of his recent misery, when, scrambling to the top of a boulder, he saw something that for the moment made him forget himself. On a rock just ahead sat Spaulding, his head sunk between his shoulders, his hands hanging limply over his knees, his face still heavy with bewilderment. The strength seemed to have been stricken from him, and Amsden felt a quick rush of pity, pity for the man's blundering, for nis humiliation. The brooding weakness behind the rugged face was suddenly revealed to him. Without any very clear purpose, he came and seated himself on a neighbouring rock, fixing his eyes on the pool under his feet. After a quick glance, Spaulding ignored him, and they sat in silence for a long time, a silence that seemed to draw out hostility as moist earth draws the pain from a sting. At last Spaulding spoke, without lifting his eyes.

"They've all turned agen me — every one on 'em. They was with me, and then they turned. That's all they're worth." Another long, healing silence brought them still closer together. Spaulding drew a picture from his coat pocket.

"That was her," he said. The cheap reproduction had reduced the childish face to doll-like blankness, but the poor finery of the little frock spoke eloquently. Amsden looked at it with a quiet sympathy that brought gruff confidences; the child's little ways and sayings, her devotion to her father. "And choked to death!" he ended with sudden fierceness. Amsden gave the picture back, and let his hand fall on the man's drooping shoulder.

"See here, Ned," he began, "I want to go off into the mountains for a few days, and they tell me that nobody knows them as you do. You come and act as guide for me. I want some real climbing." A glimmer of interest lighted Spaulding's eyes, though he lowered them as if ashamed of it.

"When did you guess you'd start?" he asked indifferently.

"Now." Amsden rose with contagious energy. "You tell me what to get for our outfit, and I will be up at your house early this afternoon. We will sleep in camp to-night. Is it a go?"

"I don't mind," was the heavy answer; but Spaulding's shoulders had straightened.

XVII

EARLY that same morning Ruth was awakened by sounds from the next room. She listened lazily for a while, wondering what Christine could be doing. When the squeak of a dragged trunk came to her, she put on a wrapper and went to investigate.

Christine was half dressed, and the bed was piled high with clothes. The face she lifted from her open trunk was curiously set.

"What are you doing?" Ruth demanded.

"I am going home to-day," was the curt answer.

"Well, for pity's sake, why?"

Christine folded a linen dress and laid it in the trunk without answering, her lips tightly compressed. Ruth closed the door, and seated herself on the edge of a chair, watching her with eyes full of distress.

"Christine, if we have hurt you in any way, or said anything, it honestly hasn't been intended," she said gently. "Please don't — be like this. I never dreamed that you were offended about anything."

"It isn't you, Ruth." She tried to stop there, but the inner tumult was too strong. "It is just that I won't stay another day under the same roof with your sister," she burst out.

"Oh, dear! I know Ellen is — but she can't help it, Christine. She isn't like us, that's all. Can't you just not mind her?"

"Oh, it isn't her rudeness! I could stand that. I could even overlook her taking possession of my private letters — yes, she did, Ruth, but it is no matter now. But I can't stand seeing what is going on here with that dreadful Philip Amsden —"

"Christine!" Ruth had jumped up, white and angry. "What do you mean!" Christine flung down an armful of clothes, and faced her desperately.

"I mean that they're both — *bad!* There, now! I won't live in the house with such things, and I don't think you ought to, either."

Ruth's colour came back and she gave a relieved laugh. "You're crazy," she said calmly.

"Very well, perhaps I am;" and Christine wrapped a hat in tissue with minute care, though her hands shook visibly.

"Plain crazy," Ruth repeated with rising indignation. "What could put such an idea into your head?"

"Well, perhaps you will explain to me why they were off together in the woods half the night when we were in camp."

"But they weren't!"

"I am sorry, but they were. I had been awake hours, and there had not been a sound; then I saw them coming back from somewhere together, she in her wrapper with her hair down. He held her hand and they whispered — oh, it made me simply sick!"

"You dreamed it," said Ruth; but her colour had gone again.

"I wish I had."

"Why didn't you speak of it?"

"It didn't seem any of my business. And everyone else seemed to think them both so perfect, I felt I ought to give them the benefit of the doubt. There might have been some explanation, though I confess I don't see —! But after last night — well, I shan't stay, that is all. And I think you ought to come with me."

"What about last night?" Ruth asked in a frightened whisper. Christine turned away from the bewildered eyes, and her voice was less hard as she went on.

"The shade rattled and woke me up very early — it was barely light. I was getting up to fix it when I heard a sound on the trail. Mr. Amsden was just going down. I saw him distinctly."

The silence lasted so long that Christine became frightened.

"I had to tell you, Ruth," she said uncomfortably.

"Of course. And it is all some mistake, some silly misunderstanding;" Ruth spoke in a tired, faint little voice, rising to her feet with an effort. "Ellen can explain it. It is absurd to think anything wrong of those two."

"Well, if she can explain all that away," began Christine, vindictively.

"Why, of course she can. She has gone out, but I will ride after her and find her. You must wait,

Christine. You can't take to-day's stage. It isn't fair not to wait till I have asked Ellen."

"I don't charge her with anything," said Christine, quickly. "I am only telling you what I have seen."

"Yes, I know. Of course it is all a mistake." Ruth pressed her hand to her forehead as though to clear her thoughts. "Ellen will tell me the truth, you know. She always does. Go and have your breakfast. I will find her."

She looked scarcely able to dress herself as she went out, but Christine was afraid to follow her. She sat huddled uncertainly among her things until she heard a horse galloping off in the direction of the village.

The fact that Ellen had not taken a horse showed that she had not gone far. Ruth meant to ask in the village if anyone had seen her, but her heart was beating so horribly that she could not trust her voice. She rode slowly down the main street, looking right and left with sick, frightened eyes that had no recognition for acquaintances. When she was almost at the bridge she saw them, Ellen and Amsden. They had paused, and Ellen was looking down into the racing water, but he was looking at Ellen. Then they went on together, and the quality of their silence fell like a garment of horror about the girl watching them. She saw them leave the road and disappear among the trees.

Turning her horse, she rode back through the village quietly enough, though she put Eve to a gallop as soon as they were outside. The mare struggled to take the home road, but Ruth struck her savagely and they flew on, anywhere, that she might get away from the wild anger in her heart. Rory, standing at the gate, saw her coming, and waved a welcome, but Ruth stared at her unseeingly as she raced past. The white face and reckless riding brought a smothered exclamation from Rory. She had a glimpse of the truth.

"She's heard, and heard wrong," she muttered. "Oh, if I had my arm, now!" The black horse whinnied suggestively to her over the bars of the corral. Rory stood biting her lower lip, her eyes on her bandaged arm; then she brought a bridle and slipped it over his head. "You ride better than you drive — or, at least, not much worse," she muttered. "I've got to look after that child."

She managed to saddle with one hand, and rode out bare-headed, avoiding the house and her mother. As the horse broke into an eager canter, she dropped the reins about the pommel and clutched her left forearm.

"It don't hurt much," she gasped.

Ruth galloped on until Eve was streaked with foam, and the wild confusion in her heart died down, leaving the place of her deepest wound uncovered to her desolate eyes. When at last she let the horse settle to a tired walk, it was not Amsden who held her thoughts, nor her own hopes and desires. Her faith in Ellen had been the big, sound centre of her life, the star by which she knew infallibly where the right course lay. She had fought her sister, resented her, at times almost hated her; but she had believed in her as she had never believed in God or creed. And now it was as though the stars themselves had fallen. She was lost in the dark: there was no right and no wrong, and no human faith was justified if Ellen was not true to herself.

"I can't bear it, I can't!" she cried at last, pressing her hands to her temples. And then she wondered with sick iteration what people did when they could not bear it. Perhaps they died? The idea brought a cool breath of relief. There was nothing to stay for, now, and to her passionate impatience of suffering another day such as this was the unbearable ordeal, not dark, quiet death. And it would hurt them, these two who had been cheating her: there was grim satisfaction in that thought. For the first time she looked to see where she was.

The shadow of a granite cliff lay over the road. Below, through a fringe of willows, shone the pale face of a tiny mountain lake, a pond in width, though no line had ever fathomed its secret depths. Ruth dismounted, leaving the horse free, and, climbing down the steep bank, parted the band of low bushes that hedged the pool. They sprang together behind her like a door closing on a hateful street, and the cool room that received her was redolent of peace and secrecy. Its silver floor was so narrow that the crowded willows kept it in shadow: at their feet about the rim ran a border of late flowers, doubled in the rippleless surface. Ruth knelt at the margin and dipped one hand into the water; its tingling cold had a welcome purity. She had not committed herself to any intention, yet some vague thought of a prayer crossed her mind. She tried to remember one, but the haunting words of the old darky song crowded it out. She crooned them under her breath:

"Sometimes I feel like a motherless chile,
Feel like a motherless chi — le,
Feel like a motherless chile —"

After all, why say prayers? If there was no Ellen, there was assuredly no God. The smothering trouble dragged its weight over her, crushing out the momentary peace. No, she could not bear it. And there was nothing left in life. She dipped her hands to the wrists in the welcome cold.

"Hello, Ruth," said a commonplace voice. Rory's face, oddly white and lined, was looking casually over the thicket. "Nice spot for a picnic. Wait till I come in there, now." She worked her way through the bushes, emerging with a set smile on her grim little face. "I saw you ride by, and I couldn't resist a ride myself, so I came along," she explained.

Ruth, sinking back on her heels, looked at her remotely, conscious only of a vague shame at being caught. But Rory seemed to suspect nothing. She seated herself on the ground, talking cheerfully of unimportant matters that required no answers.

"You didn't fasten the mare very good," she threw in. "You'd have had a good walk home if I hadn't come along. And Dr. Ellen has trouble enough on her hands without you doing yourself up." Ruth had winced and turned her head away at Ellen's name. Sure now of her attention, Rory plunged in: "Did she tell you the low trick some of the boys played on her that first night up in camp?" Ruth shrank away with a tense shake of her head, and Rory, tossing pebbles into the pond, went on with the tale of the dummy child and the moonlight burial. "Mr. Amsden dug the grave for it with the potato shovel — I wondered what had come over it the next day," she concluded. "Wasn't that the mean trick, though!" It was hard to meet unmoved the face Ruth turned to her — so tremulous and eager, so pitifully afraid of hope.

"They went off — to bury the thing?" she stammered.

"Sure. Nice job it must have been."

"But where was Mr. Amsden last night? Why was he —?" Ruth cared nothing for appearances, but Rory doggedly kept them up.

"Oh, he slep' out doors — you'd believe it if you saw his blankets, one mass of pine needles," she grumbled. "I shouldn't wonder if he was afraid Spaulding or Pocock would play some fresh trick on you, and just slep' up there near the cabin to be on hand in case of trouble. I must say 'twould be like him: he's real kind. My, that lecture's made a stir. I'm that mad I didn't get to it. Mama went, but my old arm —"

Ruth had flung herself face down on the ground, and was sobbing with a violence that racked her from head to foot. After a few moments Rory grew frightened and drew the helpless figure up against her hard little breast.

"There, now, child, don't you, now," she muttered. "It's all right. You've heard some fool talk, I'll be bound, but you mustn't mind that. There's no end to the foul tongues, but they can't touch a woman like Dr. Ellen. Steady, now — child, you'll founder yourself if you don't pull up!"

Ruth gradually grew quiet, and presently lay still but for the involuntary shudders left by the storm of tears. The look of pain deepened about Rory's mouth, and once or twice her eyes closed with a suggestion of faintness, but she did not stir until Ruth slowly dragged herself up and stooped to bathe her face.

"Oh, Rory," she said brokenly, "I shan't mind anything now, not even if he cares for her. Do you think he does?"

"No such luck," was the sharp answer. "You'll not catch a man caring for a fine woman like that so long as there's fools left free. Come on, now: we've a good twelve miles to go, and my arm don't feel any too good."

"You oughtn't to be riding yet," said Ruth, absently.

"I dare say you're right," Rory conceded.

Long before the ride was done, all traces of the storm had left Ruth's sky: she sat her saddle in smiling peace, Ellen and righteousness restored to their places, and all things well with the world. Her head ached, but she was too happy to care. Rory, who had grown very unresponsive, pulled up at her gate with a suppressed sigh of relief.

"Will you ask Dr. Ellen to drop in and look me over?" she said, dismounting with weary caution.

"You should not have ridden — but I am awfully glad you did;" and Ruth, stooping from the saddle, kissed the small brown face.

"Oh, go 'long!" muttered Rory, turning away.

It was long past lunch time, but, as Ellen had not been home, Ruth called up her office and found her there. Oh, that warm, true, strong voice! Surely she could never again be hateful to Ellen. Tears came back to her eyes as she gave Rory's message.

"Riding, was she? Well, she deserves it," commented Ellen. "I shall tell her so."

"Aren't you coming home for lunch?" Ruth's voice was warm and sweet, and Ellen responded gratefully.

"I am too busy, dear. Miss Gowdy gave me some. Have you had a nice morning?" Ruth laughed a little, but did not answer.

"Well, good-by," she said.

She started to find Christine, but was checked by the sight of a note addressed to her on the table. It was from Amsden, and merely said that he had gone off for a few days in the mountains with Spaulding as guide: he was sorry not to see her before starting. Ruth read it with a sense of relief. She did not want to feel anything more now — just to be peaceful and quiet and thankful that the world was good and true.

"Well?" said Christine's voice from the head of the stairs.

"Oh, Christine, we are two silly idiots," said Ruth. "You don't need to leave this house, my dear. But, for pity's sake, get me something to eat!"

While she was telling her tale to a very much subdued Christine, Ellen was making an indignant examination of Rory's arm. It was not injured, though the pain was great, and was likely to last some time. She relieved her mind with a severe lecture, which the girl accepted with abject meekness, though there was suppressed humour in the twist of her mouth.

"I'm a bad lot. There's no trusting me," she assented. "A horse has just got to put his nose over the bars and off I go, arm or no arm. You'd best turn me over to Pocock; I'm not worth your time and trouble."

"I certainly should, only I have a feeling that he is preparing to leave town. Really, Rory, I have always supposed you had sense: I can't understand your being such a little fool."

"I know. I'm like that — plain unreliable;" and Rory shook her head over her own depravity. Ellen eyed her suspiciously.

"Rory Dorn, you are too meek to be natural," she exclaimed. "There is something in this that I don't understand. Why don't you tell me the whole truth?"

"But haven't I told you just what happened? Ruth rides by, and says I, 'I'll join her,' so I go galloping after; and we come home together. She'd not tell you any different." Ellen was not satisfied, but she gave it up.

"You are an inscrutable young person," she commented. "I will give you something to make you sleep to-night, though you deserve to lie awake thinking of your own folly. At least, I think you do," she amended gravely. Rory's eyes fell before hers.

"Sure — you're right there," she affirmed.

XVIII

"SATURDAY, Sunday, Monday, Tuesday, Wednesday, Thursday, — I think Mr. Amsden must have fallen down a cliff or something," said Christine, dropping her book over the side of the hammock, and yawning behind a clenched fist.

"More likely Spaulding has pushed him over," commented Wallace from the bearskin close beside her, where he was stretched full length. "What did he say in his note, Ruth?"

Ruth, who was staring down the wind-swept valley, bleak and forbidding under a muffled sky, did not turn her head from the window.

"Nothing much," she answered listlessly; "just that he was going off for a few days' mountaineering with Spaulding."

"Pretty mean of him, our last week up here," Wallace said, his eyes following the path of Christine's slipper as he swung her gently by the fringe of the hammock. "Shall we go off to-morrow without him if he doesn't show up?"

"We must," said Christine, "Our rooms are all engaged at Del Monte." She let her hand drop over

255

the side of the hammock, where it swung just above Wallace's eyes.

"And I have to get to work," he added. The hammock had come to an abrupt stop.

"Ruth, Willie is holding·my hand," complained Christine, presently. Ruth turned towards them with an effort at brightness.

"Good for him," she said. "I wish someone would hold mine."

"Come on; I've got another hand," offered Wallace amiably, moving over to make more room on the bearskin. She came and sat down beside him. There was kindly understanding in his gentleness as he put his arm about her. Ruth's spirits responded at once.

"There are times," she said demurely, "when that feels very good — from most anyone."

"I like that!" objected Wallace.

"I don't think she is a nice girl," said Christine, primly, drawing away her hand. "I don't think we'd better take her back with us; do you?" She had lowered her voice, and they all glanced towards the doors.

"Have you broken it to Ellen yet?" Wallace asked. Ruth shook her head.

"I have been feeling so done up these last few days. There was no sense in bringing it up until I was sure I could go."

"Oh, the change will do you good," Christine urged. "You can't go back on that embroidered blue linen."

"I wish I didn't feel mean about it," sighed Ruth.

"You have the silliest conscience I ever knew!" Christine was indignant. "You wouldn't expect her to sacrifice every minute of her life to little sister's hobby, would you? Very well, then! I declare, it is partly your fault she's such a tyrant, you're so ever. lastingly scrupulous and polite. Honestly, I don't believe she has half known how you felt." Ruth laughed.

"Don't scold me. I am not really scrupulous, I only talk so. I may hate my sins, but I go right on committing them."

"And that is what makes you endurable," added Christine, at which they all laughed. "Ugh, isn't it a nasty day," she added, as a fiercer gust shook the cabin, and left the windows chattering.

Wallace sat up with sudden energy.

"I don't believe it is half so bad outside as it is in here listening to it," he declared. "Come on, reef yourselves as tight as you can and we'll take a walk."

"Oh, no," moaned Christine.

"Oh, come on. Don't you want an appetite for your last supper? Leaving Ying is no joke, for me."

"And we thought it was us that kept you!"

"Well, you thought wrong. Jump up, now, let's be strenuous." He tipped Christine out of the hammock with little ceremony, and presently they went off together, not visibly downcast at Ruth's refusal to join them.

She, left alone, curled down on the bearskin and presently fell asleep. When she awoke, an hour later,

Ellen was sitting near, looking at her with such troubled eyes that Ruth felt a clutch of fright for what she might have said or shown in her sleep.

"What are you staring at me for?" she asked resentfully, sitting up.

Ellen spoke impulsively. "Oh, Ruth, I shall be glad when these people are gone."

"Well, I shan't," was the curt answer. "I think it is rather unkind of you to grudge me the little fun I can get." She was twisting up her hair, with face averted. Ellen rose and turned to the door; then she came slowly back.

"I wish we could be better friends, Ruth," she said in a low voice. "You are all I have in the world, but I can't seem to — I am stupid, I say things that hurt and offend you, without in the least knowing why. We are both lonely. If you would only let me — love you."

Ruth's head had sunk till her face was wholly hidden.

"I suppose — it's this abnormal life," she said with difficulty, after a pause. "I am not happy, and so — I take it out on you. I can't help it. I can't. I do hate it so!" She was crying, but the look on Ellen's face was sadder than tears.

"You didn't hate it the first two years; at least, you seemed fairly contented," she urged. "It is only since this spring that you have been so restless. Don't you think you could — get interested in something —"

"No, I don't!" Ruth jumped up fiercely. "And I think you are mean, mean, to keep me here!" She ran up the stairs and the door slammed after her. Ellen pressed her palms to her temples, then let her hands drop.

"The minute they are gone, I shall tell her," she said aloud.

Ying's supper was half cold when Christine and Wallace came back, the former very full of laughter, very mischievous and important, the latter one broad, sheepish grin. They took their places and tried to talk as usual, but even Ying, waiting on them, had his suspicions aroused. He chuckled softly as he went out, then thrust back his bony yellow face through the narrowest possible opening of the door.

"Miss Clistine, I guess she catch 'im husband," he confided in a falsetto whisper, and vanished. Wallace's roar of laughter was a confession in itself; also an irresistible example. They all shouted. Their congratulations were offered with wet eyes and helpless relapses.

"We were going to keep it a dead secret," Wallace confessed. "I guess we'd better give up that idea, Christine. Won't old Amsden be surprised!"

"Rory won't," said Ruth, sagely.

"Good little Rory — let's all go down after supper and tell her," suggested Wallace. Christine looked dubious.

"She's such a cross little thing — you can tell her by yourself. I've worn myself out going down there, and she isn't a bit appreciative."

"Oh, yes, she is, only she's shy," said Wallace, confidently. "Isn't there someone else we can tell? I think it's fun."

"Tell what?" asked a voice from the other end of the room. The porch door swung back, and Amsden, sunburned and wideawake, stood smiling on them. His eyes went straight to Ellen; then the others, jumping up, surrounded him with joyous welcome, and brought him back to the table with a deluge of questions. He held Ellen's hand for an instant, and dropped into his chair with the satisfaction of one who returns home.

"Tell what?" he insisted.

Wallace laid one hand on Christine's shoulder, and thrust the other into his coat, the standard bride-and-groom grouping of the Gallop photographer. "This," he explained.

Amsden looked disappointed. "Is that all? I could have told you about that before I left." The two were indignant.

"Did you hear that!" exclaimed Wallace. "Isn't he the patronizing —! Man, it hadn't happened then."

"Oh, yes, it had. You were a little slow about knowing it, that was all."

"Perhaps you will be good enough to give us the correct date? It may be needed for our biographies."

"Let me see: I should say it was the night Miss O'Hara set the table in a blue-checked apron."

"You ought to have told us," said Christine. "We have lost several weeks. Just when did you give us your best wishes?" He laughed and rose to shake hands with them.

"You've had them all along," he said; "only I have forgotten my manners, living in the wilderness with Spaulding."

"Tell us about it," urged Ruth, whose face had lifted like a flower put into water during the past few minutes.

"It was great — great," said Amsden, but he seemed reluctant to talk on the subject. They got little out of him.

Presently Christine and Wallace drifted off to the other end of the long room. Amsden begged for more coffee, and when Ruth had gone to get it, he turned quickly to Ellen.

"Spaulding won't give you any more trouble. We have had it all out, and he understands now. The climbing rather cleared and steadied him, and he is sorry. He asked me to tell you so."

"It was good of you — it was fine. I shall never forget it." Her voice was warm and quick.

"I can't go away to-morrow without a talk with you," he went on. "There will be no chance to-night. Can't you manage it — meet me somewhere in the morning? Am I asking too much?"

Her eyes fell. "I think perhaps we had better not. It will only make things harder."

"Nothing is so hard as not knowing. I must see you, Ellen." Ruth's step was heard.

"I shall be at the post-office at eight," Ellen said, rising and turning away.

Amsden did not stay long. He was tired, and had to get his things together.

"But I shall not say 'Good-by' to-night," he told Ruth. "The stage doesn't start until half-past nine, so I will be up again. Or will you see us off?" She smiled, with a quick glance at Christine.

"Oh, I shall see you," she assured him.

At the cottage he was greeted with thanksgiving by Mrs. Dorn, who had daily prophesied a broken neck for him, and with a sardonic grin from Rory.

"If you've no bones broke, you can thank my mother," she assured him when he had asked about her arm. "She's not done a stroke of work — just sat at the window and concentrated on you. I haven't had a square meal."

"You do look thin," Amsden assented.

"Thin! There isn't a pick on me; you could blow me off your hand."

"Oh, Rory, be still. How you do go on," grumbled Mrs. Dorn, retreating to fill Amsden's pitcher. He seated himself on a corner of the kitchen table.

"Have you heard the news about your other lodger?" he asked.

"I can guess it." Rory's mouth drew down expressively. "If Mama could have put her attention on him, now! 'Twould have saved him worse than a cracked bone or two."

"Miss O'Hara is an easy-going sort of girl," he argued. "She will be pleasant about the house."

"A fool's a fool. He'll not get any congratulations

here. Do you wonder I've no use for the men, when they have so little sense? And Dr. Ellen there in plain sight!"

He laughed. "Rory, you are too good to spend your life in Gallop. What would you like to do? Perhaps I could help you." She wagged a negative.

"Naw, naw! If you're not after the men, one place is as good as another. So long as there's horses to handle, it's good enough for me. If they gave out —"

He wrote his address on a slip of paper. "If they give out, there I am," he said. "I am going to keep an eye out for you, anyway. Good-night."

"You're real kind," Rory admitted.

XIX

THOSE days in the mountains had been the most
wonderful experience of Amsden's life. Spaulding had
led him up and up, beyond the forests, beyond the
living earth, into a strange, bleak world of granite
domes and turrets and spires where the wind came
down from snows that never melted, and the blue of
the noon sky had the dark of night against the white
glare of the naked precipices. They had climbed and
slid and jumped chasms and struggled up sharp pin-
nacles of rock and stood clinging against the wind to
stare down a frozen sea of peaks, vast upheavals seemingly stricken to immobility in the moment of their
wildest tumult. To come down out of this blinding
savagery to the green grass of meadows and the familiar trunks of pines was to exchange awe for exhilaration. The thrust of Amsden's hands into his pockets
was equivalent to another man's shout.

Through every hour of the way Ellen had been
beside him, like a living presence against his arm.
Her sure step echoed his on the cliffs; the splendours
of dawn and sunset were for them both together; the
firelight brought her serene face out of the shadows.
He now knew what it was, this amazing experience

that had caught him out of his shell and overturned his neat scale of values, giving him the deep breath of a living man. And he used to believe that the power of love was a thing vastly exaggerated. He remembered how he had lain in the hollow on Lone Cedar coolly considering whether Ruth might not "do," and a flush of shame swept through him.

"What an ass I was, what a blind prig!" he muttered. "Ellen, Ellen!" The word seemed to be in every sound, every bird note and ripple of water and stir of wind; his feet walked to it in rhythmic repetition; he said it aloud after Spaulding was asleep, and it sent a pang through him like the humming of a plucked string. He had no plans, and he did not once despair. He was still absorbed in his wonder at the miracle.

The first day or two they talked little, though the friendliness between them grew to friendship as they learned to respect each other's cheerful acceptance of hardship. Amsden did not for a moment lose sight of his purpose in coming, but bided his time. It was not until they crossed the timber line again that Spaulding returned to his grievance.

Amsden, his back against a log and his feet to the camp-fire, let him say every bitter word that was in his mind; then he turned on him and told him, without temper or palliation, what a wrong-headed part he had been playing. Spaulding grew sullen and left him, building his own fire half a mile away, but in the morning he was back. After the long, healing day he returned to the charge, but feebly, with evident effort.

Amsden met him inflexibly, and again the man went off; but, an hour or two later, Amsden was awakened by a touch on his arm. The firelight, falling on the sharp black and white of Spaulding's face, showed it cleared of its gloomy hostility.

"I guess I ben a fool," he said. "Tell her so, will you?" Amsden grasped his hand with a satisfaction amazing in its intensity. Long after the other was asleep he lay with his head on his arm, staring into the embers, rejoicing that this man had worked out his freedom.

"I wonder if Gilfillan feels like this all the time?" was his startled thought as he settled down to sleep. Then he reached out his hand in the dark, and his fingers closed as though on another hand. "But I did it — my part of it — for Ned, not for you, beloved," he whispered.

The morning after his return the thought that he was to meet Ellen put off realization of the fact that he was to leave her. He started up, but felt a shock of apprehension at sight of a note thrust under his door. Before he opened it he knew it meant that he should not see her.

The note was as bald as a telegram, and merely stated that she had been called to a case fifteen miles away, and might not be back for several days. "So I shall not see you again," it ended. A refusal to meet him might have meant something; but this was as impenetrable as a blind wall. He flung himself down, sick at heart, and did not stir until Wallace shouted to him that he would be late. When he came out, he found a stack of luggage in the hall.

"You ought to have seen me coming down the trail with those bags last night; heard me, rather," laughed Wallace. "We had to sneak them out without Ying's seeing."

"But why?" asked Amsden, listlessly, leaning against the wall to watch Wallace's neat packing.

"For fear he'd suspect. Oh, don't you know that Ruth is going with us?"

"Why didn't she speak of it last night, then?"

"Well, she hadn't had it out with Ellen. She was just going to, after you left, when a cart came up and scurried Ellen away — I guess it's a baby. You got her note?"

"Yes." Amsden was frowning. "And so Ruth is going without telling her?"

"Had to. She will send back a note, of course. Ying would raise the deuce, she says, so we are going to put these bags on here at the gate, to avoid questions. He's a keen old boy. Guess we'd better go down to breakfast; it's late."

Amsden followed downstairs in worried silence. "I don't think Ruth ought to do it," he said abruptly, when Mrs. Dorn had served them and left the room. "It isn't treating Mrs. Roderick fairly. She ought to have had it out, and then gone openly. I have half a mind to go up and tell her so."

"Well, you're too late," was the placid answer.

267

"They were afraid Ellen might get back this morning and meet the stage — 'twould have been awkward! So little sister and Christine lit out early by the Lone Cedar trail. They will hit the stage about three miles from here — Ellen's road branches off before that. Great scheme, wasn't it?" Amsden made no answer. "I don't see why you're so grumpy about it," commented Wallace.

"Well, look here. We have been Mrs. Roderick's guests for a month — it is all hers. We know she doesn't wish her sister to leave her, and the minute her back is turned, we entice Ruth to run away. She ought at least to have had a chance to express her mind. I think it is discourteous and abominable. I won't stand for it."

"What will you do?"

"Stay here till she comes back, and explain."

"But you said this was the last day you could possibly —"

"This is more important than work."

Wallace peevishly sawed at the Dorn beefsteak. "You've gone cracked, living with Spaulding. How you can stay to make speeches to Ellen, when you might be playing with Ruth —!"

Amsden spoke sharply: "I am not going to be rude to the finest woman I have ever known!" Wallace's look grew to a stare; then he slowly laid down his knife and fork.

"Are you in love with Ellen Chantry?" he demanded.

"Yes," was the curt answer.

"Do you mean you want to marry her?"

"Yes."

"Well, I don't believe it!"

"Very well, don't."

Wallace took up his fork again, then laid it down. "Does Ruth know it?"

"I don't know; but I want her to." Wallace relapsed into gloomy silence, which lasted until nearly time for the stage. Then he heaved himself up with a sigh.

"Well, I guess you'd better stay, then," he said. "But it beats me! What shall I tell the girls?"

"Why not the truth?"

"H'm. Nice job you've given me," Wallace muttered.

The first day of his waiting did not seem long to Amsden, for a pile of letters demanded his attention, and he was tired enough to find sitting still a relief. At noon the next day he mounted to the cabin, but found it deserted, with dusty porch and locked doors. There was no sign of Ying. Amsden remembered a squalid Chinese settlement down by the creek, and wondered if Ying could consort with such of his kind. It might be natural, but the idea irritated him. The horses were not in the shed; but Ellen had probably ordered them turned out before she left. That afternoon he climbed to a point whence he could see the bald mountain, fifteen miles away, which Gilfillan had pointed out to him the day they walked down Lone

Cedar together. "Strong as a man, gentle as a woman, ready to work day and night to make it safe and sure;" the preacher's words came back to him, and stayed in his head like the burden of a song.

After that the days dragged unbearably. The exaltation of the high mountains left him, and Amsden was as moody and despairing as any other lover; he had no resource but to haunt the empty cabin, which had already taken on a look of blind desolation. Ying did not return, and he was moved to bitter reflections on the faithlessness of Orientals.

Every evening he climbed to a point whence he could see if the lights were lit. He had just given up and gone in on the sixth night when a cart put down a tired figure at the cabin door. Ellen sent a puzzled look at the dark windows, then, after knocking in vain, found a key under the mat, and let herself into the living-room, musty with stale air. Lights revealed a funereal orderliness of furniture, and a thick film of dust. The kitchen showed the same unused aspect, and a cold stove. She knocked at the door of Ying's room, then pushed it open, chilled with a sudden fear; but there was no one there, nor in the rooms upstairs, nor in the shed. Ellen had been up day and night, for her patient had needed her desperately, and the woman who was expected to come as nurse had been detained; she was hungry and cold and worn out, and the emptiness frightened her. Suddenly she sobbed wretchedly, standing with her palms pressing her cheeks. Then she took herself in hand and got together a supper of canned things and tea, and built a fire in the living-room. The absence of some of Ruth's clothes suggested that she had gone with Christine; but what about Ying the faithful? Had everyone deserted her?

Uneasiness deepened to nervous terror at the breathless silence of the place. She lit the candles all round the walls and lay down on the hearthrug with a cushion, too wretched to go to bed. Once the thought of Mr. Gilfillan brought quick comfort, and she hurried to the telephone; it was out of order, and she could get no answer. Then she cried again, scorning herself for her weakness, but too spent to fight it. Ten o'clock came, then eleven. One of the candles was sputtering, and she rose to put it out, then paused with lifted hands, her eyes fixed on the door.

There was a step on the trail, mounting steadily; now it had reached the porch, crossed it, halted at the door. It came strongly, like that of a friend, yet she could not move. The knock was repeated, then a voice, Amsden's voice, asked:

"Are you there, Mrs. Roderick?"

"Yes, yes," she called, throwing back the door. In her relief she held out her arms to him, not knowing what she did; then drew back, flushing scarlet.

"I have been so frightened — I am not responsible," she said. "Where are they? What has happened? Why are you here?"

"I waited for you," he explained, following her to the hearth-rug. "I couldn't bear that you should

271

think I had abetted Ruth in running away. I thought
you ought to have been told."

"Where has she gone?"

"To Del Monte with the O'Haras."

"And you let her go!" There was strong reproach
in Ellen's voice.

"How could I stop her? Besides, I didn't see any
harm in her going; it was her not telling you first that
I blamed."

"Why didn't Ying stop it?"

"He didn't know. He has been gone all the week,
I don't know where."

She faced him in sudden anger. "And you couldn't
trust me — that my reasons against it were real ones!
Oh, I have tried to spare her, I have tried. I thought
I could get her wholly well up here, and she need never
know. Now she has to face it."

"Face it?" he repeated.

She nodded. Evidently the word was hard to say.
She laid her hands on her chest.

"Oh, you don't mean —!" But he knew she did.

"Yes." She dropped into a chair, and leaned her
head on her hands. "It came after her illness three
years ago; but her doctor and I believed this life would
wholly cure it. Last spring she seemed really well
again. Then I let her go down to the tournament,
and when she came back I saw —" she broke off, and
presently went on from a new point: "I wanted her to
have this one good time with you all before she had to
know."

"Then it was for her, your life up here — all for her?"

"Yes, of course. But I have gained out of it immensely," she added quickly. "It was not lost time."

"Oh, and I judged you, I blamed you!" He knelt down by her chair, and bent his forehead against her knee. "Can you ever forgive me?" Her fingers passed slowly over his hair.

"It was natural. Besides, I was to blame. I ought to have told her in the first place. It was tyrannical, to try to bear her burden for her. I have made her hate me." He drew closer and took both her hands in his.

"She will love you when she understands."

"No; she will resent it. Oh, I have failed, failed everywhere." She drew her hands away and started from her chair. "She can love other people, but not me. It was the same in my marriage," she went on impetuously. "We were both very young, but my husband had always been the centre of an adoring family of women, helpless women, and my life had made me — more mature. He — hated me for it, just as Ruth does. Oh, I tried so hard not to be — it was like walking with bent knees, so as not to seem taller. I didn't care about anything on earth but keeping him — you know how one loves at twenty."

"I know," Amsden repeated, his eyes lifted to her face.

"But it was no use. It was always there, and he couldn't forgive it. He said to me once, 'No man could stay in love with you — you're too infernally strong.' That was the day before he — you knew he was killed? It isn't the sort of thing one forgets!"

Amsden had no consciousness of rising, but he found himself standing in front of her, his hands on her shoulders.

"He didn't know. I shall love you till the last hour of my life. How can I make you understand — how can I make you care for me?"

Her eyes fell. "I had put it all so far away from me," she said; but she let him draw her close and closer. The miracle had sprung to life full grown between them. It was in their hands, and their grave eyes, and their meeting lips.

"I can't believe it, that you care now! I thought it would take me years and years."

"Oh, yes, I care." Then she gently drew away from him. "But it is no use. I can't take it now — don't you see?"

"No."

"Think of Ruth. She is losing everything, everything at once. How can I?"

"But you have given up three years of your life for Ruth."

"Think what she has to face, now. How can I take you, too? Besides, I can't leave her. She will have to stay in exile."

"You can't sacrifice us both to her!"

"How can I leave the poor little soul alone!" After a long silence he lifted her hands and kissed them.

"You are right. But I shall find a way for us, now,

if I can. And if not, I will wait as many years as I must. There is one thing you must give me."

Her hands tightened on his. "What?"

"To-morrow. The day after I will go for Ruth, but to-morrow must be all mine." She lifted her face impetuously to his.

"All yours — every moment yours!"

Several candles were flaring. Amsden put them all out and piled wood on the fire until the redwood walls were aglow between the fluttering shadows. Then he threw himself on the couch and held out his arm to her.

"It begins now," he said. She came slowly, as though to prolong happiness.

XX

THE heavens were good to them, and poured a flood
of sunlight into their last day. The woods closed
after them in the brightness of the morning, and the
sky behind the western peaks was barred with fading
scarlet when they came out again. After their supper
they sat on the steps in the velvety darkness while the
stars blazed out, and the sound of little falling pine-
cones seemed loud in the stillness. The hours had
brought them heights and depths; now they had fallen
back on hope and a vast content in each other.

"I don't believe you will ever come to hate me," she
said thoughtfully. "You see, you are more terrible
in wrath than I am!" They laughed at the beloved
memory of their battle. "It's the weaker people who
hate one, for the hurt to their vanity."

"Don't think of those things," he urged. "This is
our last day."

"I can't help wondering where Ying is."

"It doesn't matter. There is nobody but us two in
the whole world, and we —" He stopped, and they
both turned startled eyes towards the trail. They had
heard the stage pass below several minutes before,
and now someone was evidently mounting, very slowly.

Ellen rose and opened the cabin door, letting a stream of light fall on the path as two figures paused on the top.

"Ruth!" she exclaimed.

"Yes;" something in Ruth's voice made Amsden spring forward to help her. Then he saw that the other figure was Ying.

Ruth, blinking in the light, dropped into the nearest chair, and smiled at them remotely.

"I bling her back," explained Ying. "She bin sick; she be al' light now."

Ruth's eyes closed. "I'm all well again, only the trip was hard," she said slowly. "I want to go to bed."

"The best thing you could do," said Ellen, warmly. "Ying will get some supper for you."

"And I will be your porter," said Amsden. "No, child, you're not too heavy." He gathered her up and carried her to her room, Ellen following with a candle.

It was an hour before Ellen came back to him.

"No; she is all right," she said in answer to his quick look. "She only seems tired — she is asleep, already. But something has happened. Do you suppose she knows the truth? I must see Ying."

"This is still my day," he reminded her. "You must do what I say."

"Oh, but you are a tyrant! What are your orders?"

"That you say good-night to me and go straight to bed without another word to anyone."

She lifted her face with tired docility.

"Good-night," she said.

When Ellen stole to her door the next morning, Ruth was sitting up in bed finishing her breakfast.

"I am all right," she said cheerfully. "I wanted food so I called Ying. Sit down; I want to tell you everything."

Ellen put the tray outside, then drew her chair close to the bed.

"I didn't write because I knew Mr. Amsden would tell you where I had gone," Ruth began, her eyes turned to the window framing the western mountains. "I hadn't slept for nights, so the excitement of getting off was too much for me; the trip was hard, and something I heard from Will — upset me. When we got to the O'Haras I felt deadly, and then — then I had a hemorrhage."

"Oh, Ruth!" Ellen's hand went out, and Ruth laid hers in it, though her eyes did not leave the window.

"It was very, very slight. I should not have thought much of it, but Mrs. O'Hara called in our doctor, and he told me — everything. He thought I knew, at first, and then he had to go on."

"I ought to have told you — I was all wrong. I wanted to spare you, Ruth, but I had no right to."

Ruth's fingers tightened on hers. "Yes; you ought to have told me. I have thought such cruel things of you, and all the time you were sacrificing everything to me. You have made me feel — like dirt." There was a hard brightness in her eyes, though Ellen's were wet.

"You know, Ruth, I believe you can get wholly well in time, if you will be patient," she said finally.

"So the doctor said, and I am going to believe it." Ruth drew her hand away, clasping her fingers behind the soft fluff of her hair. "Ying turned up the next day, and bullied me horribly. He was so funny! He waited till I was strong enough to come back. So he knew, Ellen?"

"Yes, for I wanted him to be responsible when I was away."

"He guessed I had gone to the O'Haras. Of course I did not go to Del Monte at all. Now for the practical side," she added, after a pause. "I must take up my life and run it myself, and you must go back to yours. No — wait; let me finish. Some day —" her voice faltered, then she went on strongly — "some day you will want to marry. I am not going to keep you back from that. I am afraid you will have to support me — but I know you won't mind."

"Mind, dear! But what will you do?"

"Mrs. O'Hara is not very well, and they want her to go to Arizona for the winter. Christine says she will go if I come. It is the best possible place for me, and they are not afraid to take me. Can you afford it?"

"Of course! But, Ruth, you really want to go?"

"Want to! Travel and people — I can hardly wait."

"How about Will?"

"Oh, they won't be married till spring, anyway, and Christine won't mind leaving him now that they are engaged," Ruth explained serenely. Ellen did not wholly understand, but dropped the subject.

"And what will you do next year?"

Ruth seemed suddenly the older of the two. "We will wait till that comes," she said decidedly. "I may make friends there and stay on indefinitely. I have to run myself." Then she put out both hands with a sudden softening in her eyes. "Not that I don't realize what you have done for me, Ellen! Not that I don't love you!" Ellen clung to her.

"Oh, Ruth, Ruth!" she sobbed.

"You are the biggest person in the whole world," Ruth whispered. "I am too little to belong with you — but he isn't. Don't let him go."

A step sounded on the porch below. Ruth smiled.

"Go down and tell him how noble I am," she commanded. "It won't last — I'll be nasty again in a week. But I am rather enjoying my own strength of character just now."

Ellen looked at her in wonder. The smile was an honest one; her amazing gaiety was in full possession.

"Give me that green book out of my bag before you go," she said, sitting up with energy. "It's about Arizona."

THE END

www.ingramcontent.com/pod-product-compliance
Lightning Source LLC
Chambersburg PA
CBHW020606260626
47157CB00003B/893